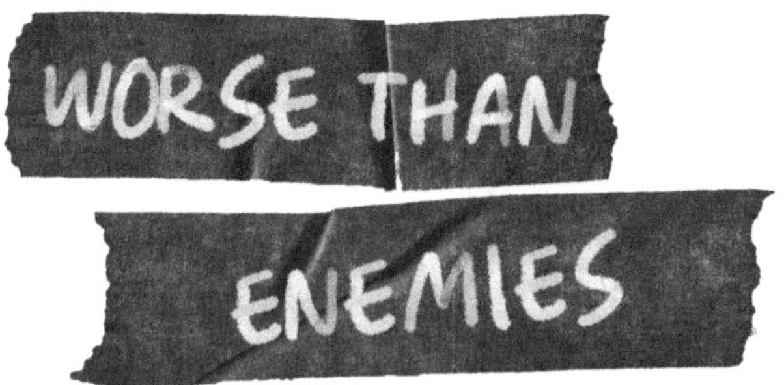

USA TODAY BEST SELLING AUTHOR

J.L. BECK

CHAPTER 1

*S*ome people get louder the quieter they try to be.

One of the many things I've learned after spending the past couple of months living in a hotel room with my mom and baby sister. Well, not a room. I think they call it a junior suite. There's a living room area with a TV and a separate bedroom with two queen-sized beds.

Like so many other mornings, Mom stumbled in a few minutes before dawn and tried like hell to be quiet so she wouldn't wake Lucy or me. The woman left us alone for two and a half days this time, but at least she tried to be quiet when she finally came back. I guess she figures that makes her a good mother or something.

Unfortunately, the quieter she tries to be, the louder she is. A herd of elephants might as well be marching through the room. I roll onto my side and find Lucy starting to stir. She's four now and should be in pre-K, but that's not my call. Next year, though, there won't be any excuses. She has to go to school, which means our mother will have to do something she's supposed to by registering the poor kid and making sure she gets to and from there every day. I hate to think it, but something tells me she's got a lot of sitting and waiting ahead of her. Mom was flaky when I was Lucy's age. Now, thirteen years later, she might as well live in a different state.

"Shh, it's okay. You can go back to sleep." I'm gentle as I draw the blankets up over Lucy's shoulders.

The door between the living room and bedroom swings open a moment later. I know better than to hold a finger to my lips. I did that once when Lucy had a rough night with an upset stomach. I had just gotten her to sleep by the time our mother returned from another weekend with her latest boyfriend, so I touched a finger to my lips to signal for quiet.

I had a swollen lip for three days after that. I won't make that mistake again.

She heads straight for the bathroom, and I exhale. How much longer are we going to have to do this? It was one thing when she did it when we lived in the apartment and there was room for all of us to move around without getting in each other's way too much. I didn't get my own bedroom then, either, but at least Mom didn't come barging in to wake us up when she had a room of her own.

"Morgan?" Lucy rubs her fists over her sleepy eyes.

"It's okay, honey. You go back to sleep. It's still super early."

"Is Mommy back?"

"Yeah, she came back. She always comes back." Though there have been times when I've wondered whether she will. Wondered if the latest loser she's dating will turn out to be a murderer or if—and I don't know whether this would be better—she'll decide to run off with him and pretend we don't exist. "We'll go out in the living room and turn on the TV."

I get up, then walk around to her side of the bed to pick her up and carry her out to the sofa. She brings a pillow, and I tuck her in with a blanket before turning on the TV. She'll fall back to sleep for a while.

Once she's settled in, I go back to the bedroom and change from pajamas to a T-shirt and shorts. It's supposed to be warm today. Spending so much time in the hotel, it's easy to lose touch with the real world. I try to get outside whenever possible to breathe fresh air instead of the stale, recycled crap blasting through the vents.

Later, I might take Lucy down to the pool. It's important to me that she has a little fun.

She's lucky. At her age, this kind of thing is an adventure. She doesn't see how incredibly fucked up it is that our mother hasn't yet found actual housing for us since our eviction.

Mom finally finishes in the bathroom, and while she stumbles her way through, changing out of her fancy dress, I wash up and brush out my long, blond hair. That's one thing all three of us share, one of the few traits I'm glad Mom passed down. My blue eyes have circles under them, thanks to another night spent lying awake and thinking. I'll be starting a new school in a couple of weeks now that we don't officially live in our old district. I won't know anybody. If we don't have a permanent residence, how am I supposed to believe they'll let me go to school anywhere?

When I asked Mom about it, she waved me off. "We'll be moving soon. You'll see. I have something in the works." In other words, she's trying to con her latest victim into paying for a place. Not that I think she actually goes out and chooses victims to con, but that's generally how it ends up. She uses them until they catch on to her or she gets bored. One or the other.

By the time I come out, she's already in bed. Only her head pokes out from under the blankets, and I see she's wearing a mask over her eyes and plugs in her ears. I wonder what it's like to live in a different world. She never even said a word to me when she came in.

"I'm going to go down and get some coffee and maybe take a walk. Lucy's on the couch with the TV on." Either she can't hear me or is pretending she can't.

Lucy is fast asleep again, just like I knew she would be. She'll sleep for at least another hour, maybe two—it's barely six o'clock. The café in the lobby opens at six, so I'll be able to get some caffeine and charge it to the room the way I do everything else.

That's something else I can't help but wonder about. How are we paying for this? What are we doing in the hotel if we can't afford rent? It's a pretty nice hotel, too, though, I can't pretend I've been to many places before this. But we've stayed in a few cheap motels over the years, and this might as well be a five-star resort compared to that. Besides the pool, there's a game room, a spa, two restaurants, and the café, which is already bustling even at this early hour on a Monday. A few guys in suits are waiting for their drinks when I get in line. I guess they're here for business.

Who's paying for this? I can't shake the question. Maybe it's because I know what it's like to have everything thrown upside down out of nowhere. One day, we had an apartment—not a great apartment, but it was ours. It was what Lucy called home, the only home she could remember. The next day, just like that, we had to throw our things into trash bags while our furniture got tossed out on the sidewalk for the garbage men to collect. I don't think anybody would blame me for feeling like I always have to look over my shoulder, waiting for the next terrible thing is on its way.

I know I stand out compared to the men waiting for their coffee. I cross my arms over myself, chilly in the air-conditioning, wishing I'd put on something that would cover me a little more when I feel the weight of their stares.

"Large iced latte, please. Oat milk if you have it." I charge it using my room card, then step aside to wait. One man, somebody who looks old enough to be my grandfather, inches a little too close for comfort.

"Aren't you a little young to be staying here by yourself?" he asks, his voice low.

I look up at him. He's staring down the front of my v-cut neckline and not bothering to hide it. "Excuse me?" I ask, playing dumb.

"You're a little young, is all. Are you staying alone?"

"And what if I was?"

"It seems a shame for a little girl to be running around by herself like that." I swear, all he has to do now is lick his chops. He reminds me of the Big Bad Wolf in the old *Three Little Pigs* cartoon. The hotel has a channel dedicated just to those old-timey cartoons, and Lucy loves them. This man could be the wolf, easy.

"Which is it? Am I a little girl, or am I the woman whose boobs you're staring at?" Somebody standing within earshot snickers, but I don't look at them. I stare at him and have the pleasure of watching his face turn almost purple, like his tie is suddenly much too tight. It's not as if this is the first time an older man has talked to me like that. When I was younger, with some of Mom's old boyfriends, I didn't know what to do about it.

Now? All it does is make me tired.

He hurries away with his drink, and I can relax a little bit. Usually, I wouldn't say boo to a ghost. But it's been a long summer, and I've spent most of it in this hotel, taking care of my sister while my mother does whatever she does until all hours of the night. So, I'm not in the mood to be sexually harassed by some guy who probably has daughters older than me.

It's good to step outside once I have my drink in hand. The hotel staff is already hard at work, trimming shrubbery and sweeping the pathways. I nod to a couple of them as I pass and turn toward the abandoned bridge spanning the North Woods River. I enjoy going there sometimes, especially early in the morning. It's peaceful, with nobody needing anything from me or demanding anything. I like to sit near the bridge and watch sunlight sparkling on the water. Sometimes I pretend I'm someone else, somewhere else. It's easier than being me most days.

Today, there's something new—no, *someone* new. I spot him sitting on the bridge with his legs dangling over the side. Even I don't usually step foot on the rotting old bridge, choosing instead to sit on the rocks overlooking the river. I doubt a car has passed over it in years. If it did, it would probably fall right through. More than once, I've wondered why they don't just tear it down, but it's probably cheaper to leave it here and use signs to warn drivers away from it.

Everything about him screams *leave me alone*, from the hunch of his shoulders to the way he stares down at the water like it offended him. Why would he be mad at the river? He's wearing a dark T-shirt and knee-length shorts. He looks like he could have been working out or going for a run.

I should turn around and go another way. Maybe I should head back to the hotel. Lucy will get fidgety once she's up, not to mention hungry. I shudder to think what Mom will do if she wakes her up, and I hate to think of her sitting there with her stomach growling while she waits for me to come back.

But I can't tear my eyes away from his short, brown curls. His chiseled jaw. Skin so tan, it's almost bronze, like somebody who spends a lot of time outside. His body tells me the same thing. His build is muscular, but not obnoxious. He must play sports. He can't be much older than me, so I guess he goes to one of the schools around here. Coming from the other side of town, I wouldn't know.

I don't even know why I'm still standing here, holding this drink, staring at him. Something about him won't let me go until I know more. The energy coming off him is so strong I can feel it from a distance.

I can either pretend not to notice him and keep walking, or I can see if he needs help. Something tells me if I don't, I'll always wonder what happened to the sad, angry boy on the bridge.

CHAPTER 2

hy am I doing this? My feet are heavy as I continue toward the bridge. I don't have a good feeling about this. That's why I can't let it go. I'm afraid he might hurt himself. It's stupid, and I know it is. I've never met this person. I have no idea why he's sitting there. But I feel it in my heart. Something bad might happen if I don't at least try to talk to him.

So I try. "Hi."

His head snaps around fast enough that I fall back half a step in surprise. I can't get the image of a wounded animal out of my head. "What do you want?" His voice is deep, filled with anger. Maybe even disgust. Why I would disgust him, I don't know. Maybe he's mad at the world, and I just happen to be the only person around.

"Nothing. I came out here to sit and look at the water. I do that sometimes."

"Did I fucking ask?"

"Actually, you kind of did. You asked what I want."

He rolls his eyes with a sigh of disgust. "Go away. Sit someplace else. Just get out of here."

I should. I know I should. He looks and sounds like he wants to rip my head off. Whatever he's angry with or hurt by, he might decide to take it out on me. With a body like his, it wouldn't be hard for him to overpower me if he wanted to.

But I don't feel like he would. I don't know why. Something in my gut, I guess. If they're cornered, a wounded animal might strike, but it's only because they're in pain. What they need is help. I wonder what kind of help I could give him.

That's what gets me moving closer to him. He stares out at the water, pretending to ignore me, but I'm not fooled. His jaw twitches, and it looks like he's grinding his teeth. Maybe that's a good thing. Instead of lashing out, he's holding himself back.

"Are you okay?" I ask.

"Yes."

"Because you looked upset."

"Did I ask you how I looked? Why are you still here?" he demands through gritted teeth. "I told you to fucking leave."

"Yeah, I know, but I guess I don't want to go yet." I shift from one foot to the other. It's difficult standing here when he obviously wants me gone. Standing up to that gross old guy at the café was one thing, but this is different.

I take my time sitting down, careful not to go over the edge. The creaking of the wooden walkway running alongside the roadway makes my blood run cold, but I don't think it's going to collapse with only two people sitting on it. "Here. You look thirsty." I hold out my latte, condensation rolling down the sides of the cup. "Do you like oat milk?"

"Oat milk? Aren't there enough kinds of milk in the world?" Still, he takes it.

"But I like this. It's really creamy. It sort of makes you feel like you're drinking something bad for you when you're really not."

"Why not just drink something bad for you?" He takes a sip anyway. It warms me inside. Like I won a tiny victory.

And it gives me the courage to keep talking. "It's pretty early in the morning to be out. Were you going on a run?"

I can practically feel him closing himself off. He sets the coffee down between us before rubbing his palms over his thighs. "I was going for a walk," I explain when he doesn't speak. "I've been staying in a hotel with my family for a little while now, and it gets claustrophobic. I'm tired of breathing all that hotel air, you know? But the windows don't open. I guess they don't want people jumping."

Ouch. Maybe that wasn't the best thing to say, since he sort of looked like he wanted to jump when I first found him. But he only snorts, shrugging a little. "Probably."

I sigh, looking out over the water. "You know, mornings like this remind me of when I was little. It always felt kind of, I don't know, special to be up this early. The sun is just coming up, and most people are still sleeping. Everything is so still. You can hear the birds waking up."

He responds grudgingly. "I guess so. I never really paid attention."

"I used to love when my dad would take me fishing. That's when I would get up early, you know? We would head out, and it would still be dark when we left the house." I swing my legs back and forth. I'm glad I wore tennis shoes this morning instead of my slides. I'd be too afraid one would fall off and drop into the water.

"Did you used to go a lot?" he asks in a flat voice. I can't tell if he's interested or if he only wants a distraction. Either way, I don't mind.

"Only sometimes. Usually in the summer. He had more time for me in the summer. We'd go out and get in the little boat, and he would take us out to the middle of the lake."

"Which lake?"

"I don't remember. I don't even think he ever told me the name of it. And I was too little to care. He always put the worm on the hook for me. I would sit there and hold my pole, and he'd, you know…" I mime reeling the little crank thingy to bring the fish in.

"What kind of fish did you catch? Were you any good?"

I bite my lip. "I don't remember the names."

"Probably minnows. They're easy to catch. Did you used to eat them?"

"Sure. He'd pull all the guts out and stuff."

"Minnows aren't fish you eat. They're too small."

"Then I must've gotten the name wrong. What difference does it make?"

He's quiet for a second. The only sound I hear is his breathing. "You know what I think?"

"No, what?"

"I don't think you've ever been fishing. Not even once in your life."

"Why would you say that?"

"Just a guess." He raises his eyebrow like he's daring me to argue. I shrug. "Fine. You got me. I've never been fishing."

"Why did you make that up?"

"Do you really want to know?"

"Now, yeah. I do. It's a random thing to pull out of your ass." He picks up the coffee and takes another sip.

"Because all I've ever been able to do about my father is make things up. Because I don't know who he was. I never met him."

It surprises me when his face falls. "That sucks."

"It kind of does sometimes. And again, maybe it doesn't."

"What do you mean?"

"I'm just saying, what if he's really an asshole? I mean, between you and me, my mom doesn't have the best taste in men. I'd probably fall over dead from shock if she actually picked a good one for once."

He snorts. "Yeah. I know that feeling."

"Does your mom date losers, too?"

His jaw works again, and the light leaves his eyes before he looks down at his dangling feet. "In my case, it's my father." He heaves a sigh that sounds like it comes all the way from down in his toes. Something is really bothering him, something deep and painful. How can I know that when we've only just met? I don't even know his name.

"Are your parents divorced?"

"Why are we talking about this?" His head snaps up. Now his

piercing blue eyes are hard and flashing. His lip curls in a sneer. "It's none of your fucking business."

"Okay. That's all you have to say."

"Fine."

"But I'm sorry you're going through that. I know how hard it is when you see a parent making stupid decisions, and you can't do anything about it."

"I don't want to talk about it."

"That's fine. But if you do, I can listen."

He takes a deep breath, and I think maybe he's going to open up for a second. Why do I care so much? "Why did you pick fishing?"

"What?"

"Fishing. Why did you decide to lie about fishing and not something you know about?"

I have to laugh a little. "I don't know. I guess I never wanted to think about my father being the dad who sits around burping up beer and watching baseball. And I don't like football. Too violent."

"Makes sense." He sounds tired now, but at least he's not so angry anymore. "Listen. You really should go. I need to get back home."

"You're leaving, too?"

"As soon as you do, since you're in the way." He nods toward the end of the bridge, where I came from.

"Okay. Thanks for talking with me." I get up slowly, carefully. For a second, it looks like he's going to help me, but then he stops himself. "See you around."

"Yeah. See you." He nods. I nod back. Something is different about him now. I think whatever he was feeling passed.

I'm at the end of the bridge before he calls out.

The wind blows my hair in front of my face as I turn around. I brush it away. "What did you say?"

"What's your name?"

"Morgan!" I wave goodbye before turning toward the hotel again. I've already been out here too long. With my luck, this is the one time my sister will decide to wake up before I expect her to. But even if Mom is pissed by the time I get back, it'll be worth it if I helped that guy. I wish I had thought to get his name.

My heart's pounding by the time I finish trotting back to the hotel and taking the elevator up to our floor. I haven't been gone all that long, but time got away from me. I hope Mom didn't take it out on Lucy if anything happened.

As it turns out, something has.

When I open the door, I discover a whirlwind.

"Good, you're back!" My mother, who less than an hour ago staggered in here probably still drunk, is now racing around. Lucy watches from a corner of the sofa, eyes wide.

"What's going on?"

"He just called." She's going through the shoes in one of her suit-cases and doesn't bother explaining who she's talking about. Too busy tossing things around. We can't fit all the bags in the bedroom, so some of them are out here. "Where are my nude slingbacks?"

"What's-his-face? Is he taking you to breakfast?"

"Better than breakfast." She finds her shoes and stands, sliding one on, then the other. Anybody who didn't know her might think she actually possesses class and sophistication. She looks great in a form-fitting cream dress, and the shoes make her already long legs look endless.

"Lunch, too?" I wink at Lucy, who giggles.

Mom clasps her hands in front of her chest. "He's going to call the store to have them open early, so I can shop alone. This is a dream come true. I'm afraid I'm still in bed, sleeping."

Meanwhile, I haven't gotten new clothes for school, but she's going on a shopping spree. "That's nice. Have fun." If anything, it'll be better if she's not around.

"You don't understand." She's glowing, I realize, and tears are welling in her eyes. "He called because he didn't want to wait anymore. We had such an incredible weekend that he wanted to wait until he's back in town on Friday and make a big thing out of it, but… he's so impulsive." Her chin trembles.

"Make a big thing out of what?"

"Girls." She looks from me to my sister and back again. "He's taking me out to buy an engagement ring. We're getting married."

CHAPTER 3

$\mathcal{M}$y heart's hammering so hard, I'm afraid I'm going to be sick. That would be a great way to introduce myself to my classmates. Throwing up all over myself, or maybe on one of them. I have dreaded this moment all summer. Walking into my new school, not knowing anyone.

But this is worse, somehow, because I didn't imagine it this way. I didn't imagine going to this school.

North Woods Prep is where the rich kids go. I would imagine myself going to Harvard one day before imagining going here. This world is totally out of reach for me.

No, not anymore. At least, not according to my mom, who insisted her fiancé pull strings to get me a last-minute registration. "And he did it because he wants you to have all the best things. Finally, we're all going to have exactly what we deserve. This is only the beginning. Just wait until you see everything he's put in place for when we move in with him."

Right. I hope she's not getting her hopes up too high. This is further than she's ever gotten with any of her guys—he gave her an enormous ring, so big I'm surprised she can lift her hand—but plans can change. She'd better hope he's okay with a quick wedding, so she can hook him before he sees who she really is.

It's a shame, because he seems like a decent guy. Kind and thoughtful. He's pretty handsome for an older man, too. Tall, dark-haired, chiseled. She won't let him do more than say *hi* to Lucy and me when he picks her up for dates, which he's done more often over the past two weeks since his proposal. But he always tries to be friendly, and he's brought a few presents for Lucy. Last night, it was a little stuffed bunny.

"I'm not so sure what a seventeen-year-old girl wants," he admitted with a laugh.

"You shouldn't be getting them gifts, anyway. You're too generous." Mom gave him a big kiss, but I heard what existed underneath her words. Jealousy. She can't allow even her four-year-old to get a little attention when she thinks it should be hers. She needs to get their names on a marriage certificate, fast, before she ruins it by being herself.

Though right now, looking at the school from inside the Uber I took from the hotel, I wish this all could have waited. Getting used to a new school would be bad enough without it being North Woods Prep. Everybody walking across campus looks like they just walked off the set of a TV show. And the cars in the parking lot! It's like a freaking luxury dealership.

Meanwhile, I'm about to climb out of a Corolla that doesn't even belong to me.

"Are you okay?" The driver checks me out in the rearview mirror.

"I'm fine. Thank you."

I have to force myself out of the car. I don't belong here. My clothes aren't nice enough, even though it's my best pair of jeans and an almost-new pair of sandals. I'm not wearing half as much makeup as most of the girls, and it doesn't look like I spent an hour doing my hair this morning—but I did. I tried my best with the few things I had at the hotel. I guess my soon-to-be stepfather's generosity doesn't extend to spa treatments or salon visits, though, it's not like I want it to. It would feel weird to accept that from somebody I don't know. But that doesn't stop my mother from taking advantage.

Once I knew I'd be going here, I looked up the campus map online. Most of the classes take place in the main building, which is more like a castle or even a fortress. A huge center section looks like it stretches a mile in both directions, but that's probably my nerves. Then there are two buildings to the sides, forming a capital letter H. Those are the buildings holding the gym, the pool, the auditorium, that sort of thing. I'm already wondering how anybody can get from one end to the other in the five minutes we have between classes.

"Look out!" I barely have time to notice someone shouting before realizing they're shouting in my general direction. Moments later, I'm scrambling, along with a handful of other kids, trying to get out of the way of a bright red sports car now tearing across the lawn and sending clumps of sod and grass in all directions. Another few seconds and I could have been run over.

The car screeches to a stop, and moments later, three guys jump out. They don't care that they just tore up the lawn any more than the driver does. He peels off the second the doors are closed. I guess, to park. What was the point of that display?

"Always trying to get attention!" a girl calls out, and one of the guys flips her off, laughing. She flips him off right back, and her girlfriends laugh and tease the guys.

"Don't need to try!" he calls back, and his buddies laugh. They join up with the girls, and together they all climb the stone stairs leading up to the big double doors.

I feel like somebody put ice in my stomach. I don't think I can do this.

But I have to. I can't run away. Besides, it's only for one year. I can keep my head down for a year if I have to. I know I'll never fit in with any of these people, so I'm not going to bother trying. I'll get my diploma, then get the hell out of here. As far away from my mother as I can. Even the thought of leaving Lucy doesn't bother me as much as it used to, now that I know she'll have a home and a stepfather. He's even talking about getting a nanny for her, which, of course, thrills Mom. Now she really won't have to pay attention to either of us.

Still, no matter how I try to encourage myself, my feet are like lead as I climb the stairs. I feel like I'm walking into my execution.

The inside of the main building is even more impressive than the exterior. It was built more than a hundred and fifty years ago by a wealthy family that founded the town. I look up, craning my neck to see the ceiling of the front lobby, which stretches two stories over my head. Tall windows allow sunshine to stream through and make the polished wood floors glow. There's artwork all over the walls, paintings of men and women who look very important and maybe a little bit bored. I go over to one of them and find a small plaque underneath. One of the school's principals, this one serving from 1952 to 1969. There are fewer women than men, but I guess that shouldn't come as a surprise.

I look for the current principal, whose portrait is the last for obvious reasons. A tall, handsome man with salt-and-pepper hair. Dominic Bradley, it says. He's been the principal for five years. At least now I know who to look for.

I should have thought of drawing myself a map to the main office when I looked over the online version yesterday. The hallway stretches out in three directions, two of which span the eastern and western wings of the main building, while the third juts out straight ahead from the front door. I'm pretty sure the office is in this direction, so I start walking while my eyes soak in everything around me. I would never guess this was a school, at least not from the entrance. It looks more like a museum.

It's a relief to see a sign hanging over one room along the hall. Administration Office. That's where I need to be. I don't have a roster yet, so I have no idea which classes I'm taking or where to find them. This whole thing is so last minute.

Phones are ringing off the hook, and staff members are hustling back and forth. Maybe ten or fifteen people are already waiting when I get there, and they all have a problem. "But my dad already called. I'm not taking Spanish with her. She's a bitch, and she failed me last year because she fucking hates me."

My eyes go wide before I can stop them as the girl at the front of the line shouts at the lady behind the counter. Do people seriously talk to grown-ups that way around here?

I guess so, because the staff member doesn't even seem surprised. "Like I already told you, Jasmine, only so many Spanish teachers in the school teach it at that level. Short of hiring more staff to accommodate you, I'm not sure what you expect us to do. Your father understood that when he spoke to the principal."

"So what? What am I supposed to do? Sit there when I know she hates me?" Before the woman can answer, the girl sweeps an arm over the counter and knocks a cup of pens to the floor. "Screw this place. You're lucky I don't sue."

For what? Meanwhile, she's already halfway down the hall, and I can still hear her shouting about the lawsuit that will end this entire school.

It seems like everybody's got problems like that. There's a guy who can't take physics because it interferes with football practice. There's another who wants to take the same English class her best friend is taking, even though it would change her entire schedule. Everything seems pretty trivial, and every single person threatens a phone call from their parents.

Who the hell are these kids? Mom would laugh in my face if I asked her to call because I didn't like my Spanish teacher or I wanted to take English with my friend. And if she ever got a call from the office saying I cursed out one of the staff, I don't even want to think about how she would react. It would make her look bad, which is the last thing she'd ever put up with.

Finally, it's my turn. I feel so bad for the woman behind the counter, and I grimace. "Sorry to bother you, but this is my first day. I don't have my roster yet."

"Oh, finally. An easy one." She flips through a bunch of papers and pulls out a thin folder. "Morgan Chambers, is it?"

"That's right."

"Welcome, Morgan. I hope you haven't already gotten a bad opinion of this place." Before I can reply, she slides the folder my way. "In there, you'll find your roster and a calendar of activities, and I've included a map to help you get around. It's easy to get lost around here, but you'll figure it out in a few days. Everybody does."

"Thank you." My first class is US history, starting in fifteen minutes.

"Hayes!" she calls out to somebody in the hallway and waves them in over my shoulder. "He's one of our student ambassadors. Hayes, would you mind showing Morgan to her first class? Maybe give her a small tour before class starts?"

"You know me. Always glad to help."

His voice shouldn't be familiar, but it stirs up my memory anyway. I look up from my roster to find a tall, muscular guy standing next to me.

And when our eyes meet, I understand why he sounded familiar. It's been two weeks, but he's never been far from my thoughts.

It's the guy from the bridge.

And judging by the way he's staring at me with those wide, piercing eyes, he hasn't forgotten either.

CHAPTER 4

Oh, my God.

He hasn't moved since he recognized me. Neither have I. In my case, I'm too surprised. I never thought I would see him again.

Him? I can't tell. He doesn't exactly seem happy to see me.

"I'll take it from here, Miss Collins." He flashes a smile her way, and even though she's probably twice his age, she laughs, almost like she's flirting. He's pretty charming when he wants to be.

I follow him out into the hall, staring at the back of his head. Should I mention the bridge? I don't think he was having one of his best moments when he was out there, so maybe I should let it go and pretend it never happened unless he brings it up.

"So you go here." He's not so charming anymore, and I realize that's an act he puts on for adults. He slides his hands into his pockets before looking me up and down. "I wouldn't have guessed." There's something snarky in the way his mouth pulls upward at one corner. I know what he means. He doesn't have to spell it out. I don't belong here.

"I'm a last-minute student. My mom—"

"Nobody asked." So we're back to that, I see. "Anyway, I have history with you, so we can walk there together."

"Should I stop at my locker first?" They listed the locker number on my roster, and there's a key taped to the inside of the folder that I guess I'm supposed to use to unlock it.

"Why are you asking me? I'm supposed to show you to your classroom. That's it." We make a left at the end of the hall, at the big entrance area that's now filled with students, and head to class. The noise is almost enough to give me a headache.

"Hayes! How was your summer?" A girl with waist-length blond hair and a killer tan falls in step next to him, then wraps her arms around his and drops her head to his shoulder. She couldn't get closer if she tried.

I glance up at him and find his jaw twitching like it did at the bridge. What's bothering him now? He's got a hot girl hanging on him. "Fine. How was yours?"

"We spent the whole time in Hawaii with my mom and her boyfriend. It was boring as shit, but the beaches were nice."

"Cool."

She cranes her neck, looking around him so she can study me. "Who are you?" she asks in a sour voice.

I open my mouth, but Hayes does the talking. "New student. I'm showing her to class." I guess I'm not allowed to answer for myself, either.

Her nose wrinkles. "Oh. Good luck." I would ask her what that means, but she stands on tiptoe to murmur something in his ear, then bursts out laughing while very deliberately looking at me. He's snickering by the time she walks away, swinging her hips in a short skirt.

That's how it is the entire way down the long hall. One person after another calls out to him, waving and slapping him on the back. I might as well not be here, and it might be better if I wasn't. Two guys who look like they could be football players practically tackle him and almost knock me over in the attempt. He laughs it off and ignores me like everybody else. Maybe it won't be too hard to hide for the entire year. I pretty much blend into the walls.

"Hayes!" A redhead in a cheerleader's uniform throws herself at him, wrapping her legs around his waist and her arms around his neck. They are obviously not strangers.

This time, he doesn't act like it bothers him. He comes to a stop, laughing, and gives her a hug. "What's up, Salem? You've been MIA for weeks." He sets her back on her feet while she laughs.

"I had stuff going on." She looks me up and down, but at least she's not nasty the way the blonde was. More like genuinely curious. "Who is this? Are you new here?"

He nods toward me. "Yeah, this is her first day. I'm showing her around."

She shoots him a dirty look. "What, she can't speak for herself? I wasn't talking to you." She gives him a playful shove.

"My name is Morgan. Like he said, this is my first day."

"Cool. Well, he's the guy to show you around. He knows pretty much everybody." She turns her attention to him, and her smile fades. "Heads-up. Madison is looking for you."

"Of fucking course she is." He rolls his eyes. "Thanks."

She smiles at me before continuing down the hall. "See you around!"

"Wow. She seems nice."

"Yeah, she's great." But his voice is flat, and he's not looking at me.

"Listen." People might surround us, but no one is paying attention to us right this second. "If you're weirded out, don't worry about it. I won't—"

"Just drop it." Something in his voice tells me I'd better do as he says. Obviously, he's embarrassed about what happened at the bridge. Maybe he really was considering jumping, the way it seemed. Looking at him as he strolls down the hall like a king, I can understand why he might want nobody to know he felt that vulnerable and lost. I can't be mad about his attitude when I look at it that way. If anything, I feel sorry he can't show his true feelings to any of these people who obviously love him.

I check the time on seeing the girl's bathroom up ahead. "We still have a few minutes. I need to..." I point at the room.

"Jesus Christ." He sighs. "Go ahead. But hurry. I'm not going to be late for class because of you."

And that's what I get for maybe saving someone's life.

I duck in and rush for the first stall, pushing the door open without thinking. It wasn't locked, but the stall was not empty.

I fall back in surprise when I realize one of two girls is cutting coke into lines on top of the metal box used to throw out tampons.

"What the fuck are you doing? Get out of here!" The second girl slams the door in my face, and this time, she thinks to lock it.

For a moment, I can only stare at the door in surprise. I've never seen anything like that before, and there were some pretty messed-up kids at my old school. But they would take edibles or soak tampons in vodka to get drunk without teachers knowing, that kind of thing. This is a whole other level.

I rush through peeing, if only to make sure I don't run into either of those girls again. Just before I flush, I recognize the noise coming from the stall to my other side. A look down at the floor shows me a pair of what can only be men's shoes—and a girl on her knees. Holy shit, she's giving him a blow job in the girl's bathroom? While other people are here? I've never done that myself, but I can't imagine kneeling in front of a public toilet is very sexy.

A quick look in the mirror as I'm washing my hands reflects wide, fear-filled eyes. I'm not sure why. Maybe it's the feeling that I got dumped into the deep end of a pool, only I don't know how to swim. I think I'm in way over my head here.

By the time I practically fly out to the hall again, Hayes is talking with another girl, who is leaning against a locker, giggling while she stares adoringly up at him. He leans in, murmuring something close to her ear, then caresses her ass before she walks away. Her mile-wide smile tells me she doesn't mind. Not even close.

He catches my eye, and a smile spreads slowly across his face. It's almost like he's challenging me to react, though, I can't understand why.

I cross the crowded hall. "Okay. Let's go."

He lifts an eyebrow. "Really? That's all you have to say?"

"What else was I supposed to say?"

His smile widens. "I saw a guy from the basketball team go in there before you did. You mean you didn't notice him?"

"No." I lift a shoulder and pretend not to care. I've perfected that over the years. It's easier to keep Mom calm when I'm bland and unaffected. "Maybe he likes peeing in the girl's room. It's probably cleaner."

"You're a good girl, aren't you?" He says it like it's a bad thing, like I disgust him.

"I guess I never thought about it before."

Now he's scowling. "What's your problem?"

I point at myself. "My problem?"

"Yeah. Like, you don't react to anything. I know damn well that guy wasn't in there to take a piss. I saw who he went in with. She's sucked almost every dick in this school."

"It's none of my business."

His eyes flicker over me, and suddenly, I know what he thinks before he even says it. "Since when do you mind your own business? I figured you'd be somebody who sticks their nose in where it doesn't belong all the time."

The hall is emptying out, with people heading into the class-rooms. That's the only reason I have the guts to stand straight and look him dead in the eye. "I didn't know being nice and caring about other people was such a bad thing. Maybe you should try it sometime."

"Oh, no. That's something I never do."

"We both know that's not true. You were nicer than this before."

His eyes go narrow, and I know I crossed a line. "I would watch what I say if I were you. I don't know how things went in the school you're coming from, but you don't want to make enemies here."

"Thanks. I'll keep that in mind."

I don't know what it is. I'm only making him angrier. Does he want to see me break down? Why? I'm about to ask when the bell rings.

"There." He nods toward a room two doors down from where

we're standing. "Class is in there. Go ahead. You don't want to be late on your first day."

Thank God. I don't know if I can stand another minute with this guy. How could I have been so wrong about him? He was sort of mean on the bridge, but I figured that was because of how much he was hurting. He's not hurting now, with people practically falling over themselves to talk to him and get close to him. Maybe I shouldn't have brought it up at all, but that would just be weird. Why should we pretend it never happened? I only wanted him to know it could be our secret if he wanted it to.

I'm still asking myself about this when I push my way through the door Hayes indicated.

"Whoa!" a tall, broad-shouldered guy wearing nothing but a towel around his waist calls out to the rest of what is obviously not a classroom but a locker room. "Looks like Coach wants to reward us for coming in early for practice!"

Out of nowhere come maybe ten other guys, and only some of them are wearing a towel or anything else. I don't know where to look with so many swinging dicks around. My face burns with humiliation, and I finally throw myself out the door again while their whistles and laughs and cheers still ring out.

I lean against the wall, my heart racing, my breath coming in quick gasps. Hayes is gone, and the hallway is almost empty. I'm surprised he didn't stick around to see what would happen.

For some reason, he's decided I'm the enemy he needs to crush under his shoe—and it only pisses him off when I don't react like he wants. I only wish I knew what I did to make him resent me.

The classroom is closer to where Hayes was waiting when I left the bathroom. I was too busy trying to figure him out to notice the number on the door. Now I know better than to trust him, or anybody else around here, to look out for me. From now on, I'll find my own way around.

CHAPTER 5

Somehow, I've made it to my second day at North Woods Prep. Yesterday didn't kill me. I'm hoping I keep the streak going today.

One thing is for sure: I'm not waiting around for Hayes to take me on a tour this time. I don't care that he's a so-called ambassador. He's not worth the humiliation. I didn't look at any of the jocks in the locker room long enough to memorize any of their faces, but I'm pretty sure two of them recognized me in the hall yesterday. There's no other reason for them to look at me the way they did.

After ignoring Hayes in history class—not easy with him staring at the side of my head whenever the teacher isn't looking—I make it to English with a minute to spare. I take a desk near the back of the room, the same one I sat in yesterday. Everybody around me knows each other, so they're all chatting. Nobody pays attention to me. I'm almost glad they don't.

Until somebody slides into the chair next to mine. She's not wearing her cheerleader uniform this time, but I would know her red hair anywhere. It's gorgeous, thick and curly. That, plus her sparkling green eyes, makes me wish I wasn't so boring looking.

"Morgan, right? We met yesterday. I'm Salem." She even sticks her hand out, smiling, her eyes warm. She seemed nice enough yesterday, so I offer a smile while shaking her hand. Maybe not everybody here is secretly a heartless bully.

"So, what do you think about the school? It can be a lot, huh?" She keeps talking as she opens a notebook and pulls out the novel we're supposed to be reading for class. "I remember when I first started here, my first day back in freshman year. By the time I got home, I told my parents I didn't want to ever go back."

"What happened?"

"It's just so intimidating when everybody knows everybody else, which is how it seemed to me. I used to live a few towns over, so I was one of the few people who didn't go to middle school with everybody."

I'm so relieved I could cry. "So it's not just me?"

"No, and now it's worse because everybody has been going to school together for the past three years. But it's okay. You'll find your place."

I recognize the kid in front of her from yesterday. He was one of the guys who got out of the sports car that tore up the front lawn—a great build, wavy black hair and eyes like onyx. If he wasn't grinning, he might look intimidating.

He taps on her desk. "Did you do the reading last night?"

"Excuse you, but I'm talking to my friend Morgan here." She rolls her eyes very dramatically before turning back to me. "This is Theo. He's a real pain in the ass."

"Don't be shocked," he tells me when I try not to laugh. "It's in all my social media bios. A real pain in the ass."

"Don't let him fool you. He's the biggest nerd I know. He even does the homework for some of the guys on the swim team when they're falling behind."

"We can't afford to lose any good swimmers because their grades are slipping." He shrugs. "I'm not the fastest, but I make sure the fastest stay on the team."

"That's really nice of you."

He shrugs again, good-naturedly. "The problem with being a genius. I get bored only doing my work."

"Don't break your arm patting yourself on the back," Salem mutters. Maybe I shouldn't laugh since I don't know either of them, but I can't help it. It finally feels like I've met normal people.

Salem makes sure I know where I'm headed after class before asking, "You have fifth lunch, right?" I nod. "Right, I saw you there yesterday. Come sit with me."

It's like she's reading my mind. I was dreading sitting alone at lunch. She remembers what it means to be the new girl. I hope I'm not a pet project or somebody she'll ditch once she gets bored with me.

* * *

"The first thing you need to know is, the football team likes to break in freshman girls." Salem gives me a look that can only mean one thing. "You're not a freshman, but you're new. So keep that up here." She taps a finger against her temple.

"Believe me. If a random football player asked me out or started acting super nice, I'd know they were full of shit."

She looks me up and down before taking a bite of her salad. "Why would you say that?"

Now I wish I hadn't. "I don't know. I'm not like you. All shiny and pretty."

"You're pretty! And shiny? Shiny, you can buy."

I almost choke on my sandwich before laughing. "Yeah. There's not enough money in the bank for that."

She frowns before spearing more lettuce. "Then why are you here? I mean, it costs a lot of money."

"My mom just got engaged to a rich guy. I don't even know his name. Can you believe that?"

She snorts. "That's nothing. A girl on the squad has never met her stepmom or her twin half-brothers. They live in London, and she keeps hoping they'll invite her out over a break or whatever, but they haven't in four years."

"Ouch. That must hurt."

"She pretends it doesn't." She leans in, waving me closer. "This school is crawling with kids who have fucked-up relationships with their families. I'm on my third stepfather already. At least five or six kids have dads in prison for financial crimes, and a bunch more pretty much take care of themselves because their families are never around. So a guy who's not even your stepdad yet but is willing to pay for your tuition is pretty cool."

"Thanks for setting me straight. You're right." I take a sip of my soda before adding, "But my mom is a complete mess who uses men until there's nothing else she can get out of them."

She laughs like she understands very well. "You'll fit right in."

While we eat, she gossips quietly about people as they pass by. "Chloe, Jasmine, Parker. Their dads are all lawyers for this huge firm, and they think it means they can get away with anything." That explains Jasmine threatening a suit yesterday. All three of them are super pretty, tall and thin, and confident.

"Do they play football?" I nod to a group of huge guys with trays almost overflowing on their way to a table.

"Yeah, and they're obnoxious assholes. They already tried to fuck their way through the entire cheerleading squad."

I can't help but raise an eyebrow.

"Oh, God, no. I have standards." She flips her hair over one shoulder, and I'm pretty sure I want to be her when I grow up.

"You know a lot of people around here?"

"I do. Some, I wish I didn't."

Should I do this? I don't think it matters whether or not I should. I have to. "You seemed pretty close yesterday with that guy showing me around."

"Hayes?" I nod. "We used to be pretty close, yes."

"You dated?"

"Sort of." When I keep staring at her, she shrugs. "We hooked up for a while between sophomore and junior year. We were already friends before that, and we're still friends."

My stomach's tight all of a sudden. "He seems popular."

"The girls want to fuck him. The guys want to be his best friend."

She tips her head to the side. "Maybe some of them want to fuck him, too."

"He was kind of rude."

"Don't let that get to you. He has this thing around him, like a wall. He wasn't always like that, but he would rather die than open up. That's most guys, though."

I notice a familiar girl walking past a few rows down. "Who's that?"

Her nose wrinkles. "Madison Clark. She's gross."

"I met her yesterday. I don't think she likes me very much."

"She doesn't like anybody, including herself." She follows Madison's progress with her eyes. "Maybe Hayes. She thinks she does, anyway."

"Is she the one you were telling Hayes to look out for?"

"I warned him not to hook up with her, but he always knows better than everybody else." She lifts a shoulder, picking through what's left of her salad. "Now she's obsessed or something. I hope she gives good head, at least."

I'm getting a real education today. It's a shame lunch is almost over.

"I better go," I say. "My chem class is, like, all the way on the other end of the school. I don't want to be late."

"Here. Give me your number." I might be glowing as I hand her my phone. Did I actually make a friend? And she seems like she'd be the right friend to have. She knows people, and she knows how things go around here. I need that.

We promise to text later before I get my stuff together and leave. The halls are pretty much empty right now. Maybe I need a hall pass, but I can always pretend I didn't know any better if anybody catches me.

I round a corner, then freeze when I recognize Hayes further down the hall. He's talking with another guy who I recognize as one of Theo's friends from outside. "Man, listen to me." He touches Hayes's shoulder, but Hayes flings his hand off.

"Don't act like you know anything about what it's like." Hayes turns away from him. I back around the corner before he sees me but can't help but peer out at him. I should walk away, but I can't. Does this other guy know about the bridge?

"I walked in and saw it happening with my own eyes. You can't let it keep happening when it's doing this to you."

"What am I supposed to do?" Hayes mutters.

"Tell somebody. Tell your dad."

"Right. When he's even in town."

"He could do something about it, though. You know he would if you would just tell him about this. You can stop it from happening ever again."

Stop what from happening? I figured Hayes had something going on. A secret something he doesn't want to show anybody who knows him. That's probably why he has a problem with me being here. I remind him of whatever made him go out to the bridge.

But this guy knows, too. Even he can't get through to Hayes. Whatever this is, it's something he's determined to keep hidden. What could it be? What's that serious—or shameful? Something somebody could walk in on.

Only one thing comes to mind. Is he being abused by somebody? Maybe sexually? No, that doesn't make sense. He's a strong, healthy guy. He could fight almost anybody off.

What if he doesn't feel like he can? Like if it's somebody who has power or authority? A teacher?

Their voices are lower now, and I can hardly hear. I lean out a little farther, straining my ears.

And I end up bumping against a locker.

Hayes' head snaps around, his eyes landing on me before I can pull my head back and run away. "Hey. What the fuck do you think you're doing?"

Shit, shit, shit. I have to get away, but there's nowhere to go. All the classroom doors are closed, and there isn't a bathroom anywhere close by to run to. There's a closet across from where I'm standing, though. I make a break for it—but I'm not fast enough.

"What the fuck are you doing?" Hayes almost slams me into the wall next to the door when he catches me. "Eavesdropping? Spying on me?"

"No. No, I didn't mean to—"

He snarls in my face, and for a second, I'm actually afraid he'll bite me. He looks that feral right now.

Instead, he does something worse.

He shoves me into the closet and follows me in, the resounding sound of the lock clicking into place.

CHAPTER 6

*I*t all happens so fast, too fast for me to react before it's too late to stop him.

The closet is dark and small, and the stench of cleaning supplies is thick enough to make me gag. All of this goes through my head in the second it takes Hayes to shove me up against a row of metal shelves, and I wince as pain radiates up my spine. Bottles and cans shake behind my head, but not enough to fall over.

"What did you hear?" His hand is around my throat, holding me in place. It's too dark for me to make out his full features, but I feel his eyes on me. We're so close our noses are almost touching. His breath is hot, coming in short bursts that make me think of an animal ready to attack. "Tell me," he grits out through his teeth.

"Nothing… I… I didn't hear anything," I stutter.

"That's a fucking lie. You were listening to us. Because you can't mind your own fucking business." He pulls me an inch or two away from the shelf before slamming me against it again, and this time, a handful of cans roll off and hit the floor. I'm sure my heart would do the same if it wasn't contained inside my body. He pays the cans no attention, and all I can think is, somebody is going to hear us eventually, right? If not, then I need a plan.

Grasping for any type of response, I say, "I was only trying to find my next class."

"And how were you going to get there when you were hiding around the corner from where I was having a private conversation, huh? Do you think I'm fucking stupid?" A part of me wishes it wasn't so dark in here so I could see his face, while the other part of me is terrified to see the look in his eyes.

"You know I won't tell anyone." A moment passes.

"So, you heard."

"You know I won't say anything," I insist. "I swear. You know you can trust me."

His growl makes the hair on the back of my neck stand up. "That's bullshit. I don't fucking know you at all. We don't know each other."

I want to tell him how wrong he is, but I don't know if he would even listen or if he's too far gone into a rage. I do know him. I understood him. And even now, I see through the mask he wears for everybody else at school. I see the real person underneath, and that person is scared and lonely. All I want is to make it so he never has to feel lonely again. Is that so bad?

He leans in closer, and now our noses are touching. More than that, too. His body presses against mine, hard and unforgiving. It isn't easy to breathe. "Listen to me. I'm going to tell you something, and you're going to do exactly as I say. You got it?"

"Yes," I gasp against the hand at my throat.

"You're not going to say anything about what you heard out there. Not to anybody. Ever. Got it?" I jerk my chin a little since I can't move my head enough to nod. "And when we see each other around school, you're not going to act like this happened. We don't know each other. We're strangers. Understood?"

This is all wrong. I understand why he'd be like this, but I can't pretend it feels right. "Is somebody hurting you?"

"Goddammit!" He pounds the side of his fist against the shelving hard enough to bring tears to my eyes. "Don't do that. Don't you fucking do that. You don't know what's going on. It's none of your fucking business."

"I only wanted to help." I don't know what I'm thinking. There has to be some way to get through to him. That's why I reach out and touch my fingertips to his cheek. "Please, just let me—"

I can breathe again, but that's only because Hayes lets go of my throat so he can take my wrists and pin them over my head. "Don't touch me. Don't ever fucking touch me." His whole body is shaking. Even his voice is. I've never seen anyone so close to going over the edge, but he's fighting to keep from falling over.

"I'm sorry."

"Didn't anybody ever tell you it's not right to touch people without asking? Or maybe you like that. Is that what it is? Do you like having somebody touch you without permission?" He crosses my wrists over each other and holds them tight with one hand while the other encircles my throat again. This time, he squeezes hard enough to make me choke a little.

And he laughs softly when I do. "Not so nice, is it?" He lets go, and I gulp in as much air as I can. He laughs again at my distress before his hand begins a slow journey down my chest. Now my heart is a hammer, thudding so hard I can barely hear anything over the sound of it in my ears.

"What are you doing?" I whisper, trembling, when a dozen different scenarios tear through my panicking brain.

"What do you think?" He cups my boob, gentle at first, but then squeezes hard enough to make me suck in a surprised gasp through clenched teeth. "Not so much fun when you're on this side of it, is it?"

"I wasn't trying to hurt you."

"And I'm not trying to hurt you either. I'm only teaching you a lesson." His grip loosens, but that doesn't do anything to make me feel better.

"I don't need you to teach me a lesson."

"Oh, but it's obvious you do. Because you can't leave well enough alone. You couldn't just turn around and go the other way, could you?" Now his hand travels lower, grazing my stomach and making the muscles jump under my skin. He chuckles. "Sensitive, huh?"

"I get it, okay? You made your point." I try to squirm away, but he won't stop grazing my stomach, almost tickling me. Only it's not funny. It's torture.

"I say when I've made my point." Just like that, his touch goes from feather-light to almost painful. He grips my hip, pressing it against the shelves, and I feel his fingers digging into my flesh, even through layers of clothing. "Understood?"

"Understood," I whisper, even though I don't understand anything. Where is this coming from? Why is he doing this?

"No," he whispers, his face close to mine again. Almost close enough to kiss, but that has to be the last thing on his mind. "I don't think you get it. I don't think you're the kind of person who learns a lesson easily. Or else you would have taken the fucking hint and left me alone after yesterday. Why won't you just leave me alone?"

"I will from now on. I swear."

"Maybe I have to make sure you will. Is that it? Do I have to scare you enough that you won't look at me anymore?" The hand around my wrists tightens hard enough that I would swear my bones are grinding together.

"Let go of me."

"Not until you learn your lesson." It's like he's possessed. Like he can't even hear me. He has only one thing on his mind, and nobody will distract him from that.

I almost sigh in relief when he lets go of my hip—only to stiffen again when he tries to slide his fingers between my closed thighs. The panic in my head turns to full-blown horror. "Stop it." I hold them closed as tight as I can, though, it doesn't matter. He works his way between them before pressing the heel of his hand against my covered pussy.

"What?" he asks when I gasp. "I'm not hurting you, am I? I can't be. I'm hardly touching you."

"I want this to stop."

"Do you?" He brushes his chest against mine, and I can't believe it when my nipples harden. What's he trying to do to me? Does he even know he's doing it? Can he feel them?

I think he can. The strip of light coming from under the door is enough to show me the outline of his face now that my eyes have adjusted, and he's smiling. "Your body's telling another story. Isn't it funny how that happens? Your brain can tell you one thing, but your body will always betray you. It has a mind of its own."

The pressure from his hand increases, and now he's rubbing a little. And he's right. I hate him for being right and for the way he's starting to make me wet. I don't want this to happen, but my body has a mind of its own, like he said.

He chuckles, and it's a nasty, knowing sound. "That's right. I told you I wouldn't hurt you, and I know this doesn't hurt. It feels good, doesn't it?"

"I don't like it."

"Liar." He comes so close to touching his lips to my throat. The feeling of his breath blowing over my skin makes me shiver while it makes him laugh softly. "Told you so. I could make you come here in this closet if I wanted to. I wouldn't even have to try."

I grit my teeth and shake my head. "No. No, you couldn't."

"Is that a dare?"

"No." I turn my face away and squeeze my eyes shut. Why won't he stop? Why won't anybody stop this? Where did his friend go? The bell's going to ring soon. Why won't it ring?

"I want you to remember this." He finally pulls his hand from between my legs so he can use it to turn my face toward his, jerking hard so I can't fight back. "The next time you decide to be where you don't belong, listening to shit that doesn't concern you, I want you to remember how easy it was for me to get you alone and do any damn thing I want to you."

He leans so close that our lips almost touch. "And I want you to remember how much you loved it." With that, he shoves me one last time, making the back of my head tap the metal shelf hard enough to sting.

That's what it takes. The haze of confusion that's kept me frozen in place breaks in time for me to get in one last thing. "Lots of people go through things that hurt them. But that isn't an excuse to hurt other people because of it."

He grunts, backing toward the door. "And you think that's why I did this?"

"I do. I know it is."

"Then I guess you don't know me as well as you thought. If you know what's good for you, you should keep it that way." He opens the door and strides out into the hall without glancing at me or saying another word.

A second later, the bell screeches, and voices fill the hall outside the closet.

But I haven't moved. I can't move. He's nowhere near me, yet I'm still frozen in fear. Not of him—I don't believe he'd ever hurt me—but of whatever makes him this way. It has to be something awful and something he's deeply ashamed of. Why else would he go to all the trouble to scare me?

I have no choice but to pull myself together and leave the closet before I get written up for being late to class. The hall's so full that nobody notices me sliding out through the barely open door and blending into the crowd. They're all laughing, talking, and shouting things to each other as they pass.

We might as well be living in two different worlds.

In their world, Hayes is a swim captain. The guy everyone likes. I bet girls are walking past me right now who wish they had the chance to spend a few minutes in a small closet with him, who wish they still felt the pressure from his hands on their bodies. Even now, I'm wet and aching, and it's enough to make me ashamed of myself. I didn't want him to be right. I still don't. But there was nothing I could do to control it.

He's right about something else, too. I need to leave him alone before he takes things too far next time.

No matter how much a part of me wants him to.

CHAPTER 7

When I reach the hotel room, the only thing I want is to put on pajamas, crawl under the blankets, and not come out until morning. I don't even want to play with Lucy, and she usually brightens up my lowest moods.

I don't think I've ever had a mood lower than the one I'm in now. I've never had somebody practically spit in my face when all I was trying to do was be their friend. I've had nobody do to me what Hayes did in that closet. The sense of being out of control, totally at his mercy, makes me shiver even now.

And when I remember how my body reacted without me wanting it too, I could die from shame. I didn't mean to get excited. I couldn't help it. Now, every time I see him, he'll remember that. I guess we both have something to be ashamed of.

Even now, I want to help him with whatever he's going through. Knowing he'd rather be cruel and hateful than let me in isn't enough to make me stop wanting to help. What is wrong with me that I still care? Don't I already get enough shit from my mother?

I slide the key card into the door lock and wait for the light to go from red to green before turning the handle. And for the second time in a little over two weeks, I step into the middle of a raging storm.

One my mother stands in the center of. "Finally, you're back. What time do they let you out of that school?" She doesn't wait for an answer before darting back to the bedroom, but then I don't think she was really asking.

"I came right after last period."

The desk drawers are open and empty. The hangers in the armoire are empty, too. Our bags are stacked on the sofa, the ones on top still hanging open with items spilling out.

Lucy launches herself at me, wrapping her arms around my legs. "We're going home!" She's practically bursting with excitement, bouncing up and down until it's almost enough to knock me off balance.

"Take it easy," I laugh, disentangling myself before following Mom into the bedroom. "Is that true? We're leaving?"

"Yes, thank the gods, and I really could have used your help getting things together." I pass the bathroom doorway in time to see her sweeping makeup into a bag. "Look under the beds. Make sure we're not leaving anything."

"Where are we going?"

"Morgan, I swear to God. For once, just do what I say." I leave her muttering under her breath, getting on my hands and knees and peering under the beds. Aside from a few of Lucy's dolls, nothing is left. I pull them out and, finding everything else stuffed already, tuck them into my backpack.

"But where are we going? Are they kicking us out?"

Mom bursts out laughing, shaking her head and giving me a funny look as she passes by. "Where do you come up with some of these ideas? No, we're not getting kicked out. Why would we? Your father is paying for everything."

Not my father. Not even my stepfather yet. It has taken her no time at all to slide into the role of his wife. I have to bite my tongue hard enough to hurt. "Does this mean we're moving in with him now?"

"There's that brain of yours."

Lucy bounces into the room. "We're going to the big house! And we'll have our own bedrooms, and there's a pool and everything!"

"That's super exciting!" I give her a quick hug, even if I feel less than excited. More like confused by how quickly this is all happening. "Now, you have to make sure you take everything, okay? I have Elsa and Anna in my backpack. You know, they were under the bed. They almost got left here."

Her eyes go round. "You saved them."

"That's right, honey. They're safe now." I wish I was her age again. The only thing she has to worry about is making sure she has all her toys. "Can you believe it? You're going to have your own bedroom. I wonder if you'll be able to pick out the furniture and stuff."

"I'm sure someone has arranged all of that." Mom goes through the dresser drawers one last time. "Honestly, Morgan. Try not to get her hopes up too high."

I can't say anything right. "I bet you'll love it," I whisper, and my sister beams. It's so easy being around her. I don't have to work to make her love me the way I do with my mother. And for all the work, it hasn't made a bit of a difference.

"All of your things are already in the bags, in case you were wondering." I don't miss the condescending tone of her voice. "Also, you're welcome." I watch as she closes the dresser drawers with a sigh, biting the inside of my cheek to stop me from responding. "That's everything. Are you girls ready to go?"

Ready to go? I just got here, I want to say, but I'm definitely ready to be out of this hotel for good. "I guess so. Right?" I look at Lucy, who nods her little head. Wisps of hair fly into her face.

Mom looks down at her, shaking her head. A look of disgust shimmers in her eyes. "You look like you just rolled out of bed." She searches through her purse and pulls out a hairbrush, thrusting it my way. "Morgan, call down to the front desk and tell them we're ready to have the bags taken down to the car and make sure her hair gets brushed. I don't want us looking like slobs."

"There's a car?" I ask, shocked, completely ignoring her insult. I learned a long time ago not to let things my mother says bother me. At this point, I'm pretty sure I've grown immune to her insults.

She rolls her amber-colored eyes. "No, we're walking. Would I say there was if there wasn't one? Yes, it's waiting, and I'm sure the driver is getting impatient." I make the call while brushing my sister's hair. I know better than to let Mom do it when she's in this kind of mood, all amped up, full of piss and vinegar.

When we walk out of the hotel, a sleek black car pulls up within minutes, and a heavy-set man climbs out of the driver's seat to grab our bags. "I'll take those," he says.

Before I can respond, my mother ushers us into the back seat, and I barely have time to take one last look at the hotel that's been our home for months. Not that I'll miss it or anything like that. I knew this was coming, but it still feels awfully sudden. I already felt shaky and unsure of myself when I got back from school, so this isn't helping.

Still, it's easy to feel happy when Lucy is practically glowing. She has a million questions, and now that there's a witness in the car, Mom is happy to indulge them. "You're going to have so much room to run around and play. And Bridget will be there. You like her, right?"

"Yeah, she knows lots of fun games and does silly voices when she reads to me."

"Her room will be right next to yours, so she'll never be far if you ever need anything." I have to bite my tongue and look out the window rather than ask where Mom plans on being when Lucy needs something. She'd rather have the nanny handle it.

She must be in a very good mood because she even turns her smile on me. "And you'll finally have all the free time you want. No more babysitting."

"But we'll still play together," I tell Lucy in case she gets the wrong idea. Our mother might be ditching her, but I'm not. She'll never have to wonder if I love her.

"Of course, of course." Mom types something on her phone. "He's so excited about this. It's adorable." She looks and sounds happier than I can remember her ever being. It's almost enough to make me think this could work. Maybe I haven't been giving her enough credit. She's selfish and self-centered, but maybe she found the right person who can wake her up and pull her out of that.

There's almost hope in my heart by the time we roll through a very fancy, expensive-looking neighborhood. Lucy's eyes are almost bulging out of her head, and I sort of feel the same way. These aren't houses we're riding past. They're mansions with three-car garages, pools, and fountains. These aren't regular people's homes. They're celebrity homes.

Just like the mansion in front of us when the driver pulls the car up a long, curved driveway.

"This is it?" I whisper. It's enormous, like something out of a movie. The outside is white, so clean it almost sparkles in the sun. Four thick columns stretch up to the roof, jutting out over the front of the house. Beautifully maintained bushes and trees are every-where. Around the side of the house, I see what looks like a garden full of roses and other colorful flowers.

But it's the size of the place that takes my breath away. "All this house, just for him?" I murmur. It's unbelievable.

"I told you there would be plenty of room." Mom cranes her neck to look at us sitting in the back seat. "Now, I don't think I need to remind you to be on your best behavior, but I will anyway. I'm sure your father will want the house to feel like yours but be polite. Lucy, no running around, screaming. And Morgan..."

"Yes?"

"Just try to stay out of trouble." She would have to say something like that just as I was starting to feel a little bit of happiness. Like I've ever been any trouble to her.

My soon-to-be stepfather strides out from the towering front door as we pull to a stop in the circular courtyard. "There you are. Welcome home." He's so happy when we get out of the car. "We've been so excited to have you here, finally. I'm only sorry it took this long to get everything settled."

Mom practically swoons in his arms. "Never mind. We were all comfortable at the hotel."

"Yes," I add with a smile. "Thank you for that. It was so nice."

Mom wrinkles her nose at me, but her face is turned away from his so he can't see her expression.

"It was my pleasure. Come in. Let me show you around."

I feel like I should play it cool, but I can't keep my mouth from falling open when we step inside the house. "Wow," I breathe, admiring the marble floor in the entry and the sweeping staircase leading up to the second floor. To my right is a big, bright room with an enormous TV that takes up half the wall. It's more like a movie screen. To my left, there's a dining room with a long, polished wooden table and more chairs than I can count as we walk past. Beyond that is a kitchen bigger than our old apartment, filled with shining appliances and a pair of middle-aged women chopping and mixing something.

"Charlotte and Sarah are our live-in chefs," he explains. "They'll prepare all the meals, and they always leave plenty of snacks in the fridge if anybody gets hungry late at night."

Both women smile, instantly charmed by my exuberant sister. Everybody is. They can't help it. Meanwhile, I can't get over the idea of somebody doing all my cooking for me. Not that I ever fixed more than the basics for Lucy when we were on our own at the apartment, but still. It's almost like being a princess or something.

"Girls, I understand you like to swim. The pool is this way." He leads us to the back of the house, where a long row of tall windows allows a perfect view of a large backyard with thick, green grass and a pool twice the size of the one at the hotel. "There's a tennis court, and the guesthouse is back there, too. Lucy, maybe we can find a swing set you'd like to have set up."

Mom rests her head on his shoulder, stroking his arm while she sighs softly. "Sweetheart, you're spoiling her already."

"Why not? I always wished I had a daughter. Now, I'll have two." I can't help but like him, and I only hope Mom doesn't find a way to screw this up. He seems genuinely happy and eager to please us.

He leads us out to the stairs, ready to show us our bedrooms. "Bridget is already upstairs, getting settled in. She'll have the room between Lucy's and Morgan's. And your brother will be across the hall."

Lucy picks up on it before I do. "Brother? We have a brother?"

I look at Mom, raising an eyebrow. She waves a hand, chuckling. "I thought I would save that as a surprise. Yes, you're going to have a brother. We're all going to be one big, happy family."

I'm about to ask how old he is, what his name is, and anything else about him, but the opening of the front door grabs my attention first.

Mom's fiancé turns toward the door, smiling from ear to ear. "Here he is. Son, meet your new sisters."

As soon as our gazes collide, my insides light on fire. *No.* This can't be happening. I'm not seeing this correctly.

Considering the way he comes to a dead stop with the door wide open, his features riddled with confusion, I'm guessing Hayes was just as in the dark as I was this whole time.

But somehow, I can't feel even a little bad for him because not only is Hayes Ambrose dead set on making my life miserable because I heard something I shouldn't have, but he's also now going to be my stepbrother. Could this day get any worse?

CHAPTER 8

"Morgan, you've been awfully quiet. Is everything all right?" Mr. Ambrose sets down his knife and fork, and his dazzling smile reaches me across the table. "I can have Charlotte fix you something else if this doesn't agree with you."

"Oh, no, this is great. It's delicious." And it is. I don't think I've ever had roasted chicken this tasty. The potatoes and vegetables are good enough that even Lucy seems to love them. "It's like eating at a nice restaurant."

"Do you eat at a lot of nice restaurants?" Hayes mutters from across the table, his remark clearly meant as an insult.

"The restaurant at the hotel was nice," Lucy chimes in. "They always had chicken fingers." Lucky kid. She has no idea. To my surprise, his lips twitch a little, like he's about to smile. He bites it back before it forms, though, glaring at me before staring down at his plate.

He's what's wrong with me right now. If it wasn't for the way he's spent the entire time glaring at me, I would eat until my stomach hurt. Right now, it's almost all I can do to chew and swallow. It's easier to push food around on my plate and wonder how the hell I'm supposed to get through this.

My stepbrother. We're going to have to live in the same house together.

"So tell me, Hayes." Mom picks up her glass of wine, swirling it a little as she speaks. "Your father told me you're the captain of the swim team. Is it true you might be in competition for a college scholarship?"

"Yeah." He doesn't even glance up at her.

"We should go to one of your swim meets. I'm sure Morgan would like to go." Mom turns my way, her lips turned up into a smile. "Right? It would be good for you to meet more people at school, as well."

"That's not necessary." Hayes shakes his head.

"Hayes, it will be a good way for Morgan to get to know everybody at school. Don't you want her to have the same experience you have?"

All Hayes does is snort at his dad's suggestion. I look down at my plate and wish I were anywhere in the world but here. I want to sink into the floor and never come back. How many of these family dinners will we have to suffer through? I'm not even sure I'll make it through this one.

"How are you liking school?" Mr. Ambrose asks in a slightly tighter voice than before. He's trying. I have to give him credit for that.

"It's big." I have to giggle a little at myself. "But I managed not to get lost so far. I met a really nice girl today, and she seems like she wants to be friends."

"Really?" Hayes interjects, his interest piques as he looks up from his plate. "Who?"

Great. Maybe I shouldn't have said anything. "Salem."

Mr. Ambrose smiles. "Salem's a nice girl. She's been here a few times, hasn't she, son?"

Hayes lifts an eyebrow, ignoring his father's comment. "You? Friends with Salem?"

I know better than to give in to his antics, but I can't help it.

"Yeah. We have English together, and we're sitting together at lunch."

"Oh, best friends forever." He rolls his eyes, then snickers before going back to pushing his food around the way I'm doing to mine.

"What else do you like to do, Hayes? Your dad makes it sound like you're pretty popular at school." Mom is turning on the full charm for her fiancé's sake, something that is painfully obvious to me but might not be so obvious to somebody who doesn't know her the way I do. The poor guy looks so happy. I can't get over how happy he looks. I almost feel bad knowing how things have ended for all the other men who thought they could hook their claws into my mother and make her stay.

Hayes, meanwhile, is anything but happy. He lifts a shoulder, not bothering to look at her. "I guess so. I know a lot of people."

"Hayes, don't act like we've never had a guest before." Mr. Ambrose grins across the table at Mom. "Even if none of them have ever been your future stepmother."

"I would love it so much if you would call me Mom," my mother adds at exactly the wrong moment.

His head snaps up, fury in his eyes. "No. I'm never calling you Mom." He pounds his fist on the table for effect, making us all jump along with the silverware and glasses. Poor Lucy whimpers, her eyes welling up with tears. Me? I've seen how quickly his mood can change, so I'm not the slightest bit surprised.

"Hayes!" his father scolds.

"No, you can sit here and play happy family, but I'll be damned if I do it. Does anybody but me see how fucked up this is?" Before anybody can call him on it, his eyes find Lucy, and it's like he realizes his mistake. "Sorry," he mutters.

"That's unacceptable. Apologize," his father demands.

"I just did."

"You know what I mean."

Hayes slides a side-eye look at Mom. "Sorry."

"I understand. It was probably wrong of me to push for that so soon. It's only that I'm so excited to have a son. A family. It's been a long time and a long road for us." I swear, if anybody didn't know better, they would think my mother was some kind of saint. She's practically glowing, sitting at the head of the kitchen table rather than the long one in the formal dining room. It's a little big in there for just the five of us. Even this table is set with candles and a floral centerpiece and what has to be a silk tablecloth. It's so nice I almost don't want to touch it.

And Mom is in her element. This is exactly the sort of life she's always wanted— o live in luxury without having to lift a finger to earn it. I'm so embarrassed that I could throw up. Why does she have to lay it on so thick? No wonder Hayes flipped out.

Mr. Ambrose clears his throat. "I hope you girls get settled in well and have everything you need. Next week, your mother and I will be taking a trip, just the two of us."

My stomach sinks as I lift my eyes, only to find Hayes looking my way. "How long will you be gone?" he asks, though he's staring at me.

"A full week."

A full week? I can't help but sputter a little as I turn toward Mom. "Where are you going?"

"Since when are you so curious?" she asks with a tight little laugh. I know that laugh. It means I should shut up and stop asking questions.

"I was just wondering. I mean, with only Bridget here..."

"It isn't as if your father and I won't be busy doing our own things most of the time, anyway. He'll be at work much of the time, and I'll have my own activities."

Activities. I have to bite my tongue and look down at my plate before my face gives me away. She means shopping, going to the spa, probably forcing her way into brunches nobody wants her to attend. I have no doubt she'll do everything she can to ingratiate herself in her fiancé's world, which she'll see as her world now. And I thought she was hard to deal with before this.

"I'm sure you'll manage just fine without us. Hayes will be busy with his swim practice, and I'm sure Morgan will have plenty of things to do with her new friends." Hayes barely stifles a snort at his father's suggestion, but I hear it. And I know what he's thinking. I don't have friends. Not yet. Not ever, if he has his way.

"I'm finished." Hayes pushes back from the table abruptly, tossing his napkin to the chair before shoving it back in place. "I'm going up to my room to do homework." The pressure in my chest loosens. If he's not here, he can't glare at me like I ruined his life or something. I might actually be able to eat a little bit.

Of course, Mom has to ruin it. She stands suddenly, blocking Hayes from leaving the room. "I'm sorry if I said something to upset you."

"Don't worry about it." He looks down at the floor, shoulders hunched up around his ears.

"It's just that your father and I want everyone to be happy. I'm sure I came on a little too strongly. Can you forgive me?"

"Yeah. Sure." Obviously, he's only doing it because his father is staring at the two of them, but at least he's trying. This can't be any easier on him than it is on me. Only Lucy is genuinely thrilled.

"Friends?" Mom opens her arms, offering a tiny smile.

"Go ahead, son," his father encourages. Meanwhile, I could just about die from embarrassment. Does she ever know when to stop? I'm sure Mr. Ambrose already thinks she walks on water. She doesn't need to keep playing this role.

Hayes opens his arms, and all I can think about is how he doesn't like to be touched. This must be killing him inside. Mom puts her arms around him, and he barely touches her shoulders before pulling away.

"He'll come around," Mr. Ambrose assures Mom as she sits back down.

Hayes leaves the room without another word.

"Excuse me. I'll be right back." I hop out of my chair and hurry out of the room, hoping to catch him before he gets upstairs. He's almost at the foot of them when I reach out to touch his shoulder just enough to get his attention without my voice carrying to the kitchen.

"I'm sorry—" I start, but I don't have a chance to say the rest before he spins on his heel and shoves me up against the wall hard enough to knock the wind out of me.

"I told you. Don't fucking touch me," he mutters through clenched teeth as he pins me to the wall with his body. "I might have to play nice with your mother, but that doesn't change anything. Got it?"

"I only wanted to apologize for her. I know she is—"

"Nobody asked you to apologize."

"But she's impossible, and I am sorry. Whether or not you want to hear it."

"I can handle my own shit. Why don't you get a fucking life and stay out of mine?" He presses himself against me so tight that I can hardly breathe. When I try to suck in air, he only sneers in disgust. How can someone so handsome make their face look so ugly when they want to?

"I kind of don't have a choice anymore," I remind him in a choked whisper. "If we have to live together, why not at least try to be friends?"

He bares his teeth in a snarl that makes my blood run cold. "How many times do I have to say it? I don't want to be your fucking friend. I don't need shit from you, and I don't want your pathetic apologies. Just leave me the fuck alone, or else you will regret it."

"I don't want to be your enemy."

"Too fucking bad. We don't always get to choose these things."

It's so frustrating that I could cry. He's determined not to hear me. "But if we have to live together, can't we at least try to get along? I did not know until I saw you come through the door that I would even have a stepbrother. I'm sorry if you were surprised, too."

He takes me by the throat like he did at school, looking down the hall to make sure nobody can see before leaning in close. "There you go again, making apologies that aren't yours to make. I'm fine. I don't need your fucking protection, and I don't want your fucking apologies. Leave me alone. The only way we'll get along is if you stay the fuck out of my life. Got it?"

"But how can I do that if we have to live here together?"

"It's a big house," he points out with a snicker. "Just stay out of my way. Or else you'll see what happens when I stop playing nice."

I can't help it. "This is you playing nice?"

His eyelids flutter like the question knocked him off balance, but he recovers quickly. "Believe me. You don't want to find out the hard way just how nice I'm being right now. I will destroy your fucking world unless you stay out of my way." He lets go of my throat but gives me another shove before stomping up the stairs.

I know better than to follow him. Instead, I sit down and put my head in my hands. I thought it was bad enough when all I had to deal with was seeing Hayes at school, but now our parents want us to play happy family. He can tell himself all he wants that we can avoid each other, but I know it's not going to be easy, not with Mom so desperate to keep her new man happy.

Besides, even with him acting the way he is, I can't help but want to get through to him. He's hurting, it's obvious, even if he doesn't want to admit it. And I've never been good at ignoring somebody when they're hurt—maybe because I know what it feels like to have my pain ignored.

I will destroy your fucking world unless you stay out of my way. I don't even want to know what that means. What I do know is our parents won't stop trying to get us to act like a family, no matter what Hayes wants.

How am I supposed to get through this without everything blowing up in my face?

CHAPTER 9

I don't notice how much my concentration has strayed until Lucy snuggles against me on the oversized, deep sofa in what Mr. Ambrose refers to as the media room. The latest animated movie is playing on the big screen. I didn't even know it was available to watch at home yet. Maybe for rich people, it doesn't matter.

I stroke her hair absentmindedly. Bridget is seated at the other end of the sofa, reading a book. I don't blame her. She's supposed to keep an eye on Lucy. That doesn't mean she has to enjoy watching Pixar movies. She seems nice enough, maybe in her mid-thirties, with the motherly vibe a four-year-old needs. She's also kind of plain-looking, a little overweight, and she wears baggy, shapeless clothes. I doubt Mom would ever admit it, but something tells me she wanted a woman less attractive than her.

I can't even blame her for that. Her fiancé is handsome and super rich and could have any woman he wanted, I'm sure. I haven't been to many places, and I know there's a lot I haven't seen yet, but even I know stories about nannies and employers having affairs. Mom would want to make sure that doesn't happen.

It's like my mother hears me thinking about her. "Don't you have anything better to do than sit here and watch a movie?" she asks on entering the room. Maybe she forgot about Bridget being there, or maybe she's so deep in the habit of criticizing that she forgot herself for a minute. I look up at her in time to see her expression change from irritation to a motherly smile. "You have this whole house to explore and a bedroom to set up the way you want it. You don't have to chain yourself to your sister."

"I know. I'll go up soon." I doubt she would understand if I tried to explain, and I know better than to waste my breath. Just because Lucy has a nanny doesn't mean I'm going to abandon her. This house seems huge enough to me. What must it seem like to a little kid? I want her to know she's still important.

Besides, even setting up my bedroom isn't enough to take Hayes off my mind. Since dinner, he hasn't come downstairs that I know of, which is a good thing. But what am I supposed to do, walk on eggshells the rest of my life? Or at least for the rest of the year, until we go to college? Always having to look over my shoulder and make sure he's nowhere near? Maybe we should set up a schedule for who gets to use the kitchen when.

That sounds ridiculous, but what's the alternative? Getting slammed into a wall every day? He's never hurt me, not the kind of hurt that lasts once the moment has passed, but when his eyes harden, it's almost terrifying. There's something dark and unpredictable inside him.

So dark, it's almost easy to forget about the boy on the bridge. His eyes were hard, too, but they softened. There was sadness in him. I almost wish we had never met that morning because it's the sadness that keeps me wanting to get through to him. I know there's somebody good inside. What I don't know is why he's so determined to hide that part of himself.

"You don't want to look ungrateful, do you?"

It's obvious Mom's not going to let this go. I shrug at my sister before getting up, grateful Mom doesn't follow me up the stairs. Another thing I'm going to have to get used to is performing for my stepfather or face her blaming me for every little thing that goes wrong between them. I've been there before and don't feel like going back.

At the top of the stairs, I can go either left or to the right. To the left are two guest rooms, and the master suite at the end. To the right, there's Lucy's room, Bridget's, and mine. In that order.

Across from my room is Hayes's. The door is closed, thank God. I tiptoe anyway, afraid to make too much noise before ducking into my room and closing the door without making a sound.

Now I can breathe. I lean against the door, looking around at what is the biggest and prettiest bedroom I've ever seen. It may be a little cliché, with its pink bedding and curtains, but it was nice of Mr. Ambrose to make it feel homey for me when I got here. If he asked Mom what I liked so he could add it, I doubt she would've known what to tell him.

There's an enormous desk, a vanity with a mirror lined in lights, and shelves I can't wait to fill with books. I unpack my clothes and change into pajamas before barely filling up half of the long dresser and walk-in closet. I wonder if I'll ever feel like I fit in this life.

I wonder if I'll ever feel comfortable trying to settle in. I can't help it. I've already seen how what looks like a good relationship can fall apart. That's what's keeping me from relaxing into this new world. That, and how it was thrown at me all last minute.

I have my own private bathroom, too. That's probably the best part of this whole thing, knowing I'll have a shower and bathtub all to myself whenever I want to use them. There's a bottle of bubble bath sitting on the shelf above the deep tub. Maybe I'll use it, soak for a little while and try to ease the tension in my shoulders and neck.

No, I doubt even a bath will help with that. I turn off the lights and go to the bed, bouncing on it a little to test it out. I'm sure it would be okay for me to buy things that will make everything feel more like mine, but it still feels awkward to even think about spending his money. They aren't even married yet, and we certainly don't have the cash.

The sound of voices outside my door gets me off the bed. I listen hard but can't make out more than mumbling, however, there's one thing I know for sure. Mom is one of the people speaking.

I turn the knob slowly and ease the door open an inch. I can just make out her back, along with a little bit of the person standing in front of her.

It's Hayes.

My chest tightens, but not because of him. It's because of her. Because she can't leave things alone. I want to warn her to lay off him before she makes things any worse. Why isn't it enough to have a man wrapped around her little finger? She has to make sure everybody loves her.

"I only want us to get along. If not for my sake, for your father's." At least she sounds gentle, though that could be because she's whispering.

"Whatever." He thrusts his hands into his pockets, looking at the floor.

"Both of us, your father and I, have been through a lot of heartache in our relationships."

"Sure."

"But now, we've found each other, and what we want more than anything is for everyone to get along. I know it's not easy, all of us being together now, but we can try. Right?"

I almost want to give her credit for trying until she makes a mistake by reaching out and running her hand over his arm. He doesn't like to be touched! I have to bite back that warning or else give myself away.

He doesn't treat her the way he would treat me, but that's not surprising. Instead of slamming her against a wall, he only pulls his arm away while glaring at her. "I get it, okay?"

"I understand if you resent our being here. Please keep your father in mind. That's all I ask." With that, she turns away and walks in the direction of her room. I let out the breath I was holding. It's not her I was worried about, but him. Why is that? Why should I care if he gets in trouble for losing his temper?

He turns around like he's going back to his room, and I start to close the door again.

I should have waited until he was gone. I should have been quieter.

The next thing I know, he's shoving my door open so hard, so suddenly, I don't have time to react. "There you are again," he snarls before closing the door and leaving us alone.

"What? What did I do?" I back away until my legs hit the bed.

His features twist in an ugly snarl. "Eavesdropping. Why won't you leave me alone?"

"I wasn't trying to. I only wanted to see who was out in the hall."

"No, that wasn't enough. You couldn't close the door and mind your own fucking business."

I have to make him understand. "When I saw it was her talking to you, I wanted to help. I know how she can be."

"Really? How can she be?"

"Pushy. She doesn't know when to stop."

"Yeah, and neither do you. You don't even fucking see it."

Is that true? "I just want to help you."

"How many times do I have to say it?" He gets in my face, and it takes everything I have not to cringe away. "I don't want your help. I don't need your help. I need you out of my life."

"We don't have a choice anymore."

His eyes dart over my face, and I think I've gotten through to him for a second. "You're right. There is no choice."

My heart swells with relief. "The only thing we can do is try to get through it together. Right?"

"No. That's not the only thing we can do."

"What are you doing?" I ask when he places his hands on my shoulders.

He pushes, and I land on my back with my feet on the floor.

Suddenly, he's on top of me, almost crushing my ribs. "Maybe this is what I'm going to do. Yeah, I think this is how I'll get through it. If you won't stay out of my life, then I won't stay out of yours." I don't have room to squirm away and trying to push him off me would be like trying to push my way through a brick wall.

"You've made your point," I gasp.

"No, because you keep coming at me no matter what I do." Like he did in the closet, he slides a hand down my body, but his touch is different this time. He's not teasing or tickling. "I might as well enjoy it, right?"

"Stop it."

A nasty smile touches his lips, making my blood run cold. "You want me to stop? Then call out for somebody. My dad, your mom. Somebody. Anybody. Maybe they'll stop me."

He stops at the waistband of my pants—then slides his hand under the elastic and sends panic shooting through me. "Go ahead," he murmurs, his fingers grazing my skin. "Scream for help. What do you think will happen? Do you think people will believe you? By the time anybody gets here, I could be across the hall."

I know he's right, too. And even if somebody came in and saw this, it would cause nothing but problems for everybody. What if we had to leave? What if he got kicked out and his dad hated me for it? That would mean Mom would hate me, too.

"See? I knew you could be smart when you had to." My body stiffens when instead of touching me over my panties, he teasingly lifts them like he wants to put his hand inside. "What's this feel like? Knowing I could do anything I want to your body, and you can't do anything about it? Go ahead. Try to stop me."

I want to. I know I should.

I know something else, too. And I don't know what it says about me. But when he touches me the way he is now, I don't want him to stop. This is stirring something deep in me I didn't know was there. Something nobody ever did to me before. Burning, almost painful heat that makes me wet. I know it's dangerous, I know it's wrong, but I want more.

"Jesus Christ." Just like that, his hand is gone, and the pressure of his body is, too. I can breathe now, but somehow I'm not relieved. More like confused.

"What's wrong?" I sit up, still breathless.

"You. You're what's wrong." He looks me up and down, lifting his lip in disgust. "I never thought I'd meet anyone as fucked up as me, but I think you might be worse. You wanted me to finger you, didn't you?"

"No." My cheeks heat, giving my lie away.

"Liar." He snorts, shaking his head. "Maybe you should be more worried about yourself than me." He leaves the room, still shaking his head, and only when I'm alone do I draw my feet up onto the bed and curl up in a trembling ball.

Is he right? Did I want him to? Does that make me fucked up like he says?

And to think, this is only the first day we've lived together. What else am I going to end up learning? How much more can he make me hate myself?

CHAPTER 10

"I don't understand. He already left?"

Mom doesn't look up from her phone. "I guess he did if his car isn't in the courtyard."

"I just checked. There aren't any cars out there right now."

"Then you have your answer. Hayes already went to school. Maybe he has swim practice or something. I don't know."

"What am I supposed to do? Should I get an Uber?"

"Whatever." We're alone in the kitchen, so she doesn't have to pretend to be nice.

"Maybe I should try to get a ride with the driver?"

"Maybe you should just handle this on your own, all right?" She looks up at me and sighs. "I have to get ready for this trip I'm going on, and all my supposedly mature daughter can do is whine because she didn't get a ride to school this morning. I swear, Lucy whines less than you do."

Great. Why did I think anything would be different? I pull up the Uber app and request a car and go outside to wait for it. I don't want to be in the house with her when there's nobody else around to keep her in check.

I don't know why I thought Hayes would drive me to school. I assumed that since we're going to the same place and he has a car, it would make the most sense. I've got to be smarter. Now, I'll be lucky if I'm not late for first period.

But I do get lucky since it's only a few minutes until a car pulls up. At least school is closer to the house than it was to the hotel, so it doesn't take long at all before we're pulling up on campus. I have time to stop at the cafeteria for something to eat and maybe some coffee since I was too busy wondering how I'd get to school to grab anything from the kitchen at the house.

The cafeteria might be my favorite part of the whole place. It's like a full-service restaurant with just about anything anybody could want. In the morning, the coffee bar is set up, and we can even take the cups to class with us if we want. It's so unlike anything at my old school that I want to keep coming back for more between classes. I would, too, if I had the time.

This morning, I need all the help I can get. My bed is comfortable, but I hardly got any sleep. I can't stop thinking about Hayes. Am I obsessed with him? Could I have picked a worse person to be obsessed with? If he wasn't so different now than he was when I first met him, I might not care so much.

If there wasn't a constant worry in the back of my head that he'll try something like he did that day out on the bridge, that would be different, too. He isn't my responsibility, but I can't help caring.

I'm not halfway through the cafeteria before I notice something. Everyone is looking at me. This is my third day at the school, so I don't know what they're so interested in all of a sudden. Aren't there any freshmen they can stare at?

It doesn't take long for a guy to walk up to me as I'm getting in line for coffee. He slings an arm around my shoulders, and I stiffen, looking up at him in surprise. "Welcome to the family, little sis."

"Excuse me?" It hits me that I've seen him before, and not only around the halls. This is the person Hayes was talking to. The one who told him to talk to his dad about whatever it is he's going through. A part of me wants to shove him away and ask why the hell he didn't put a stop to things yesterday. He must have seen Hayes shove me into that closet, right?

The bigger part of me wants to beg him to fess up. What's Hayes hiding?

His easy smile reveals none of that. I wonder if he even knows I'm the girl his friend went after yesterday. Maybe he didn't get a good look at me. "Word spreads fast around here. You're an Ambrose now."

Oh, right. I didn't even think about this. "Not yet," I remind him with a tight laugh. I feel the weight of at least a dozen pairs of eyes on me, and I hate it. Whatever happened to blending in and keeping my head down?

"But as good as. I heard you moved in and everything."

"You know a lot about my life for somebody whose name I don't know."

I hear a girl laugh, but he pays her no attention. His smile only widens. "Shit, I guess I'm not as popular around here as I thought, if you don't know my name yet. Three days in. I'm losing my touch."

Even though he has a bad habit of being overfamiliar, I can't help but like him a little. "I'm waiting."

"Franky Miller. Best friend of your brother—sorry, stepbrother."

"Nice to meet you."

"Yo, is it true? Do you really live with Hayes Ambrose?" The guy standing in front of us looks impressed, while the girl standing next to him shoots me a look that could boil ice.

"As of yesterday, yeah. We just moved in."

The girl looks me up and down before snorting. "What, is your mom the housekeeper or something?"

Franky jumps in before I can even process what she said. "Are you deaf now, Hunter? Their parents are getting married. Try to keep up."

She only rolls her eyes at him before turning around, arms folded.

He shakes his head before leaning down and whispering in my ear. "Good luck. There's a lot of girls who are going to give you shit over this."

"I didn't do anything."

"Yeah, and they'll probably hate you for not doing anything because they think they would if they were in your shoes." He grins at my confusion. "Don't be surprised if some of them try to be friendly with you."

I hadn't thought about that. It makes perfect sense. I saw the looks many girls gave Hayes when we walked through the hall together that first day. Hungry looks. And if they want to get close to him, they might try to use me as a way of doing it.

"At least I know one person wants to be my friend for real," I say.

"Who's that?"

"Salem. Do you know her?" It only occurs to me now that I don't know her last name.

His brows knit together for a split second before his forehead smooths out again. "Yeah, I know her. She's cool. You don't have to worry about her being a user." I thought so but hearing him say it makes me feel better. "So what's your story? Where do you come from?"

At least he removes his arm from over my shoulders, but he's still standing next to me as we inch our way up in line.

"I don't really have a story. I have a mom and a little sister, and yesterday I moved into a house that's bigger than I ever stepped foot in before."

"Yeah, it's a big house. His dad is pretty cool. He lets us come over sometimes."

"You'll have to do it when my mom isn't around."

"So she's like that, huh? My mom's kind of that way, too. But she doesn't care if we drink, so..." He shrugs with another lopsided grin. "Do you party a lot?"

I can't remember the last time I went to a party. "Not recently."

"So that's a no." He laughs. "Don't worry. We'll change that."

I don't have time to ask what that means before Theo strolls up. "Hey, Miller. Hands off. She's an Ambrose now."

"I'm really not," I remind him and anybody standing nearby. I'm sure they're all listening.

"As good as," Theo insists. "And that means hands off."

"I don't get it." I look back and forth between them, searching for an answer.

"It's kind of like guy code," he explains. "You don't fuck around with your brother's sister. That's not cool."

"Don't worry. It's not like that." Heat flares up in my cheeks. "I mean, not that I thought you were flirting or anything. I don't even want you to. I'm just saying. Hayes doesn't care what I do."

"You sure about that?" Theo's smirking as he turns his head to look across the room over a sea of students. I follow the direction he's looking in, and my heart skips a beat when my eyes lock with Hayes's. It's like the rest of the room goes dark, and only he is standing in the light. We might as well be the only two people here.

The illusion lasts roughly three seconds before he scowls. "See? Told you," Theo crows. "He doesn't like other people touching his things."

"I'm not one of his things. We're not even related. What's next? Is he going to brand my ass, too?"

Franky throws his head back and hollers with laughter. "I like you. You should come to my house for a party this weekend. Saturday night."

From the corner of my eye, I can still see Hayes glowering at us. What's he thinking? Why does he even care? Obviously, Franky is a friend of his. Otherwise, the two of them wouldn't have been talking about whatever secret he's hiding. Franky seemed truly concerned, too. So what difference does it make if we're standing next to each other in line?

"Well? What do you think? Are you coming, or aren't you?"

Theo must see my hesitation for what it is. "Don't worry. We'll make sure you're okay."

"Why wouldn't I be okay?"

"Your first Academy party might be a little... intimidating." For once, he's not joking around. "Things can get out of control."

"At last year's winter break party, a girl OD'd in the bathroom and passed out in front of the door so we couldn't get to her. At the last party back in May, three guys got arrested for a big fight." When my eyes widen, Franky only shrugs. "I guess not everybody's neighbors know not to call the cops."

I'm more surprised over the OD, but they talk about it like it's completely normal. I don't think this party would be a good idea. All I keep thinking about is those girls in the bathroom snorting cocaine before class started. It's not the drugs that scare me. It's the girls themselves.

"Does everybody go to these parties?"

"Everybody?" Franky exchanges a look with Theo.

"I mean, is it an open invitation? I know there's at least one person who's going to hate me once they hear about the whole stepbrother thing."

They exchange another look. "Madison," Theo mutters. I nod. "Yeah. You need to watch your back around her. She's—"

"Insane," Franky finishes. "But she's like a rabid dog with no teeth. She'll only gum you."

"I don't even want her to get that close." The guys laugh, and I have to laugh with them. It does seem kind of ridiculous.

"So? Does this mean you're RSVPing yes?" Franky nudges me, grinning.

I feel Hayes staring holes through me. Not through the guys, but through me. This has nothing to do with a bro code or whatever Theo was talking about. This is about Hayes resenting me being part of his world. He resents me breathing.

And everyone thinks they can't get too close to me for fear of what he might do. He wants to control every part of my life. I can't even sleep because I can't stop thinking about him, dreading him, wanting to help him.

That's why I reach up and put a hand on Franky's shoulder. "Yeah. I'll be there." I know he's watching. I won't give him the satisfaction of looking back, but I don't need to.

"Nice." He peels away from the line when I step up to the counter. "See you around."

"See you in English." Theo winks, grinning as he turns around. Out of the corner of my eye, I see him approach Hayes, who pushes his way through everybody to get out of the cafeteria. I was half expecting him to charge at me instead.

Shit. I just said I'd go to Franky's party, and I don't have anything to wear, which is the least of my problems. I pull out my phone and send a text to Salem. *I need you to tell me how to survive a party at Franky's because I said I'd go, and now I'm freaking out.*

CHAPTER 11

"You need some new clothes anyway." Salem meets my gaze over the top of a clothes rack. "No offense."

"None taken. I know I dress like shit."

"You don't dress like shit. Just like somebody who did the best she could with what she had. And you still look cute in everything you wear."

"Sure I do."

She lets out a frustrated sigh before pulling a dress from the rack. "If I had known it was Mr. Ambrose who your mom got engaged to, I would've warned you to buy new clothes right away. Now, everybody's watching your every move."

"Thanks. I had no idea until you just told me." I shake my head when she holds up the dress. "Too short, too low cut."

"How old are you? Seventeen or seventy-seven? I have a dress just like this, and it looks hot. At least try it on." She drapes it over her arm, telling me I have no choice.

I check out the price tag and almost fall on the floor. "No way! That's too expensive."

She tosses her red hair around and makes me jealous again. "Says who? You have your stepdad's card, right?"

I don't bother correcting her. It sounds childish to remind

people he isn't my stepdad yet, even though he isn't. "Yeah, but that doesn't mean I want to max it out."

She laughs loudly enough to get the attention of a few other shoppers. "You could shop your way up and down Fifth Avenue and not max that thing out, babe. Trust me."

"You'd know better than I would. It still makes me feel gross to use his money."

"He's got tons of it. He won't miss a few thousand." She moves onto the next rack while I try to close my mouth after it just fell open.

"A few thousand?"

"At least, to get you started."

Maybe it'll help me feel more confident? That's the only good thing I can come up with, and it still doesn't make me feel much better.

She must see that because she frowns when she looks over her shoulder. "You're lucky. He's a nice guy, and he's generous. Plus, he's still trying to impress your mom and make her happy, so he's bending over backward to make you happy. It could be a hell of a lot worse."

"You're right, I guess."

"I know." She goes through stacks of jeans on a shelf. "I mean, the guy my mom's married to now is pretty cool. He doesn't try to be the stern daddy, but he's not all distant or cold either." Her jaw tightens. "And unlike my last stepfather, he's never accidentally on purpose walked in on me when I'm in the shower."

I grab her arm. "Are you serious?"

"No, I'm joking." She shrugs it off. "It's over now. One day he walked in, and it was my mom using my shower. He didn't hide his surprise fast enough. She served him papers the next day."

I don't want to ask if he ever did more than walk in on her. "I'm sorry that happened."

"It's nothing compared to what some people go through. But like I told you in the cafeteria last week, you've got it better than most. Don't forget that. You might as well enjoy it."

She's right. I don't want to take advantage, but I can't be point-lessly stubborn either. Especially since tonight's Franky's party.

I've been dreading it for the past three days, so much that I can barely eat without feeling sick. "You're sure nobody is going to pull anything?" I take out a pair of jeans in my size to try on.

"Pull anything?" She shakes her head, chuckling. "You've watched too many stupid teen movies. It's not really like that. Nobody is going to prank you because you're the new girl."

"I'm already getting a lot of dirty looks at school."

"You're going to get dirty looks because of who you are now."

"What happens when those looks turn into something else? When we're not in school, there's nobody watching."

"You worry too much. Trust me, you'll be fine, and if you stop worrying, you'll actually have a lot of fun. I'll be there with you, right? You could do a lot worse." She holds up a skirt in front of me, tipping her head to the side. "This is cute."

I have to force myself not to look at the price tag. "Yeah, it is."

"See? That wasn't so hard."

"It's just that this is all happening so fast."

"And in all the Disney movies, there was never a scene where the princess had to adjust to her new life. All of a sudden, she's royalty and happy, and there's nothing to worry about anymore. Right?" We share a knowing laugh. "They didn't prepare us for life, did they?"

"I just wish..." I bite off the rest of it, but not fast enough. Salem hits me with a hard look that tells me she's not going to let it go until I finish the thought. "I wish Hayes liked me a little more. I think that's what bothers me most of all."

"Hayes is who he is." She brushes it off on the way to another rack. "His dad's a nice guy, but they don't really have a warm and fuzzy relationship. It's probably just as weird for him as it is for you, with all these new people in his house. It's not any deeper than that."

I wish I could tell her what I know, but it would feel like a huge betrayal, even with Hayes treating me the way he does. What would Salem think if she knew what was happening to him? Then again, I'm not even sure what it is. I only have suspicions, and I can't do much with those. I might end up getting the wrong person in trouble, and I don't want that.

Then again, if his coach is touching him or being inappropriate, and I know about it, what does it make me if I keep my mouth shut? How does Franky live with himself, knowing there's a problem but doing nothing about it?

I have to shake it off. Hayes can't be the center of my universe.

"What about you?"

"What about me?" I ask on the way to the dressing room.

"Where's your dad? Your real dad, I mean. Did your parents get divorced?"

"I have no idea who he is. I've never met him." When she continues to stare at me, I add, "The way my mom makes it sound, it was a one-night stand."

"Oh. What about your sister?"

I grit my teeth at the thought of him. "He's a prick. They dated for a little while and she thought he would take care of us, but he's even worse than her. I'm pretty sure Mr. Ambrose is the nicest person she's ever been with. At least since I was born."

"It's a hard day, the day you find out your parents don't know what the fuck they're doing." She leaves me with the clothes we—she—picked out and closes the door to give me privacy.

What she said is the truth. I never thought about it that way. Kids want to believe their parents know everything, and it's a letdown when you find out they don't.

* * *

"THERE'S PROBABLY food in the fridge if you're hungry. I'm going to take these things upstairs." It's amazing I can even lift my arms for all the bags I'm carrying. In one hand are clothes, and in the other are shoes, makeup, and all the skin care products Salem swears I need If I want to keep my skin smooth and firm or something like that. We're only seventeen. How much could we possibly need?

I'm careful setting everything down in my room since we just had our nails done, too. "The first party of the year means we have to look as good as we can," she told me, and then again when we went for blowouts. Right now, I'll take her advice on just about anything, so long as it means surviving without looking like I don't belong. It's bad enough I already feel that way.

At least the house is empty. Bridget left a note saying she would take Lucy to a park nearby. Mom is wherever she is, and of course Mr. Ambrose is out doing his thing. If he's not working, he's golfing. His clubs are always by the front door, and now that I think about it, they weren't there when we came in. I guess that answers that question.

It's funny to me, walking down the empty hall and descending the stairs, to think of this house sitting empty so much of the time. All these big, empty rooms.

No, not exactly empty. Charlotte is kneading dough when I enter the kitchen.

She looks up with a smile. "Did you enjoy your shopping?"

I like her. She's kind, which I haven't experienced a lot of before now.

"It was different. I had to keep telling myself not to look at the price tags." I don't know why I just admitted that.

"Mr. Ambrose is a nice man. He wants you to have nice things."

I wish my mother would say something that kind to me just once. "Did Salem come through here? My friend?"

"She stopped in to say hello. We haven't seen her around here for a while." She nods her head in the direction of the side door leading out to the yard. "She went that way."

"Thank you." I grab an apple from a bowl on the counter and head outside. I haven't had much time to enjoy the yard, with its big patio and pool. There's even an outdoor kitchen with a pizza oven and grill built in.

It's not the pizza oven I'm thinking about when I hear Salem's voice—along with someone else's. My heart sinks, and I almost drop my snack when it hits me. Hayes is in the pool. He must have parked his car in the garage for once, or else I would have known he was here.

Now, my feet are rooted to the ground. How does he do this to me? I have every right to be here. He doesn't own this house. And he doesn't own me.

Still, when I move, I'm careful, creeping up close to a tall hedge so neither of them can see me right away.

"Don't even pretend." Salem laughs. "If she showed up at the party tonight and dropped on her knees in front of you, you wouldn't stop her."

"Untrue."

"So true! Just like you said you wouldn't let her do it before, huh? In the end, all you guys think with is your dicks."

"She's not worth the drama."

"Sounds familiar. Almost like something I told you before she sucked you off the first time."

Ugh. I guess they're talking about Madison. I haven't run into her since the news of the engagement came out, but my luck can't last forever. It's not a pretty mental picture, that skank on her knees.

"I'm telling you. I'm not interested."

By now, I'm at the end of the hedge. I can't take another step without being seen. This feels so stupid. Sneaking around in my own backyard, even if it doesn't quite feel like mine yet.

Maybe with Salem around, he'll play nice. He sounds happy. Relaxed. In other words, the opposite of how he sounds when she's not around. I wonder if she would mind moving in.

I step out of my hiding place and take a bite of my apple.

Salem waves me over. "What do you think? I think her hair looks awesome like that."

I touch a self-conscious hand to my smooth, shiny hair and wait for his reaction.

He doesn't disappoint. "It looks like hair." He backstrokes away, and I have to tell myself not to stare at his body. I've never seen him like this before, in nothing but a pair of swim trunks. Water glistens on his abs and chest. He moves with smooth, effortless grace. I could watch him all day.

"Men." Salem rolls her eyes. "The worst."

"Are you kidding? That's nice compared to some of the things he says." Why bother hiding it? Let his friends see what an asshole he is.

"He's just playing with you. Don't let him bother you."

I want so much to tell her, but a deeper part of me knows that would only make things worse. She can't be with me all the time, and he can make my life extremely miserable in so many ways.

"Were you talking about the party when I came out? Is he going to be there?"

"Of course. Everybody will be there."

There goes my stomach, sinking further. He's swimming laps and ignoring us or pretending to. "Promise me something?"

"Sure."

"Stick around me tonight? I don't mean you have to babysit me or anything like that, but don't be surprised if I shadow you."

"Okay, weirdo." She giggles. "I don't know what the guys told you, but it's not that bad. Don't worry, though. I'll have your back." She checks her phone before wincing. "I better get home, but I'll come over later to get ready, yeah?"

"Yeah, that would be great." All I can think about is how much better it will be having Salem around so Hayes will behave himself. I can't even think about having fun. I only want to survive him.

She walks off around the side of the house to where she parked, leaving me standing by the pool while Hayes swims. I have my back to him, but I can tell when the rhythmic sound of his strokes ends that he stopped.

"If I were you, I'd stay home tonight. There's no place for you there."

"Maybe you should talk to your friend Franky about that since he invited me personally." I look over my shoulder and find him glaring at me. "Why does that bother you so much?"

"Just watch your back—and stay out of my way," he warns.

"Maybe you need to stay out of mine." It was a stupid thing to say, and I regret it the second it's out of my mouth, but it might be worth it just to see the surprise wash over his face before I go back inside the house.

This time, I'll lock my bedroom door in case he gets any ideas. I'm not playing his games today.

CHAPTER 12

Franky's house is a lot like mine—rather, the one I'm living in. It's not as big, but it has the same basic layout. That's helpful. I don't feel so much like an outsider sneaking in where she doesn't belong.

Dozens of kids are already hanging around inside and out on the lawn.

"We should go in," Salem decides, and I shrug and follow along. It doesn't matter to me. She would know better than I would.

The crowd gets thicker the closer we get to the kitchen, and once we're there, I understand why. This is where the drinks are, and there are plenty of them. Bottles are lined up along the island in the middle of the room. There's a row of kegs just beyond the open door leading outside. Everybody is hanging out, sitting around on the counters, or wandering from group to group, saying hi. I recognize some of the jocks right away. They're hard to miss bigger and more muscular than the other guys.

"Remember what I told you about them," Salem says over her shoulder. As if I could forget.

"Hey! You made it!" I'm glad to see Theo with some of the jocks. He comes over and gives me a hug like we're old friends.

"I thought I was hands-off," I tease.

Salem laughs, but Theo just narrows his eyes. "What he doesn't know won't hurt him. And there's nothing wrong with being friendly." He throws his arms around Salem, who laughs again when he lifts her off her feet.

When Franky comes over, she stops laughing. "Hey," she murmurs before grabbing a cup and pouring herself a drink.

He only has eyes for me. "I'm glad you came. Hayes was saying you might not."

I'll bet he did. "He's not the boss of me."

"That's what I like to hear. Do you want a drink?"

"Some beer, maybe?" That's as much as I trust myself to drink around a bunch of people I don't know.

Franky grabs a cup and goes out to the keg.

"See?" Theo grins before taking a swig of his drink. "It's not as bad as you thought it would be, is it?"

"I only just got here," I remind him.

"You need to loosen up. Have a little fun."

"Careful," Salem warns. "Next thing you know, he'll tell you all about the great sound system in Franky's room and how you just have to come up and listen to it."

"Hey, I only did that the one time with you, and I was a lot younger then." Theo winks before adding, "She saw through me."

"I already told her I have taste." I can tell Salem's joking with him. I like their friendship, how easy and fun it is. I hope I get to the point where I feel that comfortable around them.

"Here you go." Franky hands me the cup, now full of beer, and puts an arm around my shoulders like he did in the cafeteria. "You girls go shopping today? I think I drove past when you were coming out of one of the nail places in town."

"Yeah, it was fun. I've never been to that part of town before." I look at Salem with a grin. "She forced me to have fun."

Franky smirks. "Yeah, she knows how to have a good time."

Salem pretends like she's not listening, waving to a couple of girls who just came in from the kegs.

When the guys start talking about their swim meet tomorrow, I tap her on the shoulder. "Is it okay that I'm talking with Franky?"

"Why wouldn't it be?"

"I don't know. I just got the feeling you didn't like it."

"It doesn't matter to me." She looks over my shoulder and grins. "Hey!" she calls out to a few girls I don't recognize. She won't look at me for some reason.

"What's wrong?"

"Nothing."

"Are you sure? It seems like your mood bottomed out."

"Why would it? We're at a party." She takes a long gulp from her cup.

"Okay." She's lying. Something has definitely changed. "Is it because Franky was paying attention to me? Do you guys not like each other?"

"I don't care if you talk to Franky or hang out with him or whatever. He's cool. You'd make a cute couple." Salem sets her cup on the counter before reaching for a bottle of vodka and filling the cup halfway. She tops it with a splash of juice from another bottle before taking a long drink without even adding ice.

"Because really, he was just being nice. It's not like I like him or anything."

"Why do you think I care? No offense, but the whole world isn't, like, obsessed with the guys you're talking to."

"I'm sorry." I move aside so other people can reach in and grab what they want. What did I do wrong? She's totally different than she was this afternoon.

"I've got to go pee." The words are barely out of Salem's mouth before she gets lost in the crowd.

I try to follow her progress, but she disappears into the partially lit rooms beyond the kitchen.

Awesome. Somehow, I pissed her off. And now I'm alone.

"Hey. Here." Somebody I've never met takes my hand, turns it so my palm faces up, and drops a pill on it.

"What is this?" But he walks away without answering. I don't even know if he heard me. I leave the pill on the counter, and somebody else snatches it up right away. Good for them. Do people seriously just hand drugs out at these parties? And other people take them without knowing what they are? I'll stick to my beer.

"There you are." Franky wanders over to me again. "Sorry, gotta play the host. You having fun?"

"Sure." I take a sip of my beer like that will prove something.

"Cool. Hang around. I wanna talk with you."

I nod, trying to smile, and he goes off to tap a fresh keg in the backyard. Maybe I could leave without anyone noticing, but Salem brought me here. I don't trust her to drive us home. And I don't think she'd be happy if I told her I want to go.

I settle for wandering around a little, going from room to room. I don't know why I feel so restless. It's better than standing in one place. All that'll do is attract attention, and I don't want attention. The music is good, at least, but I don't have the confidence to jump in and start dancing with everybody else in the living room.

There must be at least a hundred people here now, and there's more coming through the front door all the time. A guy and a girl are fighting as they come in, and she slaps him once they're inside, then almost knocks me over when she marches away. That kind of drama, I'm used to. All you can do is stay out of the way.

"Where's the bathroom?" I ask nobody in particular.

The guy standing closest to me points down the hall, where there's an obvious line forming. I walked down the length of the line, and of course, Salem is not in it. Dammit. What am I supposed to do? I've never been good at randomly starting conversations with strangers.

I wonder if she saw this line and went upstairs. There must be bathrooms up there, too—there's five in my new house, and this place is almost as big. I pick my way through the crowds on the stairs, mumbling *excuse me* even though I don't think they can hear me. The hallway is pretty dark, but a few of the rooms have lights on inside and the doors are open so I can at least see where I'm going.

Smoke drifts out of the first room, where everybody is smoking weed, according to the smell. I don't see Salem in there, so I keep going, even if a few hits might calm me down. But for all I know, other stuff is mixed in with the weed. It seems pretty lightweight compared to some things I've already seen around here.

In the next room, red lights run along the edges of the ceiling, giving it an eerie sort of glow. But inside, a few guys play video games. I'm almost surprised by how chill it seems until I realize one of the guys sitting on a beanbag chair on the end is in the middle of getting a blow job. Right in the middle of everything else going on around them. I back away, eyes wide. No Salem in there. I'm wishing I had never agreed to come.

Finally, I'm so desperate to find her I just start calling her name. "Salem? Are you in here?" I stick my head into another room, but all I get is a bunch of dirty looks from everybody who's sitting around in a circle, drinking and talking.

The room across from that has its door partway open, though, there's no light coming from inside. I decide to take a quick look, just in case. The way she's drinking already, I'm a little worried. What if somebody tries to take advantage of her or something?

At first, I don't know what I'm looking at. It's enough of a surprise that it takes a second for my brain to catch up. All I see is a bunch of people and body parts moving around on, and near, a king-sized bed.

Finally, it hits me they're all having sex. I don't know how many of them there are and don't want to hang around to count them. All I can do is gasp and close the door.

"Why don't you go in?"

I jump at the sound of Haye's voice before turning around. It's the first time I've heard it tonight. I didn't know he was here yet.

"Hayes," I murmur. My heart was already pounding thanks to what I accidentally walked in on, and this makes it worse.

He's practically on top of me, leaning down, leering in my face. "You don't just look in on something like that and stay outside, you know."

I'm shaking so hard that my teeth are almost chattering. It's dark here. Maybe he can't see me well enough to know how startled and uncomfortable I am. I fight to keep myself together, at least in front of him. "Who says?"

"That's how it goes." He moves a little closer until I'm flat against the closed door. "You want to be part of things, right? One of us?" His gaze moves down to my lips before darting up to my eyes again. "We could get started out here if you want."

"Get away from me." Before I realize what I'm doing, I place my hands against his chest and shove.

His hands dart out, grabbing my wrists and tightening around them until I wince. "What did I tell you? Don't touch me."

"Then give me some fucking space, and I won't have to."

Now I've really pissed him off. His hands tighten until I'm sure he's going to break my wrists, but just as suddenly as he grabbed me, he lets go. "Fair enough." He makes a big point of wiping his hands on his shirt like I've dirtied him.

"Thank you." Before I can slide around him, he places a hand against the wall on either side of me, locking me in place.

"You still didn't answer my question." He lowers his head, and I smell alcohol on his breath, mixed with the faint scent of chlorine. I'm sure he took a shower after swimming, but it seems to stick to him. "Are you going in? Or are you going to stay out here and wonder what it would be like?"

"I'm not interested."

"Then why did you show up in a shirt that's practically see-through? And you're not wearing a bra." When he looks down at my chest, I don't know if I want to crumple up and die or if I want him to touch me.

"For someone who hates me, you care a lot about what I'm wear-ing. And like I said, I'm not interested in that kind of thing."

"In general, or what's going on in there?" His eyes flash as he gives me a nasty smile. "Because from what I remember, you can be very interested under the correct conditions."

My face is hot, and I'm sweating, but I don't want him to see he's the reason for it. I know I'm fighting a losing battle but crumbling in front of him would be too humiliating. "What about you?"

"What about me?"

"Aren't you going in? Why are you wasting time out here with me?"

"Do you hope I am? Maybe you would like to watch me in action. Is that what gets you off?"

I don't even know what gets me off. He's probably guessed by now that I'm a virgin, or at least inexperienced. I know that's why he's doing this. He sees how uncomfortable I am.

"Is this what gets you off?" I ask. "Intimidating me?"

"Do I intimidate you?"

"No. You make me sad."

Hayes frowns, his eyes narrowing a split second before he backs off. "Fuck you. And if I wanted to, I'd be in there. But I have a meet tomorrow. I can't waste my energy." He walks away, and I slump against the wall while trying to catch my breath.

How does he do it to me? And why? He's the one who keeps telling me to leave him alone, but he was practically on top of me before I even knew it.

I need fresh air. As soon as he's out of sight, I fight my way down the stairs. It's difficult with so many people sitting here and there, drinking and smoking, but eventually, I make it to the first floor and through the house and out the back door. The blast of air against my flushed face feels good. I take a deep breath, pulling in all the air I can.

People are all over the place out here, just like inside. Some are sitting on the ground, and some are hanging out by the pool. A few girls are swimming in their underwear. There's a firepit off to the side with chairs positioned around it. A familiar head of red hair draws my attention, and I make a beeline for her.

"Hey!" Salem jumps up from her chair and stumbles over to me before throwing her arms around my neck. "There you are!"

"Where have you been?" I give her a brief hug and notice the way she's kind of hanging on me. She reeks of alcohol, too, even worse than Hayes.

"Just having fun. I'm sorry I lost you." She giggles before almost touching her mouth to my ear. "Isn't he hot?" Salem slides a look toward the guy she was sitting next to before I found her.

"I guess so." That's not the first word that comes to my mind when I look at him. Scary is more like it. If he didn't look like he was planning to commit murder, he might be hot with his dark hair and eyes and a wide, square jaw. His nose is a little crooked, like it's been broken, but it makes his face interesting. A shiver runs down my spine when our eyes meet across the fire.

Salem stumbles against me again and pulls my attention away from him. "Are you okay?" I ask. "How much have you had?"

She lifts a shoulder. "I don't know. So what?"

"Maybe you should have some water." I was thinking she would take care of me tonight, but I'm now taking care of her. I don't mind. It's better than watching for Hayes over my shoulder wherever I go.

"I wanna hang out with Logan."

"We'll come back and find Logan." I offer him a shrug before putting an arm around her waist and trying to lead her toward where I know there's bottled water waiting in a cooler.

"You know what?" she asks. "Men are fucking stupid. I hate them. They act like we're the ones who play games, but it's always them."

"I know. They suck."

"I would date you if I liked girls."

"Same here. That would make everything so much easier." Not that I believe that, but it feels like the right thing to say to a drunk friend. We reach a cooler by the pool, and I bend down to grab a bottle of water, but Salem slaps my hand away and grabs the half-empty bottle of vodka sitting in the ice.

"Are you sure you should do that?" I ask when she unscrews the cap and tosses it on the patio.

"So what? I want some of this."

"You can already barely stand." I reach for the bottle, but she yanks it away, then stumbles backward. I catch her before she falls into the pool.

"Lay off, would you? God. Find a man of your own and hang out with him."

"What? What does that have to do with anything?"

Her eyes narrow. "Maybe you should find Franky."

"You're the one who said I should talk to him. I'm not even interested in him."

Her head snaps up like she's ready to accuse me of something—instead, her eyes go wide. "No, don't do it!" she squeals, and I start to turn around to see what she's talking about, but don't get the chance before a pair of hands slam into my back.

Suddenly, I'm in midair, flailing, before hitting the water.

I surface quickly, sputtering with wet hair plastered over my face. I know who did it before I brush the hair away. Only one person would be this mean.

Hayes stands at the edge of the patio, hands on his hips, while he laughs along with almost everybody else who saw it happen. "What about now?" he asks. "Is your shirt see-through now?"

Oh, my God. He's right. When I get out, it will look like I'm not wearing anything. I'm going to have to stay here all night.

Salem shoves him. "You asshole. What's wrong with you?"

"Why don't you go drink some more?" he asks before turning back to me. "You gonna stay in there all night? Or are you going to come out?"

All around me, people are pulling out their phones like they want to take a video or snap a picture. Even the water isn't enough to cool my flushed body.

I'm not going to give him the satisfaction of staying here, even if it means being humiliated. All I can do is control how I handle it.

"Get out of my way," I grunt before placing my hands on the lip of the pool and pushing up to lift myself out of the water.

"Dude, what the fuck?" Theo is standing in front of me, giving Hayes a dirty look before pulling off his shirt. "Here. Put this on."

More than a few disappointed groans sound around us, and everyone wanders off to go back to whatever they were doing before.

Hayes groans and gives Theo a little shove. "Come on. It was just a joke." He rolls his eyes and waves his friend off. "Lighten up."

"You lighten up."

Hayes stares at me over Theo's shoulder, mouthing, *I warned you.*

When Hayes walks off, Theo offers me a weak smile. "He gets this way sometimes, but he's not a bad guy. Really."

"I'm going to go. Salem's... busy." She's already back to sitting on Logan's lap with her arms around his neck.

"Do you need a ride?"

"No, thanks. I'll get one." I already have the app open. Thank God I have the latest iPhone since it's waterproof and my phone was in my pocket. Hopefully, it won't take long before a car gets here because this is the last place in the world I want to be.

Hayes got his way. I'm leaving not even halfway through the party with my dripping tail between my legs.

ould you at least let me know you got home safe? I don't even know how much you remember about last night, but I couldn't stay when I was soaking wet and embarrassed.

I stare at the phone, willing Salem to text me back, but it goes unanswered, just like the seven texts I already sent. She might not even be up yet. It's only ten o'clock, and who knows what time she left the party.

I hate to think something got ruined between us last night. It's not only that I need her to help me navigate. I really thought we were friends.

I can't stay in my room all day, no matter how much I don't want to see Hayes. What kind of mood will he be in today? Maybe he'll hate me for breathing the same air as him. He said something about having a meet, so hopefully, he'll be out for a while. Now that I'm showered and dressed and have hung out up here as long as I can without starving, I venture out into the hall and downstairs.

There's a loaf of sourdough on the counter and avocados in a bowl, so I make toast while mashing up half of the ripe fruit. I wonder where Lucy is. Maybe we could hang out today. Mom and Mr. Ambrose are going on their trip in a couple of days, so I know she'll be busy packing for wherever they're going. I heard her say something about needing to go shopping. That's probably what she's doing now.

I walk through the halls, munching on my toast, looking for my sister. She's nowhere to be found. I shoot a quick text to Bridget, who confirms she has a playdate. I didn't even know she had friends. It's been a crazy week. I wish it was as easy for me to make friends as it is for my little sister.

It looks like I have the place to myself. Rather than lock myself in my room again, I pull out my reading for English class and settle in on the sofa in the media room. It's nice here, with the sunlight streaming through the big windows. Once I'm wrapped in a blanket, I can forget all the awkwardness from last night. I wonder if anybody got pictures of me after I was out of the pool before I put Theo's shirt on. I'll need to remember to return it.

I don't know if I doze off or if the book's so good it sucked me in, but I jump at the sound of the front door flying open.

"I said I don't want to talk about it." My body curls into a protective ball before I know what I'm doing as Hayes comes into view. He storms past the stairs, muttering to himself.

I barely have time to process this before Mr. Ambrose marches in. "You heard what I said. Get your ass in my study. We're going to talk about this."

My heart sinks when Mom follows him into the house. She doesn't notice me—none of them did. They're all too busy dealing with whatever latest drama is going on.

It's only been a week since we got here, but I've never heard Mr. Ambrose sound like this.

"I'm serious," he barks, his voice echoing down the hall. "Get your ass in there. We're getting to the bottom of this."

"I fucking heard you. I'm getting something to drink. Or am I not allowed to do that anymore?"

I can't help myself. Curiosity is killing me. I get up from the couch and creep out to the hall and past the stairs. Hayes bursts out of the kitchen, but he doesn't see me since he turns in the direction of his father's study.

"I don't know who gave you the idea you get to talk to me that way, but I'm sick of it," Mr. Ambrose says. "What the hell is going on with you lately?"

I hope he gets an answer because I would like to know, too. I get as close to the study as I dare, stopping at the doorframe so nobody can see me.

"It's not even that big of a deal," Hayes says. "You're acting like I killed somebody."

"I'd say fighting in the middle of a swim meet is a pretty big deal, Hayes, and you know it."

"It wasn't even a fight."

"Really? Because that's not how your coach made it sound when he described it to me."

Mom pipes up. "He said you pushed your friend."

"We were just screwing around."

"In the middle of a meet?" Mr. Ambrose asks. "That's a lie, and you know it. He said you were already taunting members of the other team. Franky tried to stop you once it went too far, and you turned on him."

I cover my mouth to stifle a gasp. Franky? Why would he fight with Franky? They're supposed to be best friends. Did I miss something last night after I left? Dammit, I wish Salem would talk to me. I'm totally lost here.

"He doesn't know what the fuck he's talking about."

"Again with the language! Speak to me that way one more time, and you can forget having any privileges while I'm away."

"What are you going to do? Install cameras in every room to watch me?"

"Try me, son," Mr. Ambrose growls. "Though what I have in mind is more like hiring somebody to sit outside your goddamn bedroom door to make sure you don't leave the room unless you're going to or from school. Got it?"

"Right. Like you would do that."

"I said it before, and I'll say it again. Where is this coming from? This isn't the kind of thing we do, Hayes. Being aggressive. Being a bully. You're the captain of the goddamn team. This isn't the behavior of a leader."

"Now you sound like him."

"Your coach? Because we both know what we're talking about. A leader doesn't taunt the other team, and he sure as hell doesn't start a fight with someone on his own team. I thought you and Franky were better than that."

"Because we weren't fighting. How many times do I have to tell you that?"

"So your coach was lying?" Mom asks.

"Does she have to be in here? This doesn't have anything to do with her." I can't help but smile a little because she needs to hear that. She's not even his stepmother yet, but of course she has to make it seem like she's an authority figure.

"You will speak to and about her with respect. Got it?"

"It's all right," Mom murmurs in her best martyr voice. "He's upset. I know it's nothing personal."

"Hayes." His dad lowers his voice, no longer shouting. "You're so close to a full scholarship to any school you choose."

"I don't even need a scholarship. Maybe a poor kid should get it. Ever think about that?"

"You think I'd pay for your college education from my pocket if you got kicked off the team for being a bullying asshole?" Mr. Ambrose is downright nasty when he laughs. Now I know where his son gets it from. "Try again. I'm not about to reward you for bad behavior. If you lose this opportunity through your own shitty deci-sion-making, you're on your own. Take out loans. That's what the poor kids you're suddenly so interested in have to do."

"Are you fucking serious? You weren't even there at the meet. You're never there. But you're taking his word for it?"

"Yes, I'm taking your coach's word for it because he's an adult, and you're behaving like a spoiled brat who doesn't know how to keep his hands to himself. News flash: you push somebody while standing on a wet surface, and you could kill them. What if he'd struck his head?"

"Can we not be so dramatic? I shoved him gently. I hardly touched him."

"There's no such thing as gentle shoving," Mr. Ambrose growls. "Stop bullshitting me. Here's the way it stands. You fuck up again, you're off the team. So you'd better think of some way to get on Coach Greg's good side, or you're on your own once your graduation ceremony is over."

"Are you saying you want me to kiss this guy's ass for the rest of the year?" Hayes's voice grows in volume until he's almost screaming by the time he finishes the question. "Do you have any idea what you're asking me to do?"

Hearing him like this is almost enough to break my heart. Now I'm more convinced than ever that it's his coach who's abusing him —and his dad wants him to play nice, which could mean any number of things that are obviously making him crazy. I hear his feet pounding the floor as he marches back and forth. "You have no fucking idea," Hayes mutters. His teeth are clenched so tight I can barely make out what he's saying.

"Then, by all means, quit the team. It's up to you. You're a legal adult now." Mr. Ambrose's voice gets a little louder and I realize almost too late he's leaving the room. "Honey, let's go. You've already wasted enough of your day on this."

I duck into the closet next to the study with barely a second to lose.

Mom's voice is low and comforting, or at least that's how I'm sure she wants to sound. "He'll come around," she murmurs as she and her fiancé pass the closet.

I wait until the front door opens and closes before easing myself out into the hall. I should go back to the media room, grab my book, and run upstairs before Hayes hears me.

So why do I turn toward the study, instead? Maybe it's because I've already spent my whole life tiptoeing around Mom's moods. Making sure I don't wake her up—or her boyfriend of the moment. Always having to read the signs to know what kind of day it's going to be and doing everything I could not to make things worse if I could tell it was going to be a bad one.

I'm tired of that.

And I can't forget the pain in Hayes's voice. Maybe his dad couldn't hear it. I'm sure Mom couldn't. To me, it was obvious.

That must be why I take my life in my hands and peer into the study instead of hiding. I hear him opening one of his dad's liquor bottles before I see him, his back to me as he pours something into a glass.

"I know you're there," he mutters before slamming back the contents of the glass and pouring more.

Goose bumps race over my arms. "How did you know?"

"You're always there." He drinks again before snorting. "Like a rotting tooth I can't pull."

"You weren't being quiet, you know."

"I guess that's my fault, too, right?" He shoots me a filthy look over his shoulder.

I creep into the room, ready to run if I have to. "Did you guys get into a fight last night at the party, after I left?"

"You're not going to start in on me, too, are you?" He takes another drink before answering his question. "Of course you are. What am I saying? It's all you ever do. You can't help me. So don't bother trying."

I can practically feel his pain. Nobody ever told me how much it would hurt, seeing somebody else hurting and wanting so much to help but having them push me away.

I sit down on a leather sofa set against the wood-paneled wall. "I was just wondering. I'll hear about it in school tomorrow, anyway."

"Then wait until tomorrow. I don't want to talk about it. And if I did, it wouldn't be with a nobody like you."

When I draw a breath to say something else, he whirls around and throws his glass at the wall. It strikes beside the sofa, shattering, and I squeal in surprise and more than a little fear before jumping up, ready to do what I should've done in the first place.

But I'm not quick enough.

"Is this what you want?" He charges at me, grabbing me before I can get away and throwing me back onto the sofa. I beat at him with my fists, but it does nothing to stop him from taking a fistful of hair and yanking my head back.

Tears spring to my eyes as my scalp sings with pain. "Stop it. You're hurting me!"

"Is this what I have to do to make you leave me alone? Get the fuck out of my head," he grits out, so close to my face his spit hits my cheeks.

"I'm only trying to—"

"Stop trying." With his other hand, he encircles my throat and I let out a whimper of fear before I can stop myself. His eyes flash, hardening like the rest of his face. "What do I have to do to you? Do I have to hit you? Do you want me to hurt you for real? Do you get off on it?" The hand in my hair grips tighter and I whimper louder this time.

"No!"

"Then why? Why won't you stop trying to get in my head? I don't want you there. I don't want you anywhere near me, you fucking bitch."

"I only want to help," I tell him in a shaking voice. "Like I did before. Remember?"

I don't know why I brought it up. Was I hoping to shake him out of this? Stupid me. All it does is make his face go deep red.

"This is all your fault. I should've gone through with it."

"No. I'm glad you didn't."

He barks out a cold laugh. "Why?"

"Because you don't deserve to feel the way you do."

It's like I stuck a pin in a balloon. All at once, his intensity vanishes. He's still holding me in place, but he isn't hurting me. And when he speaks, it isn't through gritted teeth. "How would you know?"

"Because nobody does. You don't have to go through things alone. I know what it's like to feel alone."

He frowns, searching my face like he thinks I'm lying. "You don't know what you're talking about. Not really."

"Then tell me. What am I missing? I only want to be your friend."

"No. You only think you do."

"Isn't that enough?"

His mouth works, but no sound comes out. I sense his conflict and want so much to ease it. We're getting closer. I feel it in my soul. He's going to let me in.

His gaze drifts down to my lips like he only just realized how dangerously close he is to kissing me. My heart lodges itself in my throat as I realize I don't know if I want him to back away or lean in closer.

"I know what you want," Hayes growls, "and it's not friendship." He lets go of my hair, still holding my throat. When his free hand slides over my chest, my nipples harden to painful points.

He feels them, sneering as he does. "Told you so."

"Stop." It sounds weak even to me. Half-hearted. Because I don't mean it. Because, God help me, his touch lights me on fire. It's so wrong. I can't help it.

"You don't mean that." His mouth almost brushes against mine. So close. I bite back a whimper of disappointment. "I bet you lie in bed at night wishing I'd come to your room and do this." He squeezes one of my boobs, but not hard enough to hurt. Instead, it makes me arch my back, offering him more. I can't control myself. My body is hungry even if my heart is all kinds of confused.

"Stop flattering yourself." It doesn't even sound like I mean it, but I can't accept this without at least trying to fight back. He doesn't deserve to have this power over me.

"You're the one begging for it. Maybe not with your words, but your body?" He runs his hand over my stomach before coming to the waistband of my jeans. "You want me to do this. You want so much more."

"I don't," I whimper, even as I fight against the urge to lift my hips. To rub myself on him. I'm aching and so wet and craving more. Just like he says.

"Who are you lying to? Me, or yourself?" He unbuttons the jeans, then lowers the zipper. "I bet if I slide my hand in here, you'll be soaked. Dying to be touched. Licked. Fucked."

A groan dies behind my clenched teeth. "Stop." It sounds pathetic.

"You don't mean it." Like he predicted, he works a hand inside my panties and finds just how wet I've gotten. "Damn. I didn't think you'd be this bad. You must really be hard up for somebody to work this pussy."

I can't answer. I can't even make a sound, not when I'm trying so hard not to moan as his fingers slide along the length of my slick lips. It's so good, better than when I do it myself.

I close my eyes, blocking out the sight of his smug grin, but the scent of chlorine and the whisky on his breath won't allow me to block out his presence entirely. There's no pretending he isn't the one doing this.

"I could drown in all this. Maybe I will." My eyes fly open in surprise and his smile widens. "What? Does that scare you? The idea of my tongue on you? Inside you?"

Now I can't hold back a moan because, yes, that sounds amazing. Scary and amazing and so hot. My hips are rocking, grinding, my body trying to direct his fingers to where it aches the worst.

"You want me to make you feel better?" Hayes laughs softly at the way I whimper in response. When he parts my lips and strokes my clit, I almost explode.

"Oh, my God!" I reach up and grab his shoulders, twisting his shirt in my fists. "Oh, yes! Hayes!"

"Feels good, right?" He's breathing faster now, but nowhere near like I am. My body's rocketing its way toward an orgasm, and I know I should fight it, but I want nothing less. What I want—need—is to come on his fingers, so expertly stroking my swollen bundle of nerves.

I'm about to go over the edge when he stops.

"Why?" I ask before I know what I'm doing.

He answers by using his thumb on my clit while his forefinger teases my quivering hole. My hips jump up as fresh waves of agony wash over me.

"So tight. I bet you'd feel great around my cock."

I don't have it in me to tell him to stop saying those things. I don't want him to stop, either. I want more, more of everything.

He eases his finger deeper, and my muscles tighten around it. "Yes... Hayes, oh, God, I'm coming!" I clutch him harder, my body going stiff like an electric current's running through it for a heart-stopping second before the wave breaks and the most blissful sensations roll over me.

"Mm-hm, that's right. Come for me." He lets go of my throat, his other hand still in my panties while he frees his hard dick from his shorts. I'm still trembling and moaning softly when he strokes himself close to my face.

The opening of the front door makes us both jump.

"We're home!" Lucy calls out.

In a flash, Hayes tucks himself back into his shorts. He doesn't make eye contact before he leaves the room. I hear Lucy excitedly greeting him, and he says something that makes her giggle.

I need to pull it together for her sake, if not for my own. By the time I straighten myself out and leave the study, he's halfway up the stairs.

Lucy throws herself at me, completely unaware of what she walked in on. "We're going for ice cream later! You wanna go with us?"

I barely hear the question. I'm too busy wondering what would have happened if she hadn't come home when she did.

CHAPTER 14

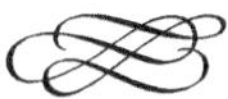

My stomach is in knots when I arrive at school on Monday morning. I don't know what to expect. I never heard from Salem yesterday, which means she's mad at me. We're going to have to see each other in English class, so she can't avoid me forever. Unless she doesn't come to school. What if that Logan guy was even worse news than I thought?

Something tells me I'd know by the time I walk into the building if Salem was missing or worse. After all, it took a few hours for word to spread about my mom's engagement to Hayes's dad.

One of the football players laughs when I walk into the building. He's tall, thick-necked, and he's wearing a smirk I'd love to slap off his face. "You looked good the other night at Franky's," he sneers while his friends laugh. "Glad I pulled out my phone in time."

Awesome. There are pictures of me looking like I came out of a wet T-shirt contest. Did he put them online? I probably would have heard about that by now if he had. It's not like I have all that much going on with my boobs, so no one would be seeing all that much. It still disgusts me, but I ignore him, going straight to my locker. I can't shake the sound of him and his friends laughing behind me.

I need to think the way Salem would. She would probably tell them to stick it up their asses or ask if they enjoyed jerking off to the picture. If she's not going to be my friend anymore, I have to figure out a way to stick up for myself.

Turns out, I don't have to worry about it.

"Hi!" Salem bounces up next to me, almost scaring me half to death with how suddenly she appears. She's wearing her uniform, telling me she had an early practice this morning. Her face glows, her eyes are bright, and she's wearing a brilliant smile.

I can only stare at her in surprise. "Where were you yesterday? Didn't you get my messages?"

"Oh, it was a whole big thing." She rolls her eyes and leans against the locker next to mine with a sigh. "My mom was super pissed when I got home from Logan's yesterday morning. She wouldn't get off my ass about it all day and took my phone. I just got it back this morning. I'm not, like, going to school without my phone."

I don't know why red flags go up in my head, but they're definitely there. "So you guys hooked up?"

"Yeah, it was amazing."

"So are you, like, a thing now?"

"I don't know. Right now, I'm just enjoying it."

She looks almost deliriously happy, so of course I want to be happy for her. She's not going to want to hear me warning her, but something feels off about him. I didn't like the way he was looking at me, or the whole vibe he gave off. But I could be making it all up in my head, too. Besides, I'm just so glad she's not mad. I don't want to ruin anything.

Her sudden pout knocks me off guard. "I was a bitch to you. I'm sorry. I get that way when I'm drinking sometimes."

"It's okay."

"I wanted to push Hayes into the pool after what he did. Theo was pretty pissed at him. I remember that much. Everything else is sort of blank."

Right, but she remembers hooking up with Logan and how amazing it was? Something about them is all wrong.

We go to the cafeteria for coffee, with Salem on her phone most of the time. I assume she's texting Logan, who she can't stop talking about.

"He got kicked out of school two years ago," she explains while she's typing.

"Oh, really?" What the hell is she doing with this loser?

"For fighting. It was all bullshit."

"Cool." I mean, what else am I supposed to say?

"Hey, Morgan! Did you have fun at the party?" Madison and her crew come our way with fresh drinks in hand. Immediately, I tense up, ready for her to throw hers in my face or something. Instead, she's actually smiling. It almost seems real.

"Yeah, it was fine," I say. "Mostly."

She shakes her head mournfully. "Brothers suck, don't they? I hate mine. One time, he put me in my toy box when I was little and sat down on the lid so I couldn't get out. I was in there for, like, an hour."

Did I walk into bizarro world today? Am I supposed to care?

"That sounds scary," I offer.

Salem's too busy texting to pay much attention. I need her to gauge this for me. Is the girl for real?

I recognize Harper standing beside her, the girl Franky told off in line last week, who assumed my mom is the cleaning lady. "You're, like, super lucky," she says. "Everybody would kill to be in your shoes."

"Why?" I look around at all of them, totally lost.

Madison laughs like it's the funniest thing she ever heard. "You're like Cinderella. Your mom marries some rich guy and now you're living in the same house as Hayes."

"Yeah, it's a big change. I'm still trying to get used to it." I bump into Salem to get her attention.

Madison ignores that. "We should hang out sometime. Maybe go shopping or, like, do homework together."

I'm getting the idea of what this is all about. When Salem finally pries her eyes away from her phone and snickers, I know I'm right.

"Come on, Madison. You don't do homework. You just have your dad get your grades adjusted for you."

Amazing how suddenly Madison's smile turns into an ugly snarl. "Was I talking to you, Salem? No, I didn't think so."

"Sure, maybe we can hang out sometime," I say. "I'll have to let you know." It's the nicest way I can come up with to tell her I'm not interested, because I am definitely not interested. She only wants to be my friend because of Hayes. I didn't see her at the party on Saturday, so I don't know if she tried to get with him then, but she probably figures this is the safer bet. If she spends enough time at the house, she'll run into him. It's sad.

It also pisses me off. Who does she think she is? He's way too good for her, even with all his problems.

"You'll have to let me know?" Madison puts her free hand on her hip, looking me up and down. "No, honey. That's not how this works. If I tell you I want to hang out with you, you thank me for the privilege."

Salem heaves a sigh. "Go choke on a dick, Madison."

"Fuck you, Salem. Last time I checked, he tired of you pretty quick."

"Yeah, except now he actually talks to me, while he only avoids you," Salem responds. "But I'm sure that doesn't mean anything."

That's when I make a mistake. I can't help it. A tiny giggle bubbles up in my throat before I can stop it.

Madison glares at me. "You just lost your chance," she warns before marching away. Harper and the other girls look at me like I'm garbage before following on her heels.

"Sorry," I call out, but she doesn't want to hear it. Not like I actually mean it, either. It feels like the right thing to say. It's not like I meant to offend her.

Though she kind of deserved it.

"Don't apologize to her." Salem's eyes are sparkling, her cheeks pink. "That felt good. I should have said that to her a long time ago."

"You're in a great mood today."

"Why not? I've got a new man, and he's got a big dick." She holds her hands at least eight inches apart. "I'm surprised I can walk. Anyway, I gotta go. I don't feel like wearing this uniform around school all day, so I have to run." She's gone before I can even say goodbye for now.

At least we're still friends, and she still has my back. That thought gives me a little courage as I walk down the hall after getting my iced latte. I don't know what I would do without these things.

A bunch of jocks come out of the locker room further down the hall when I'm a few steps away from the classroom, with their king at their center. Dammit. I almost beat him to it. Hayes's eyes narrow when he sees me. Unfortunately, I don't know the guys he's with. If it was Franky or Theo, I'd feel a little more comfortable. Instead, they sneer and elbow each other knowingly.

"Looks like you dried off," one of them says, because stating the obvious is so funny.

"Yeah, I figured I'd put on dry clothes."

"I don't know. You looked better coming out of the pool." Another of the guys waves his phone at me. "And I have the proof."

"Good for you." The idea makes me quake inside, but I'll be damned if I let him know. "Enjoy. I'm sure your hand was glad my picture did some of the work for it."

A couple of girls going into the classroom laugh when they hear me say it, which gives me extra courage. Maybe Salem is rubbing off on me.

Hayes, on the other hand, isn't laughing. He makes a move like he's trying to get around me and into the classroom, but very deliberately slams into me. Suddenly, I'm drenched in ice-cold coffee.

"Whoops," he says, while I stare down at myself in horror. "Seems like you can't be around me without getting wet."

I don't know what comes over me. Frustration? Disappointment in him? Not to mention knowing my clothes are ruined, and I'll have to wear them throughout the entire day.

Whatever it is, it inspires me to throw my empty cup at the back of Hayes's head when he turns around. "You fucking asshole!" I shriek.

"What is this?" Principal Bradley marches our way. I didn't know he was nearby. "That sort of behavior won't be tolerated in this school."

I gulp, glancing at Hayes to find him looking around like he's completely surprised. Meanwhile, everyone who surrounded us five seconds ago scatters into their classrooms like roaches when the lights come up. Now it's only me and Hayes, who rubs the back of his head for effect. Because I'm sure an empty plastic cup really hurt him.

The principal looks down at the floor, then at my coffee-soaked clothes. "What happened?"

"Uh, it's just that I—" I glance at Hayes, who watches with an arched brow. I could tell him exactly what happened, but what would it mean for him? I can't forget the fight he had with his dad.

That's why I only tell part of the truth. "I spilled my coffee, and Hayes laughed. I got upset."

"And you believe that is a reason to throw something at his head?"

"I'm sorry. I overreacted."

"To say nothing of the language you used. I understand you're new here, Morgan, but what you've done directly violates our code of conduct."

"I'm sorry."

He looks down at the floor again. "Accidents happen. I'll have the janitor clean this up. And if I were you, I would think long and hard about how I conduct myself around here. I'll let this go, but I want you to apologize to Hayes."

No. Anything but that. Of course, Hayes is the picture of innocence. Mr. Charming. Like he is to all the adults around here who can't see through him.

"Well? We're waiting." Obviously, he's not going to let this go.

This was my choice. I could've told the truth, but I shielded this idiot instead. "I'm sorry, Hayes," I murmur.

"It happens. Do you want me to get you some paper towels?" Oh, I hate him.

"Hayes, I think it would be better if you went to class. Morgan, take a few minutes to clean yourself up if you need to." Mr. Bradley walks away, using the walkie talkie hooked to his belt to summon the janitor.

Hayes is still standing there, staring at me.

"What?" I bite out.

"You could have told him what really happened."

"Yeah, no kidding."

"So why didn't you?"

"Do you really want to know?"

"I asked, didn't I?"

"Because I was afraid you'd get in worse trouble than you're already in because of what happened at the swim meet. I didn't want you to get kicked off the team."

His brows draw together, his lips almost disappearing when he sets them in a firm line. "Really."

"Yeah, really."

"Even if it got you in trouble?"

"At least I wouldn't be losing a scholarship."

Instead of thanking me, all he does is let out a derisive snort. "You're so fucking pathetic." He strolls into the classroom without a care in the world, leaving me in the middle of a puddle and wondering why I care about him at all.

CHAPTER 15

It's times like this I'm glad Bridget is here. I could never get all this studying done if she wasn't looking after Lucy.

By the time I got home from school on Monday, Mom and Mr. Ambrose had already left for their trip. The way Lucy made it sound, she was out somewhere with Bridget at the time. She was surprised when she came back and Mom wasn't here.

The look Bridget gave me over the top of my sister's head told me what she thinks about this. Sure, she's here to do a job, and she does it well. But she's not blind. At least Lucy has a caring person in her life besides me. I can't handle everything on my own.

I haven't exactly been paying a ton of attention in history class. It's practically impossible with Hayes being there. I know I can't blame him, that I should be able to pay attention, but just knowing he's in the room is too distracting. We have an exam tomorrow and since I hardly have the focus to take decent notes during class, I have a lot of reading to do tonight.

My room is dark, the curtains pulled closed. I go straight to my bed and open my laptop, using the light from the screen to navigate the darkness. I kick off my shoes, then change into pajamas. It's early, but I'm not going anywhere, and if I fall asleep studying, I might as well be comfortable.

It isn't until I stretch out on my stomach with the laptop on my pillow that I notice the lump on the other side of the bed. A big lump. Human sized.

"You little stinker!" I jump up and pull back the blanket, expecting to find my sister hiding. She likes to pretend we're in a cave, with the blankets over our heads.

It isn't my sister. It's a very almost naked, seemingly unconscious Hayes.

He's not snoring, but he's definitely asleep, lying on his back with one arm flung over his face. He's only wearing a pair of tight boxer briefs, and in the light from the laptop there's no ignoring his gorgeous body. It's wrong of me to look at him this way when he's asleep, but I can't help the heat that starts bubbling in my core when my eyes land on his chiseled abs, his thick thighs.

And oh, the bulge. Saliva floods my mouth, but that's nothing compared to what's going on in my panties.

I shake myself, shocked and a little horrified. This isn't who I am.

Who I am is the girl who leans over and shakes his arm. "Hayes. You're in the wrong bed. I need to study."

He mumbles something and I want to scream. It's bad enough I like the sight of him. Why does he have to be in my bed? I pick up my laptop and take it to the desk, determined to sit here instead if he's not going to get up.

I go back to grab my phone from where I left it on the nightstand. Just like that, his eyes pop open, and he springs forward to grab me.

"What are you doing?" I ask with a gasp before I tumble into bed.

He chuckles against my throat, and I'm pretty sure I smell alcohol on his breath. "Sorry. Guess I got the wrong room."

"Bullshit." I swat at his hands, his arms, but it doesn't do any good. "Come on, stop screwing around."

"Who says I'm screwing around?" He turns me over so I'm on my back, my wrists in his hands. He's too bare and too tempting to be this close to me, moving against me.

"Whatever this is, stop it." I'm fighting so hard I'm out of breath, but he barely has to put up a fight to hold me down.

"You know something? Half the girls in school would give up a kidney to be where you are right now." He pins my wrists over my head before draping his body over mine. Oh, God, why does he have to be so hot? Trying to fight him is twice as much of a struggle thanks to that.

"Then bother one of them. I have to study for our exam!"

"Would you relax already? There's more to life than studying." He rolls his hips and his bulge rubs against my inner thigh. "Like this."

The heat he already brought to life is feeling more like an inferno. I have to ignore it. "You know this is wrong. Why do you keep doing this?"

"I don't give a shit what's wrong or right. Haven't you figured that out?" He lowers his head until our lips are almost touching. "Besides, you don't care that it's wrong. Don't pretend. I know you want me."

"No." I turn my face away, cringing when his mouth skims my jaw. Oh, God, how much do I want to say fuck it and let him do what he wants? I don't know how strong I can be. That's why it has to stop now. "Get off me."

"You know, I could do whatever I want to you right now." With a firm grip on my wrists, he nuzzles my throat, his lips caressing my skin. "And there's nothing you could do about it."

"That's not true."

"No?" He grinds himself against me again, and this time my breath catches. He notices, the bastard, chuckling at the sound. "Then go ahead. Scream. Scream your head off, so Lucy comes in to see why you're screaming."

"You're sick."

"No, I'm thinking of her best interests. You don't want her knowing about this, do you? It would fuck her head up all over the place."

"Stop," I beg, close to tears.

"You're a virgin, aren't you? I know what it looks like when a virgin's dying to give it up. Don't you think it's been too long already?" He laughs at my nipples through my tank top. They were hard already but now, fuck me, they're like bullets.

"Not like this. Not with you."

His head snaps up, an ugly snarl twisting his otherwise handsome face. "Not with me?" He lets go of my wrists, but there's no time to be relieved because he chooses now to yank down my pants and my panties along with them. I slap at his hands, trying desperately to kick him off, but I might as well be kicking air. He's possessed. Nothing is going to stop him.

"Don't. Not like this." Adrenaline floods my system, along with pure dread, when he lowers his shorts and his erect dick springs free. I've seen it before, but not like this. Not when he's on top of me and spreading my legs and ignoring my hushed pleas.

He holds me down with his body before sliding a hand between us.

"Don't do it," I beg in a whisper, still trying and failing to buck him off me. "You said you wouldn't hurt me. You said you weren't going to hurt me."

"And I'm not," he grunts from behind clenched teeth. I feel him down there, pressing against me, and all of a sudden he fills me up.

I squeeze my eyes shut, biting down on my lip as he works his way into me. My God. I didn't think he would actually do it.

"Holy shit," he sighs, sounding almost blissful. "So tight. So tight for me. This is what you wanted? Is this what you've been waiting for?"

He pulls back a little before driving in again. I didn't know there would be this feeling of fullness, like I'm being stretched so far I might tear. What if he makes me bleed? What if he hurts me worse than that?

"No," he grunts. "I bet you wanted to be romanced and all that shit." He slams forward again, and I let out a whimper. Tears roll down the sides of my face and soak into my hair. "Is that what you wanted? Tell me."

"No." I moan, shaking my head. "I didn't. It hurts."

"You're still disappointed, huh? Don't worry. It won't hurt much longer." I barely have time to take a breath before he enters me again. Again. Filling me, stretching me, hurting me.

I close my eyes again and more tears squeeze their way out from between my lashes. It hurts, but there's something else. With every thrust, every time he invades me, it hurts a little less—and feels a little better. Every time his body is flush with mine and he grinds against my clit it almost feels good. I don't know what's going to win out, pain or pleasure.

He moves faster, harder, and I have to fight with all my strength not to scream. I have to think about Lucy. I can't scare Lucy.

"That's right," he growls. "Take it. Take my cock. Just like I knew you would. This pussy is mine now. I can do what I want to it, whenever I want." And still he's thrusting, making me feel like he's going to split me in two.

And it feels sort of good now that the worst of the pain has passed. I clamp my lips shut against a moan because I don't want him to know, but that familiar tension is building. I hate him for this. I want him to keep going, but I hate him. I hate myself.

Then just as suddenly as he started, he pulls out, taking his glistening dick in his hand and stroking it furiously. My stomach churns in disgust when ropes of cum splash onto my stomach, spurt after spurt, before he finally stops with a deep sigh.

I'm not a virgin anymore. And I didn't have any say in it. I don't even want to move. The ache in my thighs and my pussy is enough to bring tears to my eyes again.

"There," he murmurs, working his way from between my legs before getting off the bed. "Now I've got you all broken in. You're welcome." He even smiles down at me, cold and heartless, and every nasty word I've ever learned threatens to tumble out of my mouth.

And they would, too, if it wasn't for the sadness in his eyes. I'm not imagining it—I don't like him very much, especially not right now. There's not an ounce of pity in my heart for him.

But the sadness is there. Plain as anything. He can smile all he wants, but he's faking. I only wish I knew why.

"Clean yourself up. You look like a sloppy slut." He strolls out of my room, not even bothering to make sure there's nobody out in the hallway before stepping out and closing the door. How would it look, Hayes leaving my room in his underwear? Can he really not care?

I guess not, since he obviously doesn't care about me. I look down at myself, at the cum on my stomach, and bile races up my throat.

There's nothing for me to do but carefully get up from the bed and limp to the bathroom to clean myself up. There's fire between my legs, and eventually I settle on a warm washcloth held between them, hoping to ease the pain.

Here I am in this big house, with just about everything I could ever wish for, and I might as well be in hell.

Maybe that's what I deserve since, deep down inside, I can't help but wonder if it'll feel better if we do it again.

CHAPTER 16

'm barely out of a dream when one thought hits me clear as a gong: I've never been so sore in my whole life.

I wake up a bit at a time, groggy, miserable. My head is heavy and aching and I can practically feel the bags under my eyes when I open them the morning after losing my virginity.

I still can't believe it happened. I can't believe it hurt like that. I can't believe it ended up feeling good. Is it always like that? It's not like I have anybody to ask. Maybe Salem, but she'd probably want to know who it was, and I can't tell her. We're not related by blood or even by marriage yet, but it's still weird. And God forbid anybody else found out.

I tried so hard to sleep, but it was useless until probably a couple of hours ago when exhaustion finally pulled me under for good. I might have been better off if I hadn't slept at all, because now I feel like I'm moving through deep, dark water as I ease myself into a sitting position. My thighs are so sore, and my pussy throbs. Not in a good way, either.

It's only once I'm sitting up that I realize my alarm didn't wake me. I look over at the clock, confused—I couldn't have woken up before it buzzed, no way—then gasp when I see the time.

8:00? It can't be.

But it is. The alarm didn't go off.

I pick up my phone. That alarm is off, too. It's supposed to go off every morning at 6:30, but it didn't.

I'm late for school. Very.

I can't think about fatigue or pain or any of it as I request a car before running around my room, throwing on clothes, then brushing my teeth and washing my face in record time. I look like hell, but I can't worry about that right now. I'm late. I'm late for the exam.

My stomach is in knots the whole way to school.

"Sorry, but can you drive faster?" I ask the Uber driver. I really need a car. Just another thing holding me back this morning.

"You want to pay extra for me breaking the speed limit?"

All I can do is drop back against the seat and pray I have enough time to at least get through most of the exam. Otherwise, I'm going to have to pull all As for the rest of the semester to get a decent grade. How did this happen? I set two alarms every night, for fuck's sake, and I know I did last night. It's routine by now. I don't even think about it.

The halls are empty when I arrive, and I run to the classroom while checking the time. Shit. There's only fifteen minutes left in class.

And when I reach the classroom, the door is locked. Frustrated, helpless tears well up in my eyes. How did this happen? I worked so hard.

The teacher sees me through the window and rises from his desk but takes his time crossing the room. Dragging it out, the jerk. He only opens the door far enough to stick his head through. "Nice to see you today."

"I'm so sorry. My alarm didn't go off, and—"

"I really don't want to hear it. This is the second time this week you've been late for class." He means Monday, when I spent the first ten minutes trying to get coffee out of my clothes.

"But it wasn't my fault. I'm telling you, I'm ready to take the test. I overslept, is all." I have no shame at this point, so I clasp my hands in front of my chest. "Please, can I take it? I'll stay after school if I have to, or I'll come in early tomorrow."

"I think I was pretty firm when I laid out the rules for my classroom," he reminds me in a tight, prissy little voice that makes me want to scream.

"But it's not my fault. I didn't deliberately miss the test."

"And it wouldn't be fair to the rest of the class if I gave you extra time to study."

"I'm not trying to get extra time. I only want the chance to take it."

"You're going to have to learn to live with the consequences of your actions. Next time, make sure to set your alarm. I don't know what else to tell you." He doesn't look or sound sorry. If anything, he looks almost pleased with himself as he steps back, prepared to close the door.

And just over his shoulder is a very familiar face. I can't believe it took me this long to put it together. Hayes's smile and the little wave he gives me behind the teacher's back tell me why I overslept today. It's not enough what he did last night. He can't stop at taking my virginity the way he did, so hard I'm aching this morning.

He had to turn off my alarms to make sure I wouldn't get to school on time.

The fucking nerve. Making sure I know he did this.

Before Mr. Collins closes the door all the way, I flip Hayes off to make sure he knows how I feel about him. As if last night wasn't proof of how cruel he can be. He had to drive the point home. Why did I ever think he was redeemable?

"Morgan!" The teacher's voice rings out like a shot, echoing in the otherwise empty hall. "What do you think you're doing? Don't pretend I didn't see what I know I saw."

Fuck me. Hayes ducks his head but the shaking of his shoulders tells me he's laughing along with most of the other kids in class.

"I'm sorry—"

He cuts me off. "Wait here. Don't move an inch." I have to stand and endure the humiliation while he scrawls something on a piece of paper, which he then folds in half and staples closed before bringing it to me.

"Take this down to the principal's office and don't think I won't call down to see if you went. I'll be checking to make sure my message was delivered." He slams the door shut before I can tell him I will.

Dammit. Damn Hayes, damn me, damn the whole thing. This time I'm dragging my feet down the hall because I know this isn't going to be good.

It isn't.

"Is this true?" Mr. Bradley holds up the note. "You made a lewd gesture to another student?"

"Yes, I did." My face is burning, and I have to fight off tears. The sense of being powerless is enough to make me want to throw myself on the floor and weep.

"There were no reports like this in the records from your former school. By all accounts, you were an exemplary student. What's changed?"

I have to bite my tongue before I can ask how much time he has. "It's been a tough adjustment."

He tents his fingers under his chin. "I see. I imagine it would be. I should have checked in with you before now, but there's never a dull moment around here. Are you experiencing any bullying?"

Like I can tell the truth. "I think that happens to new students in every school."

"We have a no tolerance policy on bullying. If someone or a group of someones is bullying you, I need you to tell me who it is so they can be dealt with."

It's so tempting. I'd get the chance to watch Hayes's face when somebody finally holds him accountable. Maybe I'll wave at him from behind Mr. Bradley.

I'd also have an even bigger, brighter target on my back if I did that—and things would only get worse than they already are at home.

"Nobody in particular," I say. "I'm not used to being around people this… rich. They know that."

"If it's only a matter of class disparity, that will iron itself out in time. They'll forget there was a time you weren't living under the Ambrose roof."

That's the thing adults like to tell themselves so they can turn a blind eye and still sleep at night.

"I'm sure they will."

"But I have to tell you." He leans across the desk and hits me with a hard look. "Unless you come to me with claims of bullying and we get to the bottom of the situation, I'll have to look at any other outburst as the third strike. You know what happens after three strikes?"

"I do."

The bell rings and it couldn't have come at a better time.

"You'd better get to your next class. Let's not meet like this again."

I don't waste time getting out of his office. Sure, I'm still worried about my history grade—I'm not going to take the exam now, I know better than to hope he'll change his mind—but it's better than withering under Mr. Bradley's stern stare.

A part of me expects Hayes to be waiting outside the office, ready to rub it in like he rubbed his cum into my skin last night. But it's Franky, instead, and he's wearing a sad grin. "Heard you overslept this morning."

"Great. Now everybody's going to know when my alarm doesn't go off." I can't be mad at him, though. He didn't do it, even if he's treating it like a joke. He doesn't understand the depth of Hayes's hatred for me. Even I don't understand it.

"You should hide all his speedos or replace his shampoo with the kind that tints your hair," he suggests as we start down the hall. "That'll teach him."

"And you two are supposed to be friends?"

He laughs and shrugs it off. "Friends play pranks. Just, you know, try to forgive him for it. He's going through some shit." There's darkness in his voice, replacing the laughter. I won't bother asking what he means. I know he won't tell me. I don't know if it makes him a great friend or a bad one.

"Hey, there's a concert in the park tomorrow night. I know your parents are out of town, so they won't care if you go out on a school night." When I lift an eyebrow, Franky explains, "Mr. Ambrose is kind of a tight ass about that."

I like Franky a lot. He's cute—even hot—and he's easy to talk to. Hayes trusts him, which means a lot. But there's no spark on my side of things. He doesn't get me all fluttery in my stomach when our eyes lock.

Not like the guy coming our way from history class. The person whose fault it was that I missed the exam. When our eyes meet from down the hall, a shiver runs down my spine and it feels like a hundred butterflies are loose in my belly. He sets my teeth on edge, too. I can't make sense of anything he makes me feel.

"I don't know..." I look up at Franky and bite my lip.

"Come on. Everybody's going to be there. Don't tell me you'd rather sit alone in that big house."

That's different. "Who's playing at the concert?"

"Who the hell knows? It's more like a reason to hang out."

Hayes has come to a stop in front of his locker, but he's watching us and not bothering to hide it. I can almost hear him growling—his jaw twitches, his nostrils flare, and he's practically shooting flames at us with his eyes.

Fuck him if he thinks he owns me. I reach up and touch Franky's shoulder, flirting as much as I know how to. That's not saying much. "Yeah, I'd love to go. Thanks for asking me."

I shoot Hayes a look before passing him on my way to English. He'll be good and pissed when I see him again, but so what? At this point, I know there's nothing I can do to make him treat me better. I'll be damned if I'm going to let him dictate what I do with my free time. At least we'll be in a group, so he can't get away with anything.

I hope.

CHAPTER 17

"You made it!" Franky gives me a hug when I find him on the lawn at the park in town. When he lets go of me, though, he looks around like he's expecting someone else. "Did you come alone?"

"Yeah, why?" I look over my shoulder, confused.

"I just figured… never mind." He takes my hand and leads me to where a bunch of people are already arranged on blankets spread out over the grass. The sky is just going dark, and the lights coming from the stage at the rear corner of the park cast blue and purple and red beams of light over us.

I recognize one of the girls as a cheerleader I've seen Salem talking with at school. She waves me over and pats the space next to her. "I've been wanting to hang out with you," she calls out over the music. She then hands me a bottle of beer from a cooler. Nobody seems to care that we're all underage and drinking in public, so I figure I might as well do what everybody else is doing.

"Parker," she offers with a smile, which I appreciate since I couldn't remember her name. "Friends with Salem."

"Right, I'm really glad to meet you."

"Did she tell you when she's coming?"

"No, but she said she'd be here. Maybe she's coming with Logan."

Her nose wrinkles. "What's up with that guy?"

"I have no idea. But she likes him." Honestly, I'm kind of annoyed with her. She made it sound in English class like we would come out together tonight, but basically ghosted me once I texted her after school. I know people get that way when they first meet somebody new, like they forget about their friends for a little while, but it doesn't make it any easier to deal with.

"Hey, there you are." Theo wedges himself between us, lying on his side. Like Hayes, he carries the scent of chlorine on his skin. "Where's your brother?"

"I don't know. I don't care, either." I'm tired of playing nice in front of people.

"Oh, come on." He nudges me. "It was just a prank."

"And it completely fucks my final grade. I guess he doesn't care about that, since he has you to do his homework for him." I nudge him back, and he laughs it off.

"Just let me know if you ever need any help."

"How come you never offered to do my homework?" Parker asks.

"I don't know." He leans in a little closer. "What's it worth to you?"

"Get the fuck out!" She's laughing as she pushes him away, and he pretends to be hurt. From the way she looks at him, though, I feel she's not totally against what he was implying.

"You should start charging people," I suggest. "Build yourself an empire."

"I have other ideas for that." I wait for him to grin, but he doesn't. I wonder what that's supposed to mean.

Theo sits up, looking behind Parker and me. "There he is."

I don't need to ask who. Not when the hair on the back of my neck stands up. He's watching me. He's always watching me. Theo lifts a hand to wave Hayes over. From the corner of my eye, I catch him frowning.

"What's up?" I play dumb, turning my head to look behind me. There he is, standing with his feet shoulder-width apart, arms folded. The red light now washing over his frozen form is chilling. He could be the devil himself. I'm wondering if he is.

"Let me go talk to him." Theo gets up and I have to force myself not to follow his progress. I don't know why, but it seems crucial that I don't let Hayes know how he gets to me.

Franky comes over and hands me a fresh beer even though I haven't finished the first one yet. "Salem say she was coming?" He turns his head from side to side, and I can see the concern etched on his forehead.

"Yeah, I don't know what's up with her. I guess she's with Logan."

Concern turns to anger or something like it. "Right." He probably doesn't get a good feeling about Logan either. I wish Salem could see how much better she can do.

Franky sits down with us, a little closer to me than he is to Parker. I wish I could get a read on him. He pays attention to me, like opening my beer and flaring up in anger when a couple of guys from school walk too close to where we're sitting. One of them almost steps on my hand, which I pull back with a gasp.

"Hey, fuck face!" Franky barks. "Watch where you're going." Obviously, they know him, and they know better than to do anything but mutter an apology.

"Jimmy and Keith. Both probably stoned," Parker sighs, and I realize one of them is the guy who gave me a pill at the party. Sure enough, he's wandering from group to group, and something tells me he's not really just slapping hands with the people he greets. They're obviously passing something off before he jams his hand into his pocket. Money, I guess. Payment.

Franky looks like he's brooding as he stares at the stage. "Is everything okay between you and Hayes?" I ask. "I've been meaning to ask you after what happened on Sunday. Now that he won't come over here, I thought…"

"Right. That. I guess you heard about it."

"Yeah, his dad was pretty pissed. Are you guys really fighting?"

"It's complicated." When Franky looks at me, he must see something that tells him I'm not going to let it go. "It's been tough on him lately."

A quick look over my shoulder shows Hayes still talking with Theo. For once, he's not paying attention to me. "Would you tell me if there was something going on? Something bad?"

He heaves a deep sigh, and I have to wonder what it's like to carry such a big secret for somebody. He must be tired. "Here's the thing."

"Hey! Sorry we're late!" All of a sudden, Hurricane Salem tears through. She trips over my legs before Logan steadies her. "Sorry, sorry! It's dark out here."

She's drunk or stoned or both. This is not the girl I knew just a week ago. That version of Salem has her shit together. Then again, how well do I actually know her?

Parker looks downright horrified. "Girl, you okay?" She gets up and goes to where Logan is settling onto the grass like she wants to pull Salem away to talk.

Instead, Salem drops into Logan's lap. "I'm better than okay." Salem looks over at me. "Having fun?" I don't even know what to say. I don't know if she could hear me if I answered with the music this loud. Or if she's actually asking.

"Is she always like this?" I turn to Franky, but he's already getting up and going elsewhere. Maybe it's not easy for him to see her like this. I hate feeling like I walked in on the middle of everything, like there's all this history I don't know anything about.

Theo takes his place, settling in with a groan. "I don't even know why he bothered to come if he's just going to stand there by himself the whole time."

"Hayes?"

"Yeah. He hasn't sat down. He's not even drinking or anything."

I shouldn't, but I can't help looking back at him. He has his hands in his pockets, his shoulders pulled up. Everything about him screams tension, even anger. What did I do this time? I'm not allowed to have fun?

"Do you know what's going on with him? I mean, I was just

asking Franky about the fight at the swim meet. Is he under a lot of pressure right now?" I pay close attention to his face, even though it's dark enough that I can't really read it.

"I don't know. Something's up his ass. He needs anger management classes or something."

"He might just ask you to do his homework for that, too." It makes me feel good when he laughs.

What doesn't make me feel good is looking over and seeing Salem making out with Logan. He's sitting with his legs straight out in front of him and she's on her knees, straddling him. She runs her hands up and down his chest before dragging her nails across his shoulders, while his hands are up under her skirt. She rocks her hips and breaks their kiss to throw her head back. He latches onto her throat.

"Jesus," Theo says. "Why bother coming here if you're just gonna fuck in the middle of the park?" I don't know if Theo is disgusted or disappointed. Me, I'm a little bit of both. It's a little over the top, and of course they're attracting attention. A circle forms around them, mostly guys, all of them with their phones out to record the action.

I grab Theo's arm. "Franky didn't tell me when I asked him. Is this usual for her? I wouldn't know."

"No, this is a new look for her." And he doesn't sound like he likes it very much. I know I don't. When she's sober, she's going to hate knowing there's all these videos around. Should I stop it? Could I even if I tried?

She cries out, arms wrapped around Logan's shoulders. His hands are fully between her legs now, and I know what he's doing. Her eyes are closed, mouth hanging open, and her hips rock wildly. More than a few girls are grimacing, sneering, shaking their heads, while of course, the guys are cheering and asking for more.

"Let's see those tits!" one of them calls out, which starts a chant that rises in volume over the music. "Tits! Tits! Tits!"

I don't know if there's some kind of secret code around here, but I can't sit around and watch this without at least trying to do something. I scramble to my feet and dart over, blocking the view of some guys taking video.

"Back off!" I shout at the top of my lungs to be heard over the music before taking Salem by the shoulders and shaking her. "Hey, everybody is recording you. Are you sure you want to do this?"

"Get the fuck out of here." Logan gives me a shove, and all that does is infuriate me.

"You get the fuck out of here," I snap, before kicking his leg. "She's out of her fucking mind right now."

A few of the other girls come closer, like they want to help. Salem, meanwhile, is slumped in Logan's arms, her forehead touching his shoulder.

"Hey, come on. Let's take a walk or something." I try to help her to her feet along with another girl, but she shoves us both away before turning on me. A bright beam of white light hits her face, and I see her pupils are pinpoints.

"Why don't you get a life?" she mumbles before giving me a weak push that doesn't even rock me back on my heels. "Always getting in the way. Nobody asked for your help." She stumbles off through the crowd, ignoring the cheers and whistles. I look down at Logan, who snarls at me before getting on his feet. For a second, I think he's going to hit me, but he cuts through the crowd behind Salem.

"Way to go." I can almost feel Hayes's breath on my neck. "Sticking your ass in where it doesn't belong. But that's what you do best, isn't it? Or were you jealous and wanting a turn once she was finished?"

"You're disgusting."

"No, what's disgusting is how you act like you're better than everyone else." His lips brush my ear. "You know how wet I make you. You're probably wet now."

I turn my head away and try to follow Salem's progress through the crowd, but he won't let up. "Maybe eventually you'll learn to mind your own business and stay out of other people's lives."

"You know what? You're right. You already showed me what a

mistake it is to give a shit about what somebody is going through. I should have just kept walking that day."

His eyelids flutter and I know he didn't expect that. Good. Maybe I can knock him off his game for once. He's not what I'm concerned about right now. It's Salem. She could barely stay on her feet. And Logan obviously doesn't care.

I shouldn't do it, but if anything happens to her, I will never stop blaming myself. That's what gets me moving, following the path she took. Everybody has gone back to what they were doing before the amateur porn started, so it's easier to see. But I can't find either of them in the crowd.

"Did you see which way Salem went?" I ask a group sitting in a circle. One of them points over his shoulder before taking a joint from the girl sitting next to him. I jog in that direction, getting further and further away from the audience. There's equipment next to the stage, crates and amps and cables. I make a loop around them, peering into the shadows. Where could they have gone? The parking lot's the other way.

"No... no! Stop it!"

I can barely hear it, but once I do, I can't ignore it. I follow the sound of Salem's voice to where she and Logan are half-hidden between two vans.

At first my brain doesn't want to accept what I'm seeing.

She's on her back underneath him, legs kicking, fists pounding Logan's shoulders and arms. "Stop! Don't!" she sobs, while his ass moves up and down. "Please, no!"

He's raping her.

CHAPTER 18

I don't know what I'm thinking. I only know I have to make him stop. I throw myself at him, digging my fingers into his shoulders and trying to pull him off her. "Stop! Somebody help!"

"Bitch!" He swings blindly and misses me. He doesn't stop, either, driving himself into Salem while she screams and begs him.

"Get off her! You're hurting her!" I punch his shoulders, his neck, even the back of his head.

This time, when he swings, he doesn't miss. His arm sweeps back and knocks me off my feet. I land on my back and the air leaves my lungs all at once.

I sit up in time to see a blur rush past me. A blur that reaches out and takes hold of Logan and pulls him off Salem before throwing him against one of the vans. Hayes.

I scramble over to Salem on my hands and knees. She's sobbing, skirt up around her hips, her panties torn. I gather her up in my arms and she leans against me before I try to straighten her skirt out.

"You son of a bitch!" I look up in time to see Hayes pull back his fist and smash it against Logan's jaw. A thrill races through me, sick as it is. What he did was sicker, and he deserves this. And much worse.

When Logan slumps against the van, Hayes pulls him up again before landing another punch, this one against his nose. Salem is shaking in my arms, her makeup running down her face, tears dripping onto my shirt.

I'm worried about her, but I can't stop watching Hayes. He lets Logan drop to the ground before kicking him in the ribs once, twice. When Logan rolls onto his side, curling into a ball, Hayes delivers a series of sharp kicks to his lower back.

He then rolls him onto his back, straddling his midsection, when he drops to his knees. He takes him by the collar of his shirt and lifts his head and shoulders off the ground. "You wanna get rough, you raping piece of shit? Let's get rough."

He hits him again and again, until his knuckles are bloody. He drops Logan onto the ground, but keeps hitting him until his face is coated in blood and it sounds like he's choking.

Salem clutches me, screaming. "Hayes, stop!"

"You have to stop!" I get up, leaving her on the ground, then take my life in my hands by approaching. "You'll kill him! Hayes, you'll kill him!" If he's not already dead. His face is almost unrecognizable, blood glistening in what light is leaking between the vans. I can't tell if he's breathing.

Hayes's head snaps up, and the wildness in his eyes makes me fall back a step while my insides turn icy. "Stop," I say, "We have to get out of here before somebody finds him."

He's breathing heavily, and for a second, I don't know if he even hears me. Maybe he's too far gone. "Hayes," I say again, this time reaching out and touching his shoulder.

He nods slowly, shooting one more look at Logan before getting up. "Motherfucker," he mutters before taking one more kick at his ribs. Logan doesn't respond, but his chest is moving up and down.

"We have to help her." I go back to Salem, who's trying to pull herself together.

Hayes is gentle, lifting her arm and draping it around his neck. "Come on. Let's get you on your feet."

"I—I tried—" She looks around wildly, mascara-ringed eyes finding me. "I tried."

"I know you did." As I drape her other arm over my shoulders, I have to fight back tears. Her feet drag over the ground as she sags between us.

"Here." Hayes crouches a little and scoops her up in his arms. She rests her head on his shoulder, weeping, and he makes little comforting noises before looking around to make sure nobody is nearby. "Come on."

We walk around the perimeter of the park, far away from everybody. My heart's pounding and I'm still a little sick to my stomach when I remember what Logan looked like by the time Hayes was finished with him. Between that and what I witnessed happening to Salem, my stomach's churning and a cold sweat coats my skin.

"I can't go home like this." It's the only thing I understand coming from Salem before she bursts into fresh tears.

"We could take her home with us, right?" I ask Hayes. Our parents aren't home, so it's the perfect solution.

"YEAH," he says. "She can stay with us."

"But shouldn't we go to the hospital?" I ask.

"No, we can't do that." Salem lifts her head, finding me behind Hayes. "I took some stuff. And I drank a bunch."

So she would get into a lot of trouble if they tested her at the hospital. But still, I ask, "He's just going to get away with it?"

"What about..." Salem looks at Hayes before lowering her head to his shoulder again, and I understand. If Hayes shows up at the hospital with bloody hands and Logan describes what happened, everyone will know Hayes gave him that beating. If he even survives it.

On top of that, there was the scene she and Logan made in the park. It's on video, so many videos. I'm sure cops would take one look at some of that footage and say she was asking for it. If Logan had a lawyer, they would jump all over it.

She's trapped in a corner. We all are. Right now, what I need to think about is my friend, who Hayes very gently settles into the back seat of his car.

"You're okay now." I slide in next to Salem and she curls up against me. "We'll take care of you."

"Oh, Morgan, I'm sorry." She tucks her head under my chin. "I didn't mean it."

"Don't worry about it. It's fine. I understand."

"I can't believe..."

"I know." I stroke her hair, trying to be as gentle as I can.

"Thank you. I don't deserve you coming after me."

"Sure you do. Like I said, I understand."

"He got all rough with me and I said I didn't like it. And then he got so mad." She's shaking so hard, I'm almost afraid she's having a seizure at first. "And then he threw me on the ground, and I screamed, but nobody could hear me."

"You're safe now," Hayes reminds her in a gentle voice.

When I look up into the front seat, the part of his profile I can see along with his hands squeezing the wheel tell me he's not feeling so gentle. What will happen if somebody finds out what he did?

"I didn't want him to. I really didn't." She moans, curling up tighter than before. "But after what we did. With everybody watching."

Hayes grunts. "You're allowed to say no."

I almost can't believe this is coming from him, but then he seems to feel a lot different toward her than he does toward me. Almost like he's a different person.

I'm sure Lucy's in bed by the time we pull up at the house, so I'm not worried about anybody finding us. I help Salem out of the back seat while Hayes goes up to unlock the front door.

"We'll get you cleaned up," I promise as she clings to me.

"I can't believe it. I can't believe it."

"I know. I'm so sorry."

Hayes follows us up the stairs like he's ready to catch Salem if she can't make it, but she does. I take her to my room and turn on the shower. He goes to his room, where I assume he's going to clean up the blood on his shirt and body.

I can't believe any of this is happening either. I can't believe I saw what I saw. I can't get the image out of my head: Logan on top of her, ignoring the way she screamed and pleaded with him. If it didn't mean anything for Hayes, I'd be glad if Logan was dead.

While Salem is in the shower, I change my clothes and pull out a pair of pajamas for her. I hear her weeping softly in there and check on her, but she tells me she'll be fine. I hate feeling this helpless.

By the time she's finished and drying off, I've set ibuprofen and a couple of bottles of water on the nightstand by my bed. She waves off a heating pad before taking the medicine, along with half a bottle of water. As an afterthought, I go through the closet where the housekeeper keeps some of the cleaning supplies and pull out a bucket. Just in case she feels sick to her stomach.

"Thank you." Salem peers up at me as I tuck her in. Her hair is still damp, fanned out over the pillow. Her face is scrubbed clean, her skin pink enough to tell me she rubbed extra hard. I guess I would do the same thing.

"You're welcome. I'll be back in a little bit. I'm just going to go check on Hayes."

She nods before rolling onto her side, the blankets up around her shoulders. I feel bad about leaving her alone for even a minute, but she closes her eyes like she's going to try to sleep. I leave the small lamp on the desk burning just in case she needs it.

Hayes's bedroom door is open, but the lights are off. He's not in his bathroom, and the next best guess is the kitchen, so I go down there to find him holding a dish towel full of ice against the knuckles of his right hand. He's showered and changed, and aside from those knuckles, nobody would know what happened less than an hour ago.

"Is she okay?" he asks as I walk into the room, examining the bruises rising on his fist before leaning against the island, across from where he stands at the counter.

"Define okay." He nods slowly at my answer. "She's as okay as she can be. I know it's not my place to thank you, since I wasn't the one being hurt, but thank you anyway."

"Don't kid yourself. I saw you land on your back. He could've…" He shakes his head before finishing the thought. Not that he has to. Now I have a whole headful of nightmares.

"Are you worried?"

"What would I be worried about?"

"Come on. Let's be real for a minute. What if he talks to the cops?"

"What if he does? He doesn't even know who I am."

"He might be able to describe you."

"It was dark. Would you stop?"

"I'm just worried, that's all."

"You worry too much." He lifts the ice from his knuckles and winces a little, flexing his hand. How can he be so calm at a time like this? He could be in serious trouble. I hate that I even care, but I can't help it. He might've done something bad, but it was for the right reason.

"You should be like this more often," I say.

He lifts an eyebrow. "What does that mean?"

"I don't know. Like, nice. Talking to me."

It's the slightest little change. The shift in his posture. The tightening of his jaw. "Don't get all excited. This is about Salem."

"I just wish you would let me know what I did to deserve this I never tried to be anything but your friend."

"Are you really trying to start this again? Don't you know when to leave shit alone?" When he drops the ice pack onto the counter, I know I've done it. I took it a step too far.

"Forget it. I'm going to go check on her." I turn away, ready to run if I have to, but as usual, he's too fast. He blocks me in, one arm on either side of me—then, he takes it a step further by grabbing me by the waist and lifting me onto the island.

Instead of fighting, I sigh. "I don't feel like playing games. It's been a long night."

"Who said I'm trying to play a game?" He pries my thighs apart and places himself between them. "You said you want to be friends. Let's be friends."

"That's not what I meant, and you know it."

"I don't know what to do with all these mixed messages you keep giving me." He holds on to my hips, pulling me a little closer to his crotch. He's getting hard. How can he get hard right now? "Admit it. You liked watching me beat the shit out of that guy. It got you wet."

"That's not even funny."

"I'm not trying to be funny. All women like watching men assert our dominance. You can pretend all you want, but you aren't any better than the average female." He leans in until his nose brushes my neck and I have to pretend to be revolted when he inhales deeply. "I can smell it on you. Excitement. It's on your skin."

"You're sick."

"What's really sick?" He lifts his head, his lips dangerously close to touching mine. "Me talking like this, or that it's true? You're no better than me. The only difference is, I don't lie about who I am."

"I know that's not true." He's hiding himself again, trying to scare me out of getting closer. It's obvious enough to make me feel sorry for him.

"It's not?" His hands slide over my thighs, and it shouldn't affect me the way it does. It shouldn't unleash heat low in my belly, heat that spreads to my pussy and makes it throb. That's how undone I am by his touch. I'm helpless against it and it makes me hate myself. I'm leaning in before I know what I'm doing, ready for him to lead me wherever he wants to go.

In a flash, he lowers his head to my shoulder, partly exposed under a loose T-shirt. His teeth sink in, and I suck in a pained breath.

"What are you doing?" I ask with a gasp. He lets go and I press a hand to the spot. It's screaming, throbbing with every beat of my heart. "Why?"

"You know me so well, right? You tell me." He walks out of the room, whistling softly like he didn't come close to killing somebody tonight. He's right. Just when I think I know him, he reminds me I don't know anything at all.

Upstairs in my bathroom, the mark stands out like neon against my pale skin. It's red, throbbing, and it's going to turn into an ugly bruise. I wash it off before turning out the light and going to the bedroom.

Salem's asleep, snoring softly when I slide in beside her. Thank God. I hope she doesn't have too many nightmares—but if she does, I'll be here when she wakes up. There's at least one person I can help.

Hayes? I don't know if anybody can help him.

CHAPTER 19

This has been the longest few days of my life. Running out of chemistry because I'm about to throw up might as well be how I end the school week.

I barely make it, throwing one of the stall doors open and dropping to my knees maybe a second before hurling into the bowl. I barely ate anything for breakfast or lunch, but it doesn't seem to matter. My body wants to eject everything in it, fast and forcefully.

By the time I'm finished, I'm sweating and shaking and seriously wishing I was in my bathroom instead of here. But what was the alternative? Throwing up all over myself in class? As it is, I'm sure I'll catch hell from the teacher for running out. Theo's in that class with me. Maybe he'll speak up on my behalf.

How am I supposed to walk through life like nothing's out of the ordinary when all I can do is wait for the cops to show up?

Every minute, I expect them to knock on the front door at home. Or to see them striding down the hallways at school, looking for Hayes. Thanks to my frayed nerves, even a slamming locker makes me jump.

Salem's been out sick since that night. I can understand why—and if she was here, it would be too much to handle. I wasn't the one

Logan raped, and I can barely handle all the talking and the whispering and the insane stories people are making up.

After three school days worth of gossip, I've put together that Logan was eventually discovered by guys with the band. He needed surgery to fix his face. Depending on who's telling the story, he either had a broken nose and jaw or he basically needed a total reconstruction. Having watched the beating, I'm going with nose and jaw, at least.

Nobody knows for sure whether he's awake or not—and if he is, whether he can even talk thanks to his jaw being busted. But I guess he could still answer yes-or-no questions. Once he's awake, he could identify Hayes.

Meanwhile, there are who knows how many videos out there of what Logan and Salem were doing before the beating. And because I tried to stop them, I'm on those videos, too. Yelling at Logan, even kicking him once. What if somebody wants to talk to me?

What if they arrest Hayes?

Why does that bother me worse than anything else?

Is Hayes worried about any of this? That's the worst part. Nobody would ever know he laid a finger on Logan. He's still strutting around school like he owns it. Not a care in the world. Meanwhile, my clothes are getting loose because I can't eat without feeling sick.

I rinse my face at the sink and swish out my mouth. Not that it does anything to get rid of the sour taste. I hardly recognize the fear-filled eyes looking back at me. My gaze lowers to the mark Hayes left, half-hidden by my shirt and covered in makeup. That's not quite enough to hide it, but it makes a difference. I still don't know why he did it.

The door squeaks open and my heart lurches when I see who's coming in. Of all the girls in the whole school.

"Damn," Madison snickers. "You look even worse than usual."

She doesn't know I've had a lifetime of experience ignoring snarky remarks. I ignore her and make a move to walk around her so I can leave. Of course she gets in my way.

"Rude much? I'm talking to you."

"I have to get back to class." She sidesteps to get in my way again and something inside me snaps. "Don't you have something to snort up your nose? I don't want to hold you up."

Madison snarls before shoving me. I stumble back against the sinks, but don't fall. "You look like somebody who's got stuff on her mind. Like something happened and got you all fucked up inside. I wonder what that is?"

All this time I was worried about the police, when I should've been worried about vicious bitches like her.

"Get out of my way," I say.

"You know what I think?" She grins nastily. "I think you saw your new best friend fucking her guy, and you lost your shit. I think that's how he ended up in a hospital bed."

"Me?" If she only knew. I can't help but laugh. "Yeah, okay. People are saying he was almost dead when he got to the hospital. Like I could do that."

"There were all kinds of equipment behind the stage. You could've used that." She gets close to my face, eyes narrowed into slits. "I bet that's why you look like you haven't slept since. Because you got jealous and lost your shit. I wonder if the cops would want to talk to you?"

I don't know why she has to be this hateful. I don't know why the whole world won't leave me alone.

But I know why I throw my total weight against her as I shove her away. She falls against one of the stall doors and almost lands in a toilet, but stops herself just in time. Now it's my turn to lean in close, and now the surprise and fear on her face give me strength I didn't have before.

"You know what? Maybe I did. Maybe I snapped and beat a man half to death at the park." I lean closer and she flinches. "So why would you fuck with somebody capable of doing that? If I almost killed Logan, what could I do to a piece of nothing like you? Maybe you're the one who needs to watch her back before I snap again, bitch."

"You're crazy," she whispers, trembling.

"Then you need to back the fuck off." I punch the metal wall next to her head before leaving the stall, then the bathroom. I feel ten feet tall. Untouchable.

Until I see Hayes standing outside the door, arms folded. That's all it takes to bring me back to reality.

"Making friends in there?" he asks with a smirk. Did he hear any of that? He must have, or else why would he look so smug?

"I guess the rules don't apply to you, or else you'd be in class right now."

"The rules never apply to me."

"Right." I'm too sick and too tired to face off with him. Madison is one thing, but he's a different beast. "I have to get back to class." I'm about to leave when my phone buzzes in my pocket. I pull it out and read the message.

He sees the way my face falls. "What is it?"

"Mom and your dad came home early. Bridget wanted to let me know." I look up from the phone to find him pushing away from the wall and stalking away.

* * *

"It's so nice for all of us to sit down and have a meal like this." Mom is back to her benevolent saint act, sitting at the end of the table with her new tan and a warm smile. "There's nothing like coming home after a trip and finding my family here."

Because she didn't already have a family before this? I guess Lucy and I didn't count. It doesn't come as a surprise.

"I'm only sorry business cut the trip short." Mr. Ambrose is plowing through his food. He probably has to get back to whatever brought them home a few days early.

"It means I get to be with my babies." Great. As if I didn't already have trouble keeping food down.

"I'm done," Hayes says. I was so busy trying not to throw up thanks to Mom's performance, I didn't notice Hayes shoveling food into his mouth. "I've got stuff to do."

"Stay," Mr. Ambrose mutters around a mouthful of roast beef. "I haven't seen you all week."

"Seriously? This is the second time we've sat down as a family for dinner, and that makes maybe three times total for the two of us unless it's a holiday. Don't act like this is a huge tradition I'm breaking."

"We're trying to create new traditions." The men stare each other down for a beat before Hayes pulls his chair closer to the table.

So what does he decide to do next?

"Morgan's been making new friends at school since you left," Hayes says. "I heard them gossiping in the bathroom today." His smile is almost natural.

"You hang around outside the girls' bathroom a lot? Do you wish you could use it?" I ask.

Lucy bursts out laughing, which for a moment breaks the tension. Why does he have to be this way? If he heard us, he should know I was covering for him.

"Morgan," Mom warns.

"I'm only teasing my brother." I smile across the table at Hayes. "Yeah, I was having a really fun conversation with Madison."

"It sounded that way."

What is he trying to do? Get me in trouble? Why do I care about him getting arrested again? Sometimes I can't remember.

"We were talking about the concert in the park the other night," I say. "She said some crazy stuff happened. It's all anybody's been able to talk about since then."

"See?" Mr. Ambrose gestures with his knife. "This is why I'm against letting kids go out on school nights. Things happen and distract them from their work the next day."

I raise an eyebrow, daring Hayes to push it further. I'm not about to break down the way he wants me to.

"What's that?" Hayes points at my half-hidden bite mark. "Looks like a bite?"

"Yeah, a bug bite." I adjust my top to cover it and seriously wish his father had let him leave the table. "No big deal."

His nostrils flare. I don't get it. Does he want me to announce how I got this? Or am I supposed to dissolve into tears and run away from the table? It's like he wants me to break down—and when I don't, it only enrages him.

"Can I please go now? I made plans before I knew we were doing this whole family dinner thing tonight." Hayes stands, tossing his napkin to his plate.

"Let him go, sweetheart," Mom coos. "We did sort of spring this on him. At least one of the kids has an active social life." Nice way to slide in a dig at me, but I'm too relieved Hayes is getting out of here to care.

"Do you have plans tonight?" Mr. Ambrose asks me as he gets up from his chair.

"No, I have studying to catch up on."

"Hayes could take a lesson from you." He offers a wink, then goes to the other end of the table to offer Mom a kiss on her cheek before heading to his study.

I'm happy to let Lucy chatter away through what's left of the meal. I don't have much to offer right now. If either of our parents knew what happened this week... I don't even want to imagine it, though that won't stop my brain from coming up with all kinds of scenarios.

Later, in my room with my laptop and books, I keep an ear out for Hayes's return. A part of me expects him to invite himself into my room like he has before, but the doorknob doesn't even jiggle.

By the time I fall asleep, he still hasn't come home.

CHAPTER 20

$\mathcal{B}$y Sunday afternoon, Salem looks a little pale, a little drawn, and she's not as bubbly as I've gotten used to seeing her. But at least we're hanging out for the first time since she slept over.

"Here's a tip: don't mix painkillers and booze unless you're with people you trust." Salem frowns down at the fries she's moving around on her plate. "I'm not taking them anymore. I don't like who I am when I do."

"When did you start? And why?"

"Over the summer. It was something new. I didn't like who I was before I started taking them out of my mom's bathroom either. It was more fun than feeling like shit over other things."

"Like what?" When she doesn't look up from her plate, I press her harder. "What other things?"

"I really don't want to talk about it."

"You don't have to. So long as you still want to be my friend, even when you're not on pills."

She rolls her eyes but grins, too. "It didn't make me that different. Just happier. And invincible. Like nothing could bother me."

If I didn't see for myself how it ended up when she mixed the pills with a lot of alcohol, I might ask to try them. I could use a break from everything for a little while.

She takes a small bite of her sandwich and chews slowly. I sense there's still something bothering her, but I don't want to force her. Finally, she sighs. "There's somebody I was hooking up with over the summer. On and off. Not he-whose-name-I'll-never-speak-again," she adds with a grimace. "It ended before I was ready, and I didn't take it well. I thought I was over it, but when school started, it all came back."

So it's somebody from school. Hayes? They supposedly only hooked up in junior year, but it could've bled through to the summer. He flat-out almost killed somebody for her, which points to there being feelings somewhere. And he was so sweet and gentle with her afterward.

She even threw herself into his arms the first day of school and he didn't tell her not to touch him. There was no awkwardness that I could see, and I can sense awkwardness from a mile away. Mom trained me well.

Bitterness touches my heart. I hate it, but I can't help it. What if all this time he's been tormenting me, he was tormenting her at the same time?

"It's not Hayes, is it?" I blurt out. I instantly hate myself for it. What if it is and I'm rubbing salt in the wound?

She almost chokes, her face red by the time she swallows the fry she was chewing. "God, no!" She laughs. "That's ancient history. I mean, he's a good friend now, but I wouldn't fall apart over him. No offense."

"Why would I be offended?"

"Because you're almost related." She eyes me, lips pursed. "You almost bit my head off."

"I didn't mean to." I take a long sip of my soda hoping to cool my flushed cheeks. She's right. I'm on edge. "I'm just saying, if I have to kick his ass, I'll gladly do it."

"He needs an ass kicking sometimes, but not because of me. Don't worry," she adds as I mull this over. "You don't have to watch over me. I can handle my shit. I sort of… went off for a little bit, but I'm finished falling apart."

"I'm glad. And I'm always here if you need to talk."

"I know. You're the only person I trust."

It's the first time she's been out of the house since faking sick for four days after that night at the park. We haven't talked about it except for me asking how she's feeling and if she needs to talk. I'm not going to bring it up if she doesn't first.

She has to go back to school tomorrow though.

"I've got your back," I remind her when we talk about it. "But everybody's pretty much over it by now. There's always something new happening."

"I don't know. I'm dreading walking in tomorrow. I know all the guys are going to say sick things."

"Yeah, but that's what they do anyway. They know you'll kick their asses."

"That's true." It seems to brighten her mood a little. "What if we go to swim practice after this?"

My burger tastes like sawdust all of a sudden. "Why do you want to do that? I thought we were going to the movies."

"We can go see a later one. I want to get a feel for what it'll be like at school tomorrow—and there's only a handful of swim team members. So it won't be too horrible if they're acting like assholes." Salem bites her lip, eyes wide, and I understand what she means. Sort of like dipping her toe into the pool.

Does it have to be that pool in particular? I haven't seen Hayes since dinner on Friday night and I don't know what kind of mood he's going to be in. He wouldn't do anything too mean in front of his friends, would he? What am I saying? He pushed me into Franky's pool at the party. Of course he would.

But his coach will be there, too, and Hayes has to stay on his good side.

A shiver runs up my spine. I've never had the chance to see how Coach Greg treats Hayes. It might be interesting, seeing if there's a difference in how he acts around Hayes compared to the other swimmers.

"Yeah," I say. "We'll go to practice and see the movie later, if it'll help you feel better."

She doesn't need to know why I want to go.

* * *

IT'S WEIRD, being here on a Sunday. The lot is almost empty when we pull in. Hayes's car is here—its sight launches my heart into my throat. Where's he been all weekend? Maybe staying with Franky? I don't know if that's a good thing or if it annoys me. Why do I want him around when he only ever torments me?

A few other people are hanging around in the bleachers when we get there, girlfriends of guys on the team. They definitely sit up and take notice when Salem and I walk in, but they're all friendly, asking her how she's feeling after being out sick. None of them mention the concert. They seem satisfied to go along with the idea that she had the flu but is feeling better now.

All I want to do is find Hayes. He's not with the other team members standing around the pool. A few of them are in the water, swimming slow laps, while others stretch around the perimeter.

I look over all of them, wondering if I'm missing something. Where is he? I catch Franky looking up at us and give him a wave. He lifts his hand, but his expression doesn't change from blank stoniness. Did something happen earlier? Another fight? He looks pretty pissed off, and it would explain why Hayes isn't around.

Theo doesn't look like there's anything wrong. He's sitting on the edge of the pool with his legs in the water, joking with some of the other guys.

He looks up and finds us. "Hey, there she is. You better not be contagious anymore. I don't feel like shitting my brains out."

"It wasn't that kind of flu, you disgusting ass." I see the relief on Salem's face and hear it in her voice. Theo's a really good friend, maybe the best kind of friend. He's ready and willing to say exactly the right thing. In this case, he's accepting Salem's excuse for being absent like it's a fact. Who's going to disagree with him?

Apparently, nobody around the pool. They all laugh with us, and things roll along. Salem makes comments on the various swimmers and how they look in their speedos, and I'm happy to nod in agreement with her opinions.

My mind is far away, on Hayes. Why isn't he here? His car's outside. If it wouldn't look obvious, I'd go to Theo and ask about him. What would my excuse be? I'm worried about the brother I love so much, even though he's not my brother and I'm more obsessed with him than anything else? Yeah, I'm sure that would go well. He's too perceptive. I don't want him reading into it.

"Why aren't they, I don't know, swimming?" I ask. I know it makes me sound hopelessly dumb, but it's a pretty good question. We've been here ten minutes and nothing's happening but a bunch of time being killed.

Salem looks around with a frown. "I don't know. Usually the coach has them swimming themselves to death by now."

So I'm not wrong. This is strange.

"Franky looks pissed," I say. "I wonder if they had another fight."

Salem shrugs it off. "Boys are weird. I'm sure they'll be best friends again tomorrow."

I wish I believed it was that simple.

"I have to pee." I'm risking her saying she'll come with me, but she turns to one of the other girls and goes back to her conversation. I'm even gladder now that she's blending right back into things, since it means I'll get to do a little sneaking around with her.

There's a pair of restrooms across the hall from the coach's office. I've seen them before. If they're inside, I might overhear whatever's going on. I hope it's not something that'll result in Mr. Ambrose coming down here. It's hard enough living with Hayes when he has swimming and friends to take up his time. What happens if he's grounded and there's nobody but me to take his frustrations out on?

"So long as you're ready to do what it takes to be a true team player around here." Coach Greg's voice floats my way, clearer the closer I get to the office. The door is closed, but the wall facing the hallway is mostly glass, so it doesn't muffle the sound all the way.

"Like I said, I'll do whatever needs to be done." Hayes's voice is clipped, and I recognize the begrudging tone. I only heard it back on Friday night, so it's sort of clear in my memory.

"I appreciate that. I'm sure the rest of the team appreciates you giving this your all."

"You don't have to keep trying to sell me. I get it. I have to do what I'm told or else my life is over."

"I wish you wouldn't put it that way." There's the sound of metal scraping over tile, like he pushed his chair back. "There's more to being a leader than standing at the front of the group. It's about being willing to do what it takes for the good of the team. Accepting responsibility. Personal sacrifice."

"I know all about that."

"I'm sure you do, but it's one thing to know about it, and another thing to do what has to be done without complaint. That's what you need to work on, Hayes. For yourself, and for the team. You understand?"

I creep a little closer to the office, but can't see anything from where I'm standing. What do I expect to see? I don't know. There's something about the coach's voice that's rubbing me the wrong way. I feel prickly all over, uncomfortable. If that's how I feel, how much worse must it be for Hayes?

"Yeah. I get it." It's clear Hayes is ready for this conversation to be over. I don't blame him. No wonder he doesn't like having to play nice with this guy. I wouldn't want to, not if he talked to me that way.

I can't help it. I need to know what's going on in there. If I go to the bathroom, I'll be able to see from the door, so I cut diagonally across the hall and push my hand against the swinging door like I'm about to go inside.

But before I do, I cast a casual glance over my shoulder—or what I hope looks like one.

Coach Greg doesn't notice me, because he's too busy kneeling in front of Hayes, who's wearing nothing but a Speedo. "I'm glad you took my advice," the coach murmurs, placing a hand on Hayes's hip.

What the hell am I looking at? My heart stops beating, and I forget to breathe as the ugly scene plays in front of me. What are they doing? What's this man doing to him?

Suddenly, Hayes's head snaps around in time to find me standing there, gaping at him.

And there's no misinterpreting the rage burning in his blue eyes.

CHAPTER 21

"I guess I was worried about nothing. You were right."

"Sure."

"But it probably would have been different last week, like the day after. Right?"

"Sure."

"Maybe I should suck dick in public next time and really see how long it takes for people to forget something."

Salem's words finally filter through my brain fog, and I turn away from the window I've been staring out of since we left the movie theater parking lot. "What?"

"There you are." She laughs lightly as she turns onto my street. "You haven't been paying attention to anything I've said."

"Sorry. I'm distracted." I don't remember much about the movie. I was too busy worrying whether I should say something to Mr. Ambrose about what I saw.

"Obviously. What's up? Did something happen back at school? You got really weird."

She has no idea what happened, or how shaky I feel now. Having to sit through practice while the girls flirted with their guys and Coach Greg shouted instructions and encouragement to the team. It was obvious he didn't like us being there. I understand why. How is he supposed to abuse his swimmers with witnesses hanging around?

That has to be what I saw. I'm not imagining things. He was flat out on his knees with Hayes's junk practically in his face. There really aren't too many ways to interpret that. What other reason would there be?

"What's up with you?" Salem asks before pulling into the driveway. The house looks inviting and should be a haven, but I dread stepping foot inside.

"No, it's okay. I'm just…" It's so close to coming out of my mouth, all the ugliness, all my questions and fears. You can't put the toothpaste back in the tube though. Once it's out, I can't take it back. What if I'm wrong?

"Hey. You know the whole friend thing goes both ways, right? I know I've been a lot lately, but if you need help…"

"It's not me. I mean, I'm not sure anybody needs help. But I think they might."

"What's up?"

"If you thought something bad was happening, like somebody was getting hurt maybe, but you weren't sure, would you say something? Like to your parents or whatever?"

"I don't know." Salem folds her arms. "It depends on what's happening. What do you think is going on? Who's being hurt?"

"That's the thing. I'm not a hundred percent sure. If I'm wrong, or if I don't have enough proof, I could end up ruining somebody's life."

"What if you don't say anything?"

"Then I'd feel terrible if I'm right and I never spoke up. Like if I let this bad thing keep happening because I was too afraid to talk about it."

She makes a thoughtful noise. "What if it's not up to you? What if whoever this is happening to needs to be the one to speak up?"

"What if they can't? What if they're afraid to?"

"They probably have their own reasons for being afraid. And you don't get to decide if those reasons are good enough." There's an edge to her voice that makes my eyes widen in surprise. "You're not the only one who decides what's right and wrong, you know."

"I know that." I can't help but feel defensive. "But if I see something wrong and I know somebody's hurting, isn't it wrong to pretend I don't know about it?"

"Did that person ask you for help? Did they come to you?"

"No."

"Then maybe you need to mind your own business."

"Wait a second, hold on. What do you think I'm talking about?"

"Me! Like you still want to go to the police over what happened with Logan." So much for never saying his name again.

"That's not even what I'm talking about."

"Wait. It's not?"

"No. You were right about not going to the hospital. They would only have blamed it on you. This is something totally different."

"What is it?" She leans in a little, speaking in a whisper.

"No, it's not my place. You're right about that."

"But you really think somebody's getting hurt somehow?"

The image of Coach Greg on his knees flashes in front of my mind's eye. "I think so."

"That's a lot to carry around. It really isn't your responsibility to take care of everybody in your life, you know. I know from what you've told me that it wasn't easy growing up with your mom and how she kind of left you on your own. And then you took care of your sister all these years. But you don't have to take care of every single person around you."

"I know you're right. I wish it was easy to believe it."

We say goodbye and make plans to meet up in the cafeteria first thing in the morning before I drag my feet into the house. Lucy is way too busy playing a game with Bridget to care much about my being home, which isn't easy to come to grips with. I'm used to being the center of her world, or at least part of it. But this is the way it's supposed to be, I guess.

Before I go to the kitchen, I kiss her on the head. I stuffed myself on popcorn at the movies—it seems my stress reaction has turned to overeating rather than being too upset to swallow a bite. I grab an apple to at least balance things out a little before heading up to my room to finish my homework.

At least Salem didn't put things together in the car. I don't even want to imagine what Hayes would do if I let it leak that I think Coach Greg is abusing him.

It's like he hears me thinking about him. I barely have time to turn around in my chair before Hayes is in the room, locking the door behind him. His eyes flash as he crosses the room, pulling me out of my chair before pushing me up against the wall.

"What were you doing there? Why did you have to be there?"

"At school?"

"Where else? During practice. Why do you have to be in my world? Why can't you leave me alone?"

"It was Salem's idea."

"You sure about that? Was it Salem's idea to sneak around and spy on me?" He leans in, his breath hot on my face. "Or did you just want to see me in my Speedo?" He actually barks out a laugh, confusing me more than ever.

"Let go of me."

"Not until you tell me why." He catches me by the throat, holding tight. His eyes are wild, his teeth bared. "Tell me."

I lift my chin and stare straight at him. "I know you're not going to hurt me."

"Oh, yeah?" He slams his fist against the wall, close to my head. "You don't have the first fucking clue what I'm capable of."

"I do. I know this isn't who you are."

"You. Don't. Know. Me." His breathing is heavy, erratic, eyes darting back and forth over my face. "So stop pretending like you do."

"Why are you doing this? You don't have to. I have nothing against you. I've never tried to hurt you."

"You don't have to try." His grip on my throat eases until it's more of a caress. What's he doing now? Is this a game? "You don't know what you do to me."

My heart's racing, but for a different reason. This is all it takes. The slightest shift, and I find myself melting into him. "I don't mean to."

"That's what makes it so infuriating. You don't even know you're doing it." Hayes slides an arm around my waist and turns me around, backing me up against the bed where we both tumble onto the mattress.

I know what he means about infuriating because this is infuriating me, too. The way he goes from threatening me to touching me the way he is now, taking me from fear to craving.

He runs a hand down my side, then works it between my thighs. I part them, giving him room, thrusting against his fingers. Is it wrong to be this desperate? I don't care. Not when it feels this good to be touched.

"You're like a drug." Hayes kisses his way down my throat, then up again, running his tongue over my ear. "I can't keep away from you, no matter how hard I try. It's like I can't control myself when I'm around you."

"Right now, I don't want you to." I arch my back, gasping when the pressure from his hand increases. Even through my clothes, he's going to make me come.

"I didn't want to hurt you before. When I fucked you. It's just…" He trails off without finishing.

"Just what?"

He doesn't answer, choosing to slide his hand into my jeans instead. This time I welcome his touch, grinding against his fingers, working to give my body what it's craving.

"Are you gonna come for me?" he whispers in my ear, and I reach up and run my fingers through his curly hair while moaning out my response. Yes, I'm going to come. I'm already almost there.

Which is why I groan in frustration when he takes his hand away. He only gives me a teasing little laugh as he pulls his shirt over his head. I do the same with mine and take off my bra, too. I want to feel him all over me, on every inch of my skin.

"You covered it up." When his fingers skim what's left of the bite mark he gave me, he frowns. "I liked seeing it."

"Why?" I ask, but instead of answering, he only lowers his mouth to my other shoulder and does the same thing on that side. Only this time, when I'm so wet and almost ready to come, it feels good. I run my fingers through his hair, closing my eyes, wincing—but liking it, too.

"Mine." He runs his tongue over the throbbing mark, then lifts his head to look me in the eye. "If I can't get rid of you, I'm going to make sure the world knows you belong to me." I don't have time to process this—not that I could with all the blood leaving my brain and traveling south—before he's unbuttoning my jeans. I lift my hips so he can ease them down, along with my panties.

We shouldn't do this. We absolutely shouldn't. But when he covers my mouth with his and thrusts his tongue inside, the world explodes around me in shimmering light. Everything that mattered just a second ago is wiped away. I wrap my arms around him and hold on tight, my nails scratching his shoulders, running over his head while our tongues dance inside our joined mouths. I'm on fire, burning up from the inside out. And I want to. I want to be consumed.

I barely notice until he's already pressing against me that he's between my legs. He enters me while we're still kissing and I moan into his mouth, a mixture of discomfort and satisfaction. Deep, throbbing satisfaction that spreads throughout me, all of it stemming from the place where our bodies are connected.

And this time, it doesn't hurt. This time, he goes easier, rolling his hips in slow, delicious circles, grinding against my clit, bringing me back to the place I was before he stopped rubbing me.

He breaks the kiss and I gulp in air before straining upward to meet his lips again. But he has other ideas. He kisses his way down my throat again, this time sweeping his tongue over my skin until I'm whimpering helplessly. Needfully. He goes lower still, running his lips across my collarbone, his hips still rolling, still driving me crazy.

He takes one of my nipples between his lips and sucks on it, flicking his tongue over the tip before releasing it with a popping noise. He does the same to the other one and I have to bite the side of my hand to keep from making a sound. I want to scream, I want to moan his name, I want him to know how incredible this feels.

"So good," I whisper, and he groans in agreement before driving himself deeper than before.

He kisses me again, again, nibbling my lips, sucking them, brushing his tongue against mine. I'm lost in sensation, lost in him, pushing away everything else—every thought, fear, doubt—in favor of what's building in me. In both of us. I feel the change in him, the way he's losing control.

Over me. Losing control over me, because of me.

And that's what does it. What finally pushes me over the edge into that sweet, dark, blissful place. I cry out inside his mouth when it hits, then shake in his arms while my arms wrap around him and hold tight until the strongest tremors pass.

I'm still trembling when he pulls out, taking himself in his hand and jerking until he comes across my stomach like he did before. Only this time I don't feel so used. So dirty and confused. This time, there's something right to it.

He kisses me once more—slowly, almost tenderly—before getting up. "Stay there," he tells me, so I stay where I am while he goes to the bathroom. He comes back with a washcloth, and I watch, fascinated by him, while he cleans me up.

Our eyes meet and he chuckles softly. "Maybe next time I'll take it and put it up inside you," he suggests, wearing a devious grin. "What about that? Pregnant with your stepbrother's baby."

I shudder, shaking my head. "No, thanks."

"What?"

"I'm not trying to have a baby, especially not by my stepbrother." It's almost laughable, the idea. "Honestly, now that you mention it, we probably shouldn't do this anymore. I mean, obviously I like it, but it's pretty risky. I don't want to have a baby."

He looks away, and I'm afraid I might have said the wrong thing even if I can't imagine what. It's only common sense. The last thing we need is to ruin everything that way.

"What's wrong?" I ask when he turns his back on me and bends to pick up his shorts off the floor.

I'm halfway to a sitting position when he spins around, holding up his phone. I don't have time to cover myself before he snaps a picture of me still practically splayed out, naked. "Why did you do that?" I whisper, horrified.

"I like seeing you like that." Any trace of warmth or gentleness is gone from his voice. It's back to being flat, almost lifeless. "And now, it'll be a reminder."

"A reminder of what?"

"If you let Frankie or any other guy anywhere near you, I'm sending this picture to everybody you know. Including your moth-er," he adds when my mouth falls open in dismay. "So, keep that in mind."

"You can't do this. It's not fair!" All he does is laugh, barely waiting until his shorts are on before he gathers up the rest of his clothes and leaves the room.

CHAPTER 22

$\mathcal{I}$ hate feeling like I have a secret. Maybe some people like knowing things nobody else knows about. Maybe it makes them feel special. I'm not one of those people.

As I walk through the cafeteria, I can't help but wonder what people would think if they knew the real Hayes. I'm sure there isn't a single student walking in this morning who wouldn't know exactly who I meant when I said his first name. And if I asked what they thought about him, it would depend upon the person I asked, but the answers would be the same. Cool, popular, athletic, hot. An all-around great guy. Sure, he has an attitude problem, but it only adds to his mystique. He's a talented athlete who pulls great grades seemingly without trying, so he can be allowed the occasional outburst or display of ego.

I'm sure not a single person waiting in line for coffee or to get a breakfast sandwich has the first idea of what really goes on in his head. What he's capable of doing.

And how damn addictive it is. Because as much as I hate the way he uses me, I only end up wanting more.

"Salem. Good to see you. You feeling better?" I hear the question being asked before I notice her approach. She only gives the guy who asked it a thumbs-up, though, it's pretty obvious from his tone how he meant it. She's not taking the bait. I have to give her credit.

Instantly, Salem frowns at me. "Did you get any sleep at all last night?"

So the makeup wasn't enough to cover up the bags under my eyes. "Is it that obvious?"

"It's really bothering you, isn't it? What we talked about last night?"

Right. I almost forgot about that. "A little." That's not a lie, even if it's not what's at the forefront of my mind. There's a certain photo of me living on Hayes's phone, and I still don't know if I can trust him not to spread it around. I can't ask her whether I can trust him with something like that without having to admit to a lot of other things I would rather she not know about. I'm not exactly proud of myself for letting this go on, especially since I end up liking it every time he uses me.

"Maybe you should talk to the school counselor. You don't have to use any names, but they might be able to give you advice."

"You might be right." I need more than that. Much more.

He's broken inside. I guessed it, but now I know for sure. It doesn't take a genius to see he acts out against me whenever his coach touches him—or worse. It's his way of venting his pain.

I look like hell this morning because I spent the night wishing he would open up and let me help him in a way that's healthier and doesn't involve me living naked on his phone.

My phone buzzes while Salem's ordering her coffee. The site of Franky's name makes me feel guilty. I don't know what Hayes's problem is with him lately or why he'd be jealous of the time we spent together, but now I understand why he wouldn't sit with us at the concert. I figured the guys were joking about the bro code or whatever they were talking about. Maybe it's a real thing.

You left too early yesterday. Theo decided to throw a party Saturday night. You in?

There goes the guilt again. I deserve to have fun without wondering what Hayes will think about it. It's more than that. Like wondering if Franky likes me. I don't feel that way about him. Am I leading him on when I accept an invite like this?

"What's up?" I didn't realize Salem was watching.

"Something about a party at Theo's this weekend."

"Oh, yeah, he texted me about it last night when I got home. Do you want to go?"

"Sure." So long as Franky doesn't think this is a date or anything, it might not piss Hayes off too much. "We'll go together."

* * *

THEO'S HOUSE is even bigger than Franky's. It's bigger than mine, too, and built to look like a villa or something. Very opulent. I wouldn't be surprised to see armed guards at the doors. There's fancy artwork on the walls with lights shining on them to show them off.

"Is it a good idea to have a party in a house like this?" I ask Salem as we walk through the very grand foyer.

"Everything is insured."

I guess that makes it all better. There are still so many things I don't understand about this world. If I were throwing a party with all this artwork around, I wouldn't be able to enjoy a minute. I'd be too busy trying to make sure no one breaks anything.

"I guess this is a pro-coaster house." When all Salem does is quirk an eyebrow at me, I shake my head. "Never mind."

It takes a while to find Theo, who's hanging out on the back patio. And I thought Mr. Ambrose's patio was nice. There's a big screen set up on one end, with couches and pillows and chairs where a bunch of people are hanging out and watching porn, of all things. A pair of girls I recognize from chemistry class currently flank Theo. They're sort of draped all over him.

"Hey, you're here." Theo looks a little disheveled, and I'm wondering how much fun he's already had with them tonight.

"Seriously?" Salem rolls her eyes at the gangbang currently going on in front of us. "Charming entertainment."

"It's my job to keep my guests happy." Theo disentangles himself from the girls and gets up. "Drinks, ladies?"

There's a huge bar set up out here, and on the other side of it is the pool. You can swim right up and get yourself a drink if you want to. Obviously, his parents know how to party.

I'm about to ask for a beer when Hayes climbs out of the pool. I didn't see him until now. I didn't know he was already here and wasn't expecting him this soon. There goes any hope of actually enjoying myself tonight. Not when he has this look in his eyes, like he wants to light me on fire from across the patio.

"Morgan?" Theo prompts.

I walk over to the bar, nodding. "Yeah, I'll take a beer."

"You sure you should be drinking?" Hayes walks over, toweling off.

"Is it any of your business?" I ask before regretting it. All it takes is a twitch of an eyebrow and I remember the picture. I can't piss him off.

"Come on, man. Nobody wants to hang around with the over-protective brother." Theo winks, holding out a bottle, but Hayes intercepts and takes it for himself.

Theo opens his mouth like he wants to argue, but I shake my head. "Don't worry about it. It's fine."

"You're in a mood tonight," Salem observes with a sour look. "What's your problem now?"

"Hi, to you, too, Salem." Hayes isn't looking at her. He's too busy staring hard at me as he takes a gulp of the beer that was supposed to be mine.

"What did I miss?" Franky strolls out, already holding a plastic cup full of something or other that I guess he got from the kitchen.

I glance at Hayes in time to see him give Franky a death stare. Is he seriously that hung up on us being friends?

Theo answers the question before anybody else gets the chance to. "Family drama. It's not boring at all."

"No drama here." Hayes takes another swig of beer. "Right?" he asks me.

"No drama on my end." I love how he thinks he can break me down. All he's done since the first day of school is strengthen me. He's shown me I can take what he hands out, and I get the feeling it drives him nuts.

He lowers his brow. "I didn't even know you would be here tonight."

"Why wouldn't I be?" It's easy to forget there are other people around us in a moment like this. He might as well be the only other person in the world.

"It's just I thought we had an understanding," Hayes reminds me in a tight voice.

"What would that be?" Franky asks. I wince, wishing he wouldn't have said anything.

"Seems to me that's not much of your business, is it?" Hayes says in a deceptively smooth voice.

I bite my tongue rather than tell him to leave Franky alone. I don't know which comment is going to be one comment too many, so it's better not to say anything.

Salem does the talking for me. "What is it with the two of you lately? It's getting really boring to hang around with you."

"Who told you to hang out with us?" Hayes counters. She looks genuinely hurt.

"Why are you taking this out on her?" I demand. "She didn't do anything to you."

Hayes's smile is chilling. "You're right. I should take my feelings out on other people instead."

Theo scratches his head. "Am I the only one who's completely lost?"

"No, I am, too. I'd like to know what the fuck I did to piss you off so bad," Franky growls. By now, people are paying attention.

I shouldn't do it, but I feel like I have to. "It's not about you, Franky," I inform him, turning my attention back to Hayes. "Is it?"

"You don't know what it's about."

"I'm sure we would all like to know," I tell him with a sweet smile.

"You're killing the mood here." Theo turns up the volume on the movie, and the sound of grunting and squealing fills the air.

Hayes shrugs it off, then turns to a chair covered in clothes, which he slowly puts on. Even now, when the sight of him brings an unpleasant taste to my mouth, I wish he wouldn't bother putting on his jeans and T-shirt.

He slides a hand into his back pocket and pulls out his phone. The glow from the screen casts eerie shadows over his face as he taps it a few times. He then looks straight at me, grinning.

No. No, he didn't. He said he wouldn't. I didn't do anything wrong!

Suddenly, everybody's reaching for their phones. No, it has to be a coincidence. Right. Everybody out here just got a message at the exact same time?

A few people laugh, followed by more, until the sound is almost loud enough to drown out the gangbang activity.

This is a nightmare. I can't be living through this right now.

His smile widens as I rush over to him. He even lets me yank the phone out of his hand to see what he sent everybody.

It's just a dumb cat meme. It's not a picture of me. Everybody is already drunk enough to think it's hilarious, I guess.

The only thing I can come up with is to shove the phone at him and run for it, cutting my way through the house, ready to go home. I was wrong to think I could stand up to him. Not knowing what he'll do next is too much to deal with. I'd rather sit home alone than be afraid.

"Wait, Morgan!" I don't realize until I've woven my way through dozens of people that Franky is following me. Why does he have to do this?

I'm outside by the time I call out over my shoulder. "Just go back inside. I'm fine."

"Just hang on." He reaches me and grabs my arm. "Don't run out like this. He's just fucking around with you."

"And in what universe is this okay? He's made his point. I don't belong here. He doesn't want me here, so I'm going to go home."

"What the fuck?" Hayes bellows. "This is between me and Morgan." Hayes followed Franky it turns out. Salem and Theo and a bunch of others are right behind him.

"You know what, Hayes?" Franky asks. "You take shit too far. Why can't you just let her enjoy her life a little? We all get it. You don't like the situation with the whole blended family thing."

Hayes bares his teeth. "You don't know what the hell you're talking about." More kids are pouring out of the house, wanting to see what happens next.

"You sure about that?" The two of them lock eyes and the tension is thick enough to cut with a knife. Franky reaches out again and takes me by the hand. "I'll take her home, since you ran her out of the party."

"Get your fucking hands off her." Hayes takes my other hand, and now I'm being pulled back and forth. "If anybody is going to take her home, it'll be me."

"You're the reason she has to go home now."

"Leave her alone," Salem calls out. I'm not sure which one of them she's talking to.

Franky gives me a tug. "It's not bad enough you have to let personal shit ruin everybody else's lives?"

Hayes drops my hand in favor of shoving Franky hard enough that he stumbles back and almost hits the ground. "What the fuck is your problem?"

Franky throws himself at Hayes, who fights to stay on his feet.

"Stop!" I shout, horrified. "Don't do this!"

Either they can't hear me, or they don't want to. Hayes cocks his arm back and catches Franky's chin with his fist. Salem screams along with me as Franky hits the ground. I can't help but flash back to the night he beat Logan, and horror turns my blood to ice even as I lunge forward, hoping to stop them.

"No, no, don't do that." Theo grabs me around the waist with one arm. He's already holding Salem back. "You'll just get in the way. You don't want to get hurt."

Meanwhile, Hayes is leaning down over Franky, shouting in his face. At least he's not hitting him anymore. But I'm sure it's only a matter of time.

Red and blue lights wash over the front of the house, causing everyone to scramble away. Somebody called the cops. Of course, we're on the front lawn, for God's sake. Salem goes running for her car, and I'm left wondering what I'm supposed to do before Hayes finds me and takes hold of my arm. "Come on." It doesn't even occur to me to fight. I need to get out of here just as much as anybody else does.

He peels away from the house, tires squealing. I hold on to the door handle so tight my hand hurts as he takes the curve leading down from the driveway. Only this isn't the way Salem came onto the property.

"Where are we going?"

"There's a back exit," Hayes informs me through clenched teeth. I'll take his word for it. So long as we get out of here before we get caught.

And we do. The winding path leads down to a dark road. I turn around to look behind us and can't see the flashing lights anymore. I let out a sigh of relief and slump against the seat.

But not for long.

"What the hell was that about back there?" I ask. "Why do you have to do this? I wasn't trying to bother you. I was only trying to hang out. You started things."

"Do you know what a whiny little bitch you sound like right now?"

"Fuck you."

"Is that any way to talk to me when you know what I have on my phone? Don't act like you don't, because you sure as hell freaked out when I sent that meme around."

"Which you knew would make me freak out. Why are you doing this to me? Is it really only because you don't want your dad to get married, like Franky said? We're supposed to be adults now."

"Franky doesn't know what the fuck he's talking about. He only thinks he does."

"He sure seemed like he did. What's your problem with him? I thought you were supposed to be best friends."

"It's none of your business."

"It sort of is, since he's the one you don't want me talking to." We're still rolling down this dark, empty road, and it's creeping me out. "Where are we? Are we going home?"

"We'll go wherever I want to go. I'm the one in the driver's seat, not you." The engine revs as he presses against the gas pedal, and the glance I dare take at the speedometer tells me we're coming up on seventy miles an hour. On an unlit road with woods on either side.

"Slow down." I'm amazed I can sound so authoritative when my heart is racing as fast as the car.

"Pussy. This is nothing." The car seems to jump forward, and now we're closing in on eighty. Eight-five. "Wait until you see what this baby can do."

"I want to get out!"

"Going this fast? You wouldn't have skin left by the time you came to a stop on the road. But be my guest." He leans over like he's about to open my door. I want to beat his arm away, but I can't risk it when he's going this fast.

"Stop it!" I beg in a voice that doesn't sound like mine. "You're going to kill us!"

"And?" He laughs when I let out a broken sob. "Should've let me jump, huh? Now, I'm going to take you with me."

"You're crazy! Stop this! You win, okay? You win."

"What do I win?"

"I'll do what you want." The needle creeps up toward ninety. "Please, just slow down. Don't do this."

"Whatever I want?"

"Yes! Please, slow down!"

He does, finally, and I cover my face with my shaking hands. If a deer had come running out, or even a raccoon, that might've been it. We could both be dead.

A lit road comes into view when I lower my hands. He would've had to slow down once we hit traffic. I recognize the intersection as being close to the park in town. At least I don't feel so disoriented now.

Rather than pull up at the red light, Hayes pulls to the side of the road. "Get out."

"What?"

"Get out of the car. You wanted out? Go."

Is he bluffing? It doesn't look or sound that way. "But we're a couple of miles from home."

"My home. It's not your home. It'll never be your home." Hayes opens the door this time. "Go. I don't want you anywhere near me."

What am I supposed to do? I get out and slam the door for good measure, then watch him race off in the opposite direction of the house. Where's he going? Why do I still care?

It's too late and too dark to walk home. I cross the road once the light turns green, then sit down on a bus stop bench to wait for an Uber while taking deep breaths to calm my shredded nerves.

I only thought Hayes hated me before.

Now? I'll be lucky if I live through him.

CHAPTER 23

eet me at the pool at lunch. Alone. H.

He slid the note my way after history class. By the time I unfolded the paper and looked up at him in surprise, he was on his way out the door.

What is it this time? How is he going to torture me? This is the first contact we've had since that terrible night in the car, after Theo's. He wants me to meet him at the pool? Why? To drown me? Or maybe he wants me to watch while he drowns himself. Either way, I'm not interested.

Or so I tell myself as I walk to English class. What's he going to do if I don't go? That's a question I'm not sure I want the answer to. He's going to get angry with me, frustrated, and that never ends well. Maybe it'll be better to get it over with. He can't do anything to me here at school, right?

"Don't expect me at lunch time," I tell Salem after class.

"Why, what's wrong?"

"Nothing. I just have to go to the library." Whether or not she believes me, I can't tell. One thing about her is, she doesn't push for answers when they aren't offered. Probably because she doesn't like being questioned herself.

By the time lunch rolls around, I doubt I could've eaten anything

169

if I tried. My stomach is in knots from trying to figure out what Hayes has in mind. I open the heavy door leading to the pool, almost wincing at how loud the sound is when there's nobody else here.

No, that's not true. There's one other person already here, and he offers a smug little grin when I walk in. "I didn't know if you would come."

"I figured it was the safer choice." I look around rather than look at him, standing with his back against one of the ladders leading up to the diving boards. He's so proud of himself. Getting exactly what he wanted once again. "So? Why did you want me to meet you here?"

"There's something up there. I need you to see it."

He points up and I tilt my head back, back, looking all the way up at the highest board. "Up there?"

"Yeah."

"What could be up there that I need to see?"

"You'll know when you see it."

"Can't you go up and get it and bring it down?"

"What, are you afraid?"

"Most people would be. How many feet up?"

"It's seven-and-a-half meters, so around twenty-five?"

"Twenty-five feet? No, thank you."

"Coward."

I fold my arms. "Fine. I'm okay with that."

"I promise you'll be glad you went." When I roll my eyes, Hayes mimics me by doing the same thing. "What, you think I would push you off the board in the middle of the school day?"

"It would not surprise me."

"Just trust me. I only have good intentions this time."

Maybe it's the sincerity in his voice—either that, or I'm a complete glutton for punishment. No, it's probably that I don't want him to win. I want to show him I can be brave. I'm not the coward he thinks I am.

Whatever the reason, I leave my backpack on the bleachers

before taking hold of the ladder. This is probably the dumbest thing I've ever done.

"I'm right here behind you. You're not going to fall."

"Great. I wasn't worried about that until you just said it." He laughs softly but doesn't say anything else, allowing me to climb while suffering silently. Why am I doing this? Why do I let him push me into things like this?

Everything seems so far away by the time I'm a few rungs from the top. "This better be good," I mutter, willing myself not to look down.

"It is. Trust me."

I get to the top of the ladder and look out over the board. "There's nothing here. Son of a bitch, why are we doing this?"

"Keep going. Unless you want me to fall."

"Right now? Don't tempt me." I hold on to the railing running along the outer edge of the platform. My knees are shaking, my stomach flip-flopping around. "I think I'm going to faint."

"No, you won't. Take deep breaths. In through your nose, out through your mouth. You'll be fine." He's standing in front of me now, but my eyes are closed, so I can't see him. Right now, I don't want to. I'm too irritated and, frankly, scared out of my wits.

"Why am I up here?" I ask in a whisper once it feels less like I'm going to wet myself.

"I wanted to get you alone. Someplace exciting."

"Exciting?" I blurt out a laugh that echoes around the cavernous space. "That's a word for it."

"Excitement makes everything better. More intense." Am I dreaming, or is he touching my ass? I'd jerk myself away, but where can I go?

"You're joking, right? You can't mean it."

"I do." His caress turns to a grope, and a rough one at that. "I've been teaching you all about what to do with this body of yours. What it can feel like. It's time for another lesson."

"What would that be?" I ask. My heart's fluttering so fast I have to take deep breaths again or else pass out.

"On your knees. I'll show you." When I hesitate, he goes from groping my ass to gripping my shoulders and pressing down. I don't have a choice. He must really have a death wish if this is his idea of a good time.

"Good girl." Hayes runs his fingers over my cheek, letting them fall away so he can use them on his zipper. It should set my teeth on edge, him calling me a good girl. Like I'm something he can own. The way he marked me with his bite and all that.

So why doesn't it? In fact, the familiar tingles are building between my thighs.

"Pull your lips over your teeth," he instructs while he pulls himself out of his shorts. "That's the first lesson. No teeth."

I nod, my heart hammering now. I'm seriously supposed to do this? I know better than to think he's only messing around to see how far I'll let him go before I refuse. No matter how much I wish that was exactly what he's doing.

"Take it slow. Relax your throat. I won't fuck your face up here."

"Thanks."

He snickers before taking my hand and wrapping it around him. He's been inside me more than once. I shouldn't be so surprised it feels like this. Stiff, but delicate. I don't think he'd like hearing that, so I keep my thoughts to myself.

"Now start slow." Hayes coaxes me by using a hand on the back of my head. "Use your tongue on the underside." He inches into my mouth, and I do as he says with my tongue. He lets out a deep groan and, dammit, the tingling intensifies. I want to please him. I actually do.

"Somebody could come in any time." He doesn't let up on the pressure, holding my head with one hand and easing himself in as deep as I can take him. "Doesn't that get you a little wet? You can admit it."

I moan with him in my mouth, and he groans louder. "Fuck. That feels good. Keep going. Don't let up the pressure." It's a lot to keep track of all at once, but I think I'm getting the hang of it. I'm not even as scared of being up high. The platform is sturdy.

His hips move and the hand on my head takes hold of my hair. "Don't stop. Fuck, yeah. Suck my cock." I'm choking and can't help gagging, but he won't stop. I can't pull my head away with him holding so firmly.

"I'm going to come," he grunts. My eyes go wide, but I can't see him. I can't tell him not to. "You're gonna swallow it. Let it go down your throat. Don't fight it."

Don't fight it. That's easy for him to say. I try like hell to loosen my throat while his thrusts get shorter, sharper.

Then he pushes all the way back to my throat and suddenly my mouth is flooded with a slightly salty, warm fluid. I gag on it but force myself to swallow it down with the sound of his happy groans ringing in my ears.

"Good job." He sighs. "Not bad for your first try. You'll get better with practice." He loosens the grip on my hair, now stroking it. I can't help but feel proud. Glad he's happy with me. How much more fucked up is this going to get?

I should know better than to ask, even in my head.

"Now, to return the favor," Hayes says.

"Oh, no. I want to get down now. You don't need to."

He gets on his knees the way I am. "Either you're going off the platform into the water, or you're going to give me what I want. And what I want is to taste that sweet pussy."

"I've… I've never…"

"No shit." He extends an arm toward the diving board. "Lie back."

"On that?" I squeal before clapping a hand over my mouth.

"On that. Trust me." He gives me a devilish grin. "Nerves make it better. You'll see."

I can't believe I'm doing this. I sit on the board and lie back slowly, gripping the sides with both hands. When Hayes spreads my thighs, I stiffen, and the motion makes the board tremble a little. "Oh, my God!" I whisper, closing my eyes—not that it helps me forget where I am or what's happening.

"Relax." He lifts my skirt and eases my panties to the side. "Wet. I knew it. Does having my cock in your mouth get you wet? Or is it the thrill of being up this high?"

"Shut up," I mutter. He only laughs softly before running a thumb over my slit. I gasp, arching my back before I remember to stay still.

"That's nice, huh?" He strokes my slit again, this time easing his thumb between my lips. "Perfect little pussy, shaved clean the way I like it. Smells sweet. I wonder what it tastes like…"

I realize I'm holding my breath, waiting. He's not holding his. It spreads over my wet lips and makes me shiver.

The first touch of his tongue is magic. It sets my nerve endings on fire, makes the ache in my clit turn to something painful. But I'll kill him if he stops. Even gripping this board, which vibrates with every gasp I take.

"You better hold on tight," he advises in a low voice before driving his tongue deeper, until it's inside me. I have to bite down hard on my lip to keep from screaming out how good it feels. How right.

"You taste incredible." Hayes moans before running his tongue along my slit again. This time, he flicks against my clit. Teasing me. I have to force myself to stay still and silent and damn him, it makes this better. The fear of what will happen if we're caught. Of what would happen if I fall.

I'm not falling. I'm flying—soaring—with every brush of his tongue.

"More…" I whisper. "More, please…"

He groans before treating me to rapid, short little flicks that make fireworks explode in my head before they do in my core. It all happens so fast, all at once. My body goes stiff, while I fight back the screams trying to tear themselves from my throat.

"I told you it would be good." He's so proud of himself when he raises his head.

I barely raise mine, just enough to watch him sit up on his calves. "I have a problem," I admit in a choked whisper.

"What?"

"I can't move. I'm afraid to even breathe too deep."

He takes pity on me. "Here. Let go with one hand. I'll pull you up."

"No fucking way."

"Trust me. I haven't done anything to fuck with you yet."

No, except for tricking me into coming up here. But it's either trust him again or stay up here for the rest of my life, so I force my fingers away from the edge of the board and reach out. He takes hold with a firm grip and pulls me to a sitting position.

"Not so bad, huh?" He starts down the ladder but waits for me. "Come on. You'll be fine. I'll be right behind you the whole way."

And he is. That's the weirdest part of all. He's behind me all the way, coaching me down. Like I imagined the cruel, heartless part of him all along.

CHAPTER 24

S aturday morning, there's a note taped to the front of the refrigerator. *Away for the weekend. Be good.* It's in Mom's handwriting. She didn't sign it.

At least she let me know. It's not like I see a lot of her anyway. I sort of make it a point to avoid her. One good thing about living in such a big house is we can coexist without having to see each other. I'm sure she doesn't mind that either.

Lucy and Bridget had plans to go to the library today for a play-group kind of thing, so I guess they've already left. I miss spending time with my sister—I never minded it in the first place. What I minded was not having a choice and having to keep her alive when I could barely manage myself.

Just when I think I'm alone, I hear footsteps. Now I know what a deer in headlights feels like. I freeze, waiting, even as my heartbeat picks up. We have the house to ourselves, except for the staff. What is he going to do?

Turns out it's only Charlotte coming in with what looks like a shopping list in one hand. "Good morning. Can I make breakfast for you?"

"That would be great. You don't have to go to any trouble though." I pull out my phone and scroll TikTok while waiting, absently answering Charlotte's pleasant questions. It's kind of nice. Peaceful.

Until there's another set of footsteps.

"Good morning." Hayes looks around, confused. "Where is everybody?" he barks out.

"They didn't tell you?" I point at the note on the fridge, which Hayes reads with his back to me.

Then he turns around, grinning from ear to ear. "So the house is ours."

Charlotte shakes her head, chuckling softly. "No parties. You know the rules."

"What Dad doesn't know won't hurt him." Hayes pours himself a glass of juice, still smiling. "This could end up being a better weekend than I expected."

I can never tell if he's being serious or not, so I say, "You know I wouldn't tell, but what about Lucy and Bridget? You'd have to pay them off to keep them quiet."

He only laughs. It's the most genuine laughter I've ever heard from him, except maybe when he has his brief little chats with my sister.

"Lucy is easy," I say. "Take her out for ice cream and she's yours. But Bridget? That would be a tough one."

He meets my gaze over the rim of his glass and snickers. "I'm kidding. I know better."

He joins me at the island, straddling a stool. He drums on the countertop with his fingers, and I almost wonder if he's taking some of those pills Salem was on. He's bright, happy, upbeat. The opposite of what I've come to expect.

Once we're alone, with Charlotte leaving to go to the store for supplies, the energy in the room shifts.

"I guess they'll be back before Theo's Halloween party on Tuesday night," I offer. "Are you going to sneak out?"

"Are you going to tattle on me?" he counters with a nasty little grin.

"No. I was hoping maybe I could stay over at Salem's as an excuse not to be home."

"What a genius plan," he mutters. Why do I even bother talking to him?

As usual, he changes topics fast enough to give me whiplash. "So, what are you doing today?" he asks while buttering a piece of toast. For an athlete, he really slaps it on. I guess he can afford the calories.

"Since when do you care what I do on the weekend?"

"I was just wondering if you had plans." He's looking at his plate, so I can't quite check his face to see if he's serious or not.

"I don't know. Every time I go anywhere, somebody ends up ruining things."

"You know what? You're right."

I almost choke on my eggs. "Seriously?"

"I'm just saying. I've been a real piece of shit." I'm not going to argue with that. "Maybe I need to, like, make a peace offering."

"That would be a good start. What are you planning to do?"

Instead of answering right away, he pulls out his phone and taps a message to somebody. "I have to start by making things right with Franky. This is longer than we've ever been on the outs."

A few moments later, his phone buzzes. I watch out of the corner of my eye and see him smile. "Great. You're on this afternoon."

"I'm on what?"

"You have a date with Franky later on."

"Wait. What?"

"I told him you want to go out, but you were too shy to say anything."

"You can't do that!"

"Seems I just did."

"But I'm not something you can use to barter. You don't own me."

"You said you would do anything, didn't you?"

I know exactly what he means. "That was in the car when I thought you were trying to kill us."

"So you're taking it back? Because, you know, I still have this picture of you on my phone…"

He's got me where he wants me. I don't know why I bother fighting the inevitable. "Fine. What time?"

* * *

It's weird being one-on-one with Franky. Usually we're around other people, in a group. I don't know what to say after I get in the car, and we ride off only a few hours after the text from Hayes.

What does Franky expect is going to happen? He accepted the idea of us coming out together pretty fast, which makes me wonder again if he likes me more than I like him. I don't want to end up hurting anybody's feelings.

"They're doing a double feature at the drive-in, old horror movies from the 80s. *Friday the 13th* and *A Nightmare on Elm Street*." He shoots me a grin. "What do you think?"

"That sounds great." It's a gray, gloomy day, so hanging out and watching horror movies sounds kind of perfect. Especially this time of year, with Halloween around the corner. "I love horror movies."

"Me too. I figured maybe we could go out for something to eat after." He chuckles ruefully. "This is weird, isn't it?"

"A little," I admit. "I mean, not like I don't want to hang out with you."

"I get it. Hayes has a funny way of trying to make up after a fight."

"Does that mean you two are going to be okay after this?"

"That's up to him, isn't it?" He has a point. "Don't worry. I'm not going to try to, you know, force you to do stuff. Not that you're not hot or anything."

The only hot thing about me right now is my cheeks, which are burning. "Thanks?"

He bursts out laughing, and I can't help but join him. "You know what I mean. If things were different, maybe this would be a more romantic date."

"I get it." And I'm so glad. All that anxiety I've wrestled with ever since Hayes announced I had a date dissolves. We can hang out and be friends. "I hope you're not breaking more important plans for this."

"I've been trying to get to know you for weeks. It's cool."

On the way to the drive-in, I gain a little more insight into what makes him who he is.

"I can't wait to graduate and get the hell out of here," Franky says.

"Where are you going to go?"

"I already applied to, like, eight schools on the other side of the country. I'm just killing time until then. My dad can't stop going through wives who only want his money. I'm tired of having to watch them take what's supposed to be mine when the time comes." He winces a little, turning my way. "Does that sound selfish?"

"I'm sure that would piss me off, too."

"You're too nice for us. You're a good person."

"You're a good person, too." He only grunts like he doesn't believe me. For the first time, it occurs to me he might hide things the way Hayes does. Is everybody around me hurting all the time? Maybe everybody is in their own way, and all we can do is try to get through it.

Either way, it's nice to talk like two normal people without having to worry about what Hayes will think about it.

The drive-in is newer and nicer than I expected.

"I can't believe so many people came out," I say.

"Everybody wants to prove how old-school they are," Franky says with a shrug before turning his radio to the signal the movie's audio is being broadcast on.

Right now, they're only showing the trailers that went with the original *Friday the 13th* when it first came out, and that's kind of neat. I wonder if it makes me a total nerd that I'm actually into this—but who am I kidding, I already knew I was kind of a nerd.

"Would it be totally gross of me to say I could really go for some popcorn?" I ask.

"Are you kidding? I planned on asking if you wanted some. I can't smell it without wanting it." Franky makes a move to open the door, but I insist on picking this up. If it's not a real date, he doesn't have to pay for everything.

It's drizzling a little, so I make a run for the concession stand and duck under the awning that stretches along the front. A part of me wants to text Hayes and tell him we're having a great time, because I know it will drive him crazy, but I don't want him showing up. Probably a better idea to tell him about it once I get home, if he's even there.

A few people are ahead of me, but it's not like I've never seen the movie before, so it doesn't really matter. It surprises me to see so many families together in their cars. Is this the kind of thing families do together? I always used to wonder. Mom rarely took us to the movies, if ever.

"You look familiar."

I didn't notice the man standing behind me until hearing his voice close to my ear. "Excuse me?" I mutter, scooting forward a little so he's not so close. But he follows me, pressing in at my back.

"I know I've seen you somewhere before."

"You probably haven't." I try to turn around to look at him, but he grabs my arm to hold me still. "Get off me!"

The girl in front of me turns around, confused. I'm about to ask her for help when the guy speaks again.

"Not since that night at the concert. You interrupted a special moment for me."

Ice-cold fear replaces the adrenaline pumping through my veins. "Oh..."

The girl rolls her eyes and turns around again, going back to whatever she was doing on her phone.

He chuckles, stirring the hair at the nape of my neck. "That's what I thought."

I twist my head around to get a look at him, and what I find isn't exactly surprising—but it is chilling. He looks just enough like the guy I first saw at Franky's party to confirm this is Logan, but his face looks a little rearranged. There's still swelling, stitches above both eyes and down his left cheekbone. I guess his jaw wasn't wired shut like they said, though his voice is thick and slurred. He's wearing sunglasses even on this cloudy day, but when he turns his head to the side like he's looking to see if anyone is watching, I see the whites of his eyes are dark red.

"What do you want?" I whisper.

"What I deserve."

"Are you sure you didn't get what you deserved that night? Because I know what I saw."

"Then how come nobody went to the cops?"

"How do you know we didn't?"

"You're cute but stop fucking around. We both know you didn't."

"You didn't go either."

"I could. I've been thinking about it." He's still holding my arm, and now his fingers dig in until I have to grit my teeth. "I'm wondering what it's worth to you."

My heart lifts into my throat. "Don't do it. We can all agree on what was happening out there."

"Please. There's no proof, and everybody saw what we were doing before that. Nobody would buy it. I could get that stepbrother of yours locked up for a long time."

I gasp. "No!" That was a mistake. I know it right away. The second his mouth twists in a nasty smile. I did exactly what he wanted.

"So it means something to you. I wasn't sure until now. You want to make sure he doesn't go to prison, don't you?" Logan lowers his head, and a shudder of revulsion runs through me. "So I'll ask you again. How much is my silence worth?"

"I don't have any money. I'm not rich. I don't know what I could give you."

"Are you so sure about that?" I shudder again when his lips graze my ear. "You smell nice. I bet we could come to an agreement, since you're so desperate to keep your brother from getting what he deserves."

It's my turn to order, but I'm afraid to move.

"Come on," the girl behind the register calls out. "Next!"

Logan growls in my ear. "I'll find you again. Start thinking about what would happen to that pretty boy brother of yours in prison and how much you want to make sure that doesn't happen." And then he's gone like he was never here. So suddenly I would wonder if I imagined the whole thing if it wasn't for the ache in my arm and the taste of bile in my mouth.

I order the food and drinks without thinking, rattling off the order. Completely calm on the outside.

Losing my shit on the inside.

CHAPTER 25

"No fair! You can't mix the colors!" Lucy's voice rings out when I enter the house.

I feel dazed, like I'm in another world. It was exhausting to pretend everything was okay when I was out with Franky. I've been pretending for hours. At least I could quietly freak out during the movies, but I had to make conversation at the restaurant.

What am I going to do? What happens when Logan shows up again? I should tell Hayes, shouldn't I? What happens if he freaks out and loses control again?

"But that's how you make new colors." I didn't expect to hear Hayes's voice answering my sister. I figured she was playing a game with Bridget. Now I rush into the media room with my heart in my throat, unsure what to expect.

Play-Doh. They're playing with Play-Doh on the coffee table. Lucy is being her bossy self, making sure Hayes doesn't mix the colors.

"She's kind of a purist," I explain, making them both look up.

"Come play with us!" Lucy pats the floor next to her. I don't have the heart to make an excuse when she looks so happy.

Hayes looks happy, too.

"I figured you would be out," I say, sitting cross-legged on the floor with Lucy between us.

"Yeah. Bridget wasn't feeling good, so I told her to take it easy. We don't ever get the chance to hang out." Hayes winks at Lucy, who grins back. Is this for real? It seems that way. I'm afraid to believe it, but I want to.

"What are you making?" I ask my sister while I open a can of blue. The smell takes me back to my childhood. I can almost forget all the fear I've been wrestling with.

"I'm making a big diamond ring like the one Mommy has."

I exchange a look with Hayes, who looks like he's trying not to laugh.

"I think I'll make a necklace," I decide before rolling out a handful of dough. "What are you making?" I ask Hayes.

"I don't know. A snake?"

"Anybody can do that." Lucy shakes her head. "Didn't you ever do this before?"

"It's been a long time," Hayes says.

He's so gentle with her. So kind and patient. It's easy to let go of everything bothering me when it's just the three of us. I can remember what it was like to be her age and not have anything to worry about. I wonder if he feels the same way.

And I wonder what people at school would think if they saw him now. It's nice to have a fun secret about him instead of the secrets I've carried around so far.

I turn on a movie and let it play as background noise while we build things. Hayes tries to make a car, while I try to sculpt a little bicycle. Neither of us does a very good job, which leaves Lucy shaking her head mournfully. "You both need practice."

"I guess we do." Hayes meets my gaze over the top of her head, and smiles. And oh, my God, my heart just about bursts open. It's like the boy on the bridge finally came back to me. This is him, the real Hayes. He's who I keep trying to reach. I knew he was in there.

Until his phone buzzes. It's face down on the floor, but the sound is loud enough to catch my attention. I glance over while he's reading the message that came through.

And I would swear the temperature in the room drops twenty degrees. He shoves the phone in his pocket, then stands.

"Don't you want to play?" Lucy asks, oblivious.

"No, I've got to do some things." He leaves his would-be car on the table and leaves the room without another word. He slams his feet on the stairs as he climbs them.

Lucy's chin trembles. "Did I make him mad?"

I have to grit my teeth to keep from saying what I feel. "No, sweetie. I guess he didn't like the message he got. Maybe it reminded him of something he was forgetting to do."

"That's why I don't want to grow up. You can't just have fun when you want to."

"Yeah, believe me. Take your time with the whole growing up thing."

I deliberately put more energy into keeping things upbeat and happy for her sake. Another good thing about being a kid is how quickly your mind can go from one thing to another. It doesn't take long for her to forget all about it. Me? Not possible.

We clean up the mess and I let her snag a couple of cookies before we go up to her room. It's the kind of room I used to dream about when I was her age, with a big dollhouse and all the toys she's always wanted. Her bed is under a canopy with twinkling fairy lights.

"Read me a book?" she asks, and I'm happy to agree.

We settle in once she's washed up and in her pajamas, and she munches her treat while I read. I almost don't want to leave. I wouldn't mind falling asleep in a bed made for a fairy princess.

But I don't get the luxury of forgetting my problems.

Once she's asleep, I tuck her in and turn on the night-light before gently closing her door. Across the hall, Hayes's bedroom door is partly open. I see the light from his bathroom spread across the floor. Once I get a little closer, I can hear the shower running.

I poke my head in, then tiptoe to the bathroom. It's full of steam billowing out from over the top of the shower door. From this angle, I can't see inside, and he can't see me. Should I say something? Ask him if he's okay? I'm still debating whether to tell him about Logan finding me at the drive-in. Does he need to hear about that right now?

I jump a little when his phone buzzes. I didn't realize it was right here on the counter, close to the door. It's a new message. I shouldn't look, should I? But maybe it will help understand why his mood changed so suddenly down there. I know he'll never tell me.

It's from a contact labeled only as C. *There's that gorgeous cock. I can't wait to get my lips around it again.*

I cover my mouth, horrified. So that's what this is about? C. That has to stand for coach, right? Who else could it be?

I tap the screen, unable to help myself. I need to know. This could be proof. This might be enough to change things for him.

There's the new message I just read, and the one before it is from Hayes. It's a picture of his erect dick, the message before it is a request for a picture. *I need a dick pic. Give me something to think about when I'm in bed later.*

Now I'm too sick to my stomach to scroll further.

Besides, a noise from inside the shower steals my attention. The flow of the water is loud, but I can't pretend not to hear sniffling. Crying.

I close the app before approaching the shower door. "Hayes? Are you okay?" I round the tiled wall and come to a stop in front of the glass doors.

He's in there, only he's not washing up. Instead, he's naked, sitting in the corner with his knees pulled up to his chest and his arms wrapped around them. I've seen nothing so heartbreaking. He's in so much pain. I only want to help him.

So I do the only thing I can think to do. I take off my shoes, open the door, and step inside fully clothed. He doesn't stop me from kneeling next to him and wrapping my arms around him as far as I can.

I don't say a word. What is there to say? He wraps an arm

around one of mine, sobbing softly, and I let him. I don't bother offering empty promises or assurances or anything like that while the water falls on us. I'm not even supposed to know why he's doing this. I only want him to know he isn't alone.

The water is turning from hot to only lukewarm by the time I let go of him. I'm soaked, of course, but I don't mind. When I hold out a hand, he places his inside and lets me help him to his feet. He follows me out of the shower, where I hand him a towel before taking one for myself.

I wait until he's dried off, then watch him pull on a pair of shorts and a T-shirt. He won't say a word or look me in the eye. I'm sure he doesn't know I saw his phone, but he's still hurting enough to act this way. I can't even imagine the pain he's in, feeling forced to do something like that. He must hate himself for going through with it. If it's Coach Greg he sent it to, I understand why he might feel like he had no choice.

He gets into bed even though it's still kind of early. Once he's settled in, I cross the hall to my room and peel off my wet clothes. My heart is heavy, hurting. There has to be a way to help him in the long term. But how? I've seen the messages, but they're not on my phone. They're on his. And I doubt I'll ever get a chance to look at his messages again. What if I could convince him to come forward? But that would mean I saw the dick pic, and while he's still a mystery in so many ways, I know it would kill him. He would be too ashamed. He's been cruel to me in the past, but I can't be that cruel to him.

By the time my hair is dry, and I've washed what's left of the makeup off my face, I don't feel any better and I know trying to read or study will be a waste of time. I have too much on my mind. Instead of getting into bed, I tiptoe across the hall to check on Hayes.

The door opens silently, but as it turns out, I didn't need to worry about disturbing him. He's disturbed enough, tossing and turning, muttering something I can't understand.

I go over to the bed and lean down, placing a gentle hand on his forehead. "It's okay," I whisper. "You're safe. You can rest."

He whimpers, turning his head away. I have to bite back tears after seeing him like this. Is this what he's feeling all the time? How does he survive?

When all else fails, I do the only other thing I can come up with. I pull back the covers and slide into bed next to him. His back is to me, so I curl my body around his with an arm around his waist.

"You're safe. I'm here."

His breathing slows. The muttering fades to silence. Soon, the only sounds in the room are our breathing.

I have to help him. I only wish I knew how. How can you help a person when they don't want to be helped?

I'm still wondering about that when I fall asleep.

CHAPTER 26

This is the most vivid sex dream I've ever had about Hayes, which is saying something. I dream about him a lot.

He's pulling off my shorts and thong. I'd try to stop him, but I don't want to. I don't want to give up his nearness. The scent of soap barely covering up the faint chlorine smell he carries on his skin no matter how he tries to wash it off. I've come to love it—now, I breathe in deep, drinking it in the way I drink in the sensation of his touch.

My skin sizzles with every kiss. He runs his mouth over my throat, and I throw my head back to encourage more. My fingers tangle in his thick hair. "Mm…" I moan in approval, closing my eyes and melting against him when his tongue laps at me. It's so much easier to give myself to him when I know it doesn't matter. None of it is real. There's no doubting myself or wishing I could be stronger. No hating myself for craving him.

"What do you want?" he whispers in the dark.

Now I can speak the words buzzing around in my head. I've wanted it ever since he did it to me over the pool.

"Go down on me," I beg, spreading my legs and pressing his shoulders like I can put him where I want him.

His knowing laughter warms my stomach, which in the back of my mind seems odd, but this is a vivid dream. "You liked that, huh?"

"I like what you do to me." No shame, no nerves.

"What do I do to you?" He lifts one thigh and drapes it over his shoulder, hooking an arm around the other leg to hold it in place. "What do I do to your pussy?"

I flush all over when he says it. It's so dirty, but I love it. Is this who I really am inside? "You make it wet. You make it feel so good." Right now, there's slickness running down my crack and soaking into the sheet, and he hasn't done anything yet.

When he runs his tongue over my lips, my hips shoot up and I cover my mouth to hold back a moan. It feels too good. How can anything that feels this good be right? He holds me firmly in place, his hand moving up and down my thigh as he settles in to eat me. His little grunts and moans only make the already burning heat in my core turn into something I'm afraid will consume us both. I'm almost afraid of it.

I would be if this was real.

His tongue moves deeper, piercing my dripping hole before sliding up to the place where the ache is the worst. He teases my clit and I want to cry because oh, my God, it's so good. Like torture. Only I never want it to end.

My eyes open and at first my heart sinks because no, no, I don't want it to stop. I want it to keep going. I don't want to wake up.

Only it hasn't stopped. I'm looking around the dark and his head is between my legs and I'm awake. Holy shit, this is actually happening. I take hold of his head like I'm about to pull it away from my pussy because I should, right? I should stop this.

Except my fingers thread through his hair instead of pushing him away. He grunts before pulling my clit between his lips and sucking. His tongue darts over it and fireworks explode in my head and there is no way I'm stopping this, not when I'm so close—

"Hayes!" It comes out in a breathless burst before the tension breaks and there's nothing left but sweet release. I shudder again, again, wave after wave rolling over me. I'm still trembling when he lifts his head. I look down over the length of my body but can't read his expression in the dark.

"You have the sweetest pussy." His lips graze my hip, my stomach, my nipples as he climbs over me.

I whimper softly, knowing he's not finished. Not wanting him to be, but knowing he should be. This should stop.

He hovers over me, breathing hard. As hard as his erect dick now pressing against my mound. His hips move and he runs it over the fresh slickness now coating my lips. His groans match my own. Groans of hunger. Need. I need him inside me.

When he nudges, parting my lips and dragging his head through my wetness, I lift my hips in silent agreement. No, I'm begging. Begging him to fill me up. I need him to fuck me until none of this seems wrong. Until I don't think about anything but the way he feels.

It still surprises me when he pushes inside and stretches my walls. I bite down on my lip to keep from making too much noise. "So fucking tight." He almost sounds like he's in pain, but that doesn't stop him from pulling back and pushing forward again, this time grinding against my clit and making me whimper.

He doesn't wait for me to adjust. He takes what he wants, which is what I want, too. With one hand on my hip, holding me still, he sets a fast pace. Like he's already close to finishing. Hot bursts of air hit my face with every sharp exhale. I close my eyes and welcome the tension that's building again.

He's so beautiful. I can almost see him now, the outline of his perfect body. The way his muscles bunch and flex every time he rolls his hips forward. I reach out to touch him, to feel his warmth under my hands. I don't think I could ever tire of it.

When he lowers himself to his forearms and buries his face in my neck, I welcome that, too. I wrap my arms around his shoulders and run my fingers through his hair, panting the way he does. His hips move, his ass bounces, and I climb a little higher with every slap our bodies make when he crashes against me.

"Fuck... yes..." He moves faster, harder, almost frantic, and that's good, too. So good.

I hold on as tight as I can, almost as tight as the muscles now squeezing his dick with every stroke. He grunts and I grunt back. Encouraging him. Showing him how much I love this.

The tension builds, builds, until I'm sure it'll kill me if my racing heart doesn't do it first. I want to scream but know I can't, so I bite down on his shoulder before everything explodes inside me. Another few hard, deep thrusts and he roars in my ear, his body tensing, his dick still buried deep inside when he lets go. When he fills me with his cum.

The briefest, brightest red flag goes up in my head, but it's too late now. It's done. And I'm too out of breath and too blissed out to care very much.

He lifts his head as his hips pull back and he leaves me. Looking down between us, he grunts his approval. "That's what I want to see. My cum dripping out of you." It should make me wince or feel ashamed, but there isn't that nasty little bite to his voice this time. Nothing about this time is the same as before. He isn't so cold or cruel.

He even gets up and goes to the bathroom to get me a towel so I can clean up. No, that doesn't make him a prince, but compared to some other things he's put me through...

By the time I finish, he's on his back, sprawled out without a stitch of clothes on. I wish the lights were on so I could see all of him, but I can see enough to know he's perfect. I almost don't dare to stretch out next to him, even though it feels right. When his arm winds around me, my heart sings.

For a long time we lie silent, with me too afraid to speak and too nervous to relax. I wonder if he might've fallen asleep until his whispers cut through the silence.

"Can I tell you something? Do you swear to never tell anybody, ever?"

"Yes. Whatever it is, you're safe with me."

"Safe," he repeats with a snort. "Is there such a thing?"

"With me? Yes. I mean it. You can tell me anything."

His chest rises and falls under my head. "Somebody… makes me do things I don't want. To them. And I have to let them do things to me." His voice is so choked. So full of pain. "It started a few months ago. During the summer."

I hold my breath. My heart hammers. This is it. What I've been waiting to hear.

"At first, I thought I was imagining things," he murmurs. "That kind of thing doesn't happen to guys. Girls, yeah, but not guys. Getting stared at. Getting asked uncomfortable questions. I used to brush it off and act like it was joke but it never stopped."

He shivers. "It only got worse. More, all the time. It wasn't enough to touch me. I had to touch back. I couldn't say no. I still can't."

"Oh, Hayes. I'm sorry," I whisper.

"I just want it to stop. I want it to be over. That's…" He lets out a shuddering sigh. "That's what I was thinking about when you found me that day. How much I want everything to end. I feel so dirty all the time. And weak."

"You're not weak."

"Then I should stop it, right? If I'm not weak, how come it keeps happening?"

"Like you said, you don't feel like you can stop it."

"I can't stop it. Things will get so much worse if I do. I know it. They made sure I know it. I'm trapped. There's no way out." It sounds like he's on the verge of tears again.

Maybe that's what gets me crying. I can't stop it from happening. Tears roll down my cheeks and drip onto his bare chest.

"Are you crying?"

I lift my head, nodding, straining to kiss him. It's all I can think to do. To kiss him, to show him I'm here with him. That he could admit the truth to me and I'm not going anywhere. I don't blame him. I only want to help.

Except he pulls his head back, his eyes narrowing. "What is this? Pity?"

"No," I mumble, confused. "I only wanted to kiss you."

"While you're crying over me? Is that what you think I want? Somebody feeling bad for me, pitying me? I knew I shouldn't have told you."

"No, I'm glad you did."

"Right. So you can feel sorry for me." He practically shoves me away, folding his arms over his chest and angling his body away from mine. "Get your shit and get out of here."

Everything in me cries out in pain. This isn't what I wanted. "I don't want to leave you when you're like this."

"I don't fucking care what you want. It's my room. Get out of here and take your fucking tears with you. I don't want them."

Now, the tears are falling harder than before, and not only for him. For everything he's pushing away, everything I want to give him. He won't let himself have it.

Or else he doesn't want it. He doesn't want me, not really. I'm only a way for him to make himself feel better.

I practically crawl away in humiliation, gathering my clothes in the dark. I don't bother taking the time to get dressed, choosing instead to peek out through the door to make sure Lucy isn't wandering around before darting across the hall so I can be alone with my misery.

CHAPTER 27

It isn't until I wake up on Sunday morning that I realize what happened last night. Not the part about Hayes admitting what's happening to him—how could I forget that? I cried myself to sleep thinking about it, wishing I hadn't screwed everything up. Not like I did it on purpose. Not like I was trying to insult him. It doesn't matter if I meant it or not, because the result was the same.

Now, I'm a little more worried about something else. What happened before that when I first woke up in his bed.

He came inside me. No condom.

My chest tightens when I consider what this means. Where am I in my cycle? I lost track. Could I end up pregnant? God, my life would be over. His life would be over, too. He's going to be my stepbrother. This is why I told him I didn't want us having sex anymore. This is exactly what I didn't want to happen.

I can wait around and see what happens, or I can get Plan B at the pharmacy. Obviously, I know what I need to do. Thank God, Mom is away for the weekend, or she'd kill me.

Instead of going downstairs to have breakfast with Lucy, I sneak out when I hear her chattering with Charlotte in the kitchen. Bridget's there, too, so I guess she's feeling better. I'm glad, because otherwise I wouldn't be able to do this.

It's not a long walk to town—besides, I need to clear my head. This doesn't have to be a big deal. I'll get it taken care of, do the responsible thing, all that. Nobody even needs to know.

That's what I'm telling myself as I walk down the family planning aisle in the store. I thought Plan B was carried out in the open, but I don't see it anywhere. I have to go to the pharmacist's counter, I guess.

I'm going to have to announce out loud what I need. This was a lot easier in my head, before I couldn't just walk down an aisle and grab a box.

He's waiting for me, too, eyebrows raised. "Yes? What can I do for you?"

Here goes nothing. "I need... Plan B." There. I said it and I didn't burst into flames.

"I see." He gives me a penetrating stare. Is he judging me? "Can I see ID?"

"Why do you need that? I thought this was a standard product."

"ID, if you want to buy." He lifts his open palm, curling his fingers upward. I have to dig through my purse and grab my wallet, opening it and sliding my driver's license out before thrusting it his way.

He takes one look at it and hands the card back. "You're a few months shy."

"No, I need it right now. I can't wait a few months."

His expression softens. "What I'm saying is, I'm not allowed to sell that to you until you're eighteen."

"That's not true. I looked it up."

"Recent state legislation," he explains with a shrug. "It might be overturned, but for now you need to be a legal adult, or you'll need a parent or guardian to come in and make the purchase for you." I can tell he's uncomfortable, and maybe he feels bad for me.

Maybe I can use that to my advantage? "But I can't do that. Come on. Do I have to spell it out?"

"No, you don't, but I'm not allowed to make the sale to anyone under eighteen."

"What difference does it make? Like you said, it's only a few months."

"My hands are tied."

My desperation is rising along with my heart rate. My stomach has that weird feeling, like I just dropped over the first big hill of a roller coaster. "How do they know? Like, do you have to scan my ID?"

"No, but I need to enter your birthdate into the system."

"So, can't you change the date? Please, I'm desperate."

"I wish I could help you, but I can't risk it. I'm sorry." The phone rings, and I've never seen somebody look so glad to answer a call. He even angles himself away, silently dismissing me.

"This is bullshit!"

A pair of women shopping further down the aisle turn around and give me dirty looks, which I give them right back. Smug bitches. Maybe they should try being in my place for five minutes and see how well they do.

There's another pharmacy three blocks down. Maybe this guy is one of those pharmacists who thinks it's their job to bring morality into dispensing medications.

But no. I get the same stupid excuse there, too. I'm not old enough to buy it on my own. What am I supposed to do?

When I step outside, my head is spinning. I've never felt so alone in my life. That's saying something since I've been alone for so much of it.

One thing is for sure: I can't wait and see what happens. I have to take care of this now.

Which means I need somebody to buy it for me. But who? Salem's still seventeen. I doubt I could convince her to get her mom to do it. Like she wouldn't think it was for Salem instead of for me. There's nobody else I trust.

Including Hayes, but he's my only option. Otherwise, even if I ask Bridget and made her swear never to tell, I could never trust she wouldn't. And I would probably have to explain how I ended up in this situation. No, thank you.

Instead of walking to the house, I get an Uber. Fear and frustration are exhausting when combined, it turns out. What if he says no? What if he is a bastard and refuses? He can't, that's all. There has to be some grain of self-preservation in him.

Thankfully, Bridget and Lucy are out when I get back to the house. I don't need to risk either of them overhearing the groveling I'm about to do. His car is outside, so I know he's home.

"Go away," he barks when I knock on his door.

"I need to talk to you."

"I said go away."

"It's really important. Like, an emergency."

"Too fucking bad. Figure it out yourself."

"I tried to." Tears are dangerously close to welling up in my eyes, making my sinuses sting and my voice shake. "But I can't. I need you."

"Sucks to be you."

That's it. The final straw. Everything goes red before I kick the door. "Goddammit, open up! This is all your fault in the first place. If it wasn't for you, I wouldn't be in this mess. The least you can do is open your fucking door and listen to me!"

A few seconds pass. He can't possibly ignore me now, can he? He's not that heartless. The lock disengages and I let out a sigh of relief before reminding myself I haven't won, not yet. Not until he agrees to run the errand for me.

He's still wearing the pajamas he put on last night before going to bed. He must really be in a bad place. That makes two of us.

"What?" he snaps.

I look up and down the hall just in case one of the housekeepers is sneaking around. "Let me in."

"No."

"Then come into my room. I need to talk to you in private."

"For fuck's sake." He steps back, opening the door wider and ushering me in with a sweep of his arm.

"Thank you," I mutter, rolling my eyes.

"So what did I do this time? What mess have I gotten you into?"

"You came inside me last night," I whisper, wrapping my arms around myself. "And I'm almost midway through my cycle."

"Meaning?"

I'm going to kill him. He can't put it together on his own? No, he'd rather drag it out of me. "Meaning chances are higher that I could get pregnant. Mid-cycle is ovulation time, genius. Even if it wasn't, I'd still be freaking out—and you should be, too."

"What do you want me to do? Take my cum back?"

"No, you insufferable prick. I need you to buy Plan B for me. The morning after pill," I add when he scrunches up his face in confusion.

"What, because it's my responsibility or something?

"No, because you're eighteen or something. I just went to two different pharmacies, and they both told me the same thing. I need to be eighteen or have a parent or guardian buy it for me."

Finally, he gets it. His shoulders slump, his brows knitting together. "Oh."

"Yeah, oh. Get it now? If you got me pregnant, I'm not having the damn baby. And don't think I won't tell everybody whose it is because I will."

"Calm down."

"You calm down. This is all your fault. I told you I didn't want to do that anymore, and this is exactly why. Maybe you think this is a joke, but it's my life. I would rather take care of this now than wait until I miss my period or something. By then, I'll need an abortion."

"I get it. You don't need to keep going."

"Obviously, I do, or else you'd be getting dressed and getting your car keys and going down to the damn pharmacy for me. Not standing there, staring at me the way you are now."

He lifts an eyebrow. "What's in it for me?"

"You can't be serious. Did I not just tell you? Do you want everybody knowing you fucked your stepsister and got her pregnant? You should thank me for doing this."

"But if you're not pregnant? Then I went to all this trouble for nothing."

"All this trouble? It's, like, not even a five-minute drive."

"I'm still going out of my way. I have a meet at school in an hour. I was about to get ready when you knocked on the door."

"So can't you get it after the meet? Hayes, come on. Please, stop fucking around. I need this. It's the least you can do. You're the one who wasn't careful."

"Yeah, yeah."

Finally, I'm desperate enough to make a last-ditch effort. "I'll leave you alone from now on. I won't bother you. I'll stay out of your way."

He arches an eyebrow. "You're serious?"

"I'll ask permission before I go out to a party or anywhere I know you might be. I swear. I'll do that, so long as you do this for me. This is my whole life we're talking about. Please."

"I'll see if the pharmacy is open by the time I have a chance to go." I let out a choked sob, but he ignores it in favor of pushing me out of the room. "I've gotta get ready. Don't make me late for the meet."

I can't believe he would be this way. Doesn't he see how important this is? God, if I end up pregnant, what am I going to do? I don't even want to let my brain go that far down the road. All I can do is pray Hayes does the right thing.

Yes, because he's so good at doing the right thing.

It's hours before he comes home. Hours I spend wondering if I'm going to have a nervous breakdown. Salem keeps texting me, and I don't even have it in me to care. Everything, all my concentration, all my fear, everything I have is focused on this. What I need.

Otherwise, my life could become so much more complicated than it already is. I'd have to wait until I'm eighteen if I need to get an abortion, which would mean waiting three months. Would I even have enough time to get one by then, or would it be too late? God, I can't handle this. I'm going to crack.

It's almost dinnertime when I hear Lucy call out downstairs. "Hayes! Where have you been? I wanted to play."

I run for my bedroom door and open it in time to hear his reply. "Sorry. I had stuff to do. Maybe we can hang out after dinner. Play a board game or something?"

How can he sound so calm and casual? Right, because his life doesn't have to be affected. He still thinks this is a big joke.

I'm about to run downstairs and demand he tell me where he's been and why he had to take so long getting back, but I find him halfway up the stairs by the time I reach the landing. He pauses when he sees me, then goes from jogging to meandering.

"Well?" I whisper, chewing my lip. "Did you get it?"

"Get what?" He stops, frowning. "What was I supposed to get?"

"You better hope you're joking." I can't imagine why he would be, but I shouldn't be surprised at his twisted sense of humor.

"Jesus. Here." He opens the gym bag slung over his shoulder and pulls out a bag from the pharmacy, which he almost throws at me in passing.

"Thank you." I clutch it to me like it's some rare treasure.

"Whatever. Enjoy the side effects." He's in his room, slamming the door shut before I can ask what he's talking about. Why would he know about side effects? Unless he looked it up.

Or this isn't the first time he's had experience with this.

Right now, I don't care. I'm too relieved to give any thought to why he would begrudge me this, something we both need whether or not he thinks so.

I take the box to my bathroom and pop the pill before chasing it with a glass of water. My eyes close and I offer a silent prayer of thanks to whoever or whatever is watching over me. I feel like my life has been handed back to me.

Though I know now, for sure, that this is the end of my physical relationship with Hayes. I'm never putting myself through this torture again.

CHAPTER 28

Hayes was right about side effects. I have them. A lot.

I can barely pry my eyes open Monday morning, the day after taking the pill. The nausea didn't hit until after midnight. Even then, I fought like hell not to throw up. I didn't want to throw the pill up along with everything I ate for dinner. Eventually, I couldn't hold it back anymore and spent a good part of the night on the bathroom floor between long periods of dry heaving. I finally dragged myself back to bed at dawn.

I'm still pretty sure the pill did what it's supposed to do. Somewhere in the middle of all that, I read the insert that came along with the medication. As long as it was in my system for two hours or more, I should be okay, and it was way longer than that before I got sick.

I still feel like hell by 8:00. I guess I'm not making it to school today. It feels like there's a jackhammer in my head, and every time I try to sit up, I get too dizzy and have to lie back down.

What I want more than anything is to go back to sleep, but I can't rest until I call school. It's going to be hanging over my head all day if I don't.

"Hi," I murmur, eyes closed. "This is Morgan. I'm sick. I'm not going to be able to come to school today."

"I'm afraid that's not enough."

I open one eye, staring at the ceiling. "What do you mean?"

"We require a parent or guardian to make a call like this."

They've got to be kidding. "My mom is out of town. Mr. Ambrose, too."

"You're going to have to get one of them to call."

This is a bad joke, right? I can't handle this right now. "But they're not here. That's what I'm trying to tell you."

"Until one of them calls, this will not be considered an excused absence."

"I am sick in bed. If somebody wants to come to the house, they can see it for themselves."

"I'm sorry, but that's not going to happen."

"Well, I think this whole thing is pretty dumb." I end the call before I say something I can't take back, then squeeze my eyes shut before any tears can fall.

Can just one person be on my side for once? Why does everything have to be a struggle? Yeah, I might like a mom who gives a shit about me, who doesn't randomly take weekend trips without any indication of where she's going or when she'll come back. I might like a mom who actually cares when I'm sick and does all those nice things moms are supposed to do, like make chicken soup and put on my favorite movies. Isn't that how it's supposed to be? What's so wrong with me that I couldn't have that?

I'm barely asleep again when the phone buzzes. I expect it to be somebody from school calling to yell at me for hanging up, but it's worse than that. "Hell, no," I whisper when I see MOM on my screen. If I ignore the call, it will only get worse.

She doesn't give me time to say anything before laying into me. "What do you think you're doing? Get your ass out of bed and get to school. Do you think I enjoy getting calls like that while I'm on a trip?"

"Good morning to you, too."

"Oh, no. You're not going to give me any of your attitude when you're the one ruining my vacation." Vacation? From what?

"Mom, I'm sick."

"And what's wrong with you? Were you out last night? Did you go to a party?"

"No."

"Are you lying?"

"No. Call Bridget and ask her. I was home all night."

"So, what's the problem?"

"I don't know. Jesus. I'm just sick to my stomach. I guess I picked up a bug."

"Well, that's just terrific. Your timing has always been impeccable."

"I'm not asking you to do anything for me."

"It's a little too late for that. I already got a phone call from school telling me my kid didn't bother showing up today. Do you know how that made me look? I didn't even know you were sick. I had to pretend."

"Am I supposed to apologize? Sorry, next time I'll get sick when it's more convenient for you."

"I know you think you can get away with your smart-ass attitude because I'm not there, but I will be soon enough. And I'll remember this."

Terrific, something to look forward to. "I really feel sick. I was up all night throwing up. I just want to go back to sleep."

"Are you sure you haven't been doing anything you shouldn't?"

All I can see in my head is the empty Plan B box in the trash can under the bathroom sink. "I'm sure."

"Don't make it so I can't trust you when I'm away. Don't ruin this for me."

"Mom, I told you. I'm not doing anything I shouldn't do." I've lied to her so many times, always because I had to protect myself. From her temper, from her boyfriends, whatever. I'm protecting myself from her temper now, too, only there's a difference. This time, I have been doing things I shouldn't do. I am in the wrong. I can pretend all I want that this is all Hayes's fault, but it isn't. Because I wanted it. He hates me, but I still want him.

"You'd better not be, because we won't be home for another few days."

Good. It doesn't seem right, being this relieved that she won't be home. "Why not? I thought you were only away for the weekend."

"He extended the trip to make up for coming home early last time. He's so impulsive, but once he sets his mind to something, there's no changing it."

"That's nice."

"And when we get home, we're going to have a big surprise for you. So you'd better be on your best behavior. I don't want anything to ruin this."

"Nothing will."

"You'd better hope not. That Bridget is nice, and I'm sure she does a good job, but you know I expect you to keep an eye on your sister. Make sure she isn't running around like a wild animal when we get back. I want her freshly washed and dressed in clean clothes and on her best behavior. Understood? And as for you, no sulking around, no arguments with your brother."

I don't have the energy to deal with this. I can barely muster up the strength to say anything. "Mm-hmm."

"And you better hope I don't get another call from school. Whatever this is, it better be a twenty-four-hour bug. The last thing I need is for them to tell me you have to repeat a year. You know your stepfather isn't going to pay for your second senior year. You're lucky he insisted on paying for this one. And now I'm late for my massage. You always find a way to ruin my plans."

She finally stops to take a breath, and not a second too soon because I can't take any more of this. My head's already pounding. So, I end the call, punching the red button to disconnect us. I then leave the phone face down on the nightstand and roll over, turning my back on it.

I doubt she'll call again. It would ruin her plans. I already ruined all her plans by being born. I wonder if they had Plan B back in the day. Would she have taken it? I might not have been born.

Right now, with the way I'm feeling, that doesn't seem like such a bad thing. I've never been sick like this. Am I having a bad reaction? What would I even do if I was? Go to the hospital? Right. And they would ask why, and if I had any medication in my system. I would have to say yes. And then what? I don't even want to think about it. All I can do is close my eyes and hope I feel better by the time I wake up again.

* * *

"Here. Take this." There's a hand under my head, lifting it off my pillow.

"Hm?" I try to turn my face to the side. "No. Leave me alone." My voice is weak, and even that much is enough to exhaust me.

"It's just aspirin."

I can't even open my eyes. I'm so drained. Probably dehydrated, too. My head is splitting open worse than earlier.

"Here's some water." I try again to turn my head away, since I haven't been able to hold water down since last night, but the bottle follows my mouth. "Just take a few sips to wash down the pills. It'll be okay."

I'm too tired to fight. I open my mouth and allow some of the cool water inside to wash down the aspirin. The water feels good in my mouth, going down my parched throat.

"There you go." My head rests against the pillow again, and all I can do is groan in misery. "I know you're hurting. Just relax."

The voice is barely a whisper. Bridget? Maybe.

"Here you go." I wince when something cold touches my forehead, but once the shock wears off, it feels good. Very good. Some of the throbbing eases, too. I try to open my eyes again, but it's like they're glued shut.

"Try to get some sleep." A hand strokes my hair, then it adjusts my blankets until they're pulled up around my shoulders. "There's a sports drink on the nightstand to help rehydrate you. Try to drink that if you can. It'll make you feel better a lot faster."

"Thank you," I rasp. Even my lips are dry.

"It's nothing." One more stroke of my hair, and the hand is gone, along with the person it's attached to.

If I were completely naive, I would think it was my mother treating me this way. The mother I always wanted. When I was little, I used to think it was my fault she was never nice to me. I know better now, just like I know better than to think she would come home early in case there was something seriously wrong.

It's easier to be asleep than it is to be awake, so I don't bother trying to fight it off when it tugs at me again. The last thing I process is the faint smell of chlorine before I sink back into darkness.

CHAPTER 29

'm surprised Theo's parents let him have a party here so soon after the last one ended with the police showing up.

Salem only laughs at my worries as we walk up the brick path from where she parked. "Please, that was nothing. I'm sure his dad gave them some money or donated to a cop charity or something. No biggie."

I keep forgetting these aren't the same kind of people I grew up around. Theo probably has never heard of being grounded.

I'm starting to think I'm underdressed. All I did was pick up a headband with cat ears attached, then drew some whiskers on my cheeks and dressed in all black. I know Halloween is supposed to be for dressing up sexy, at least when you're our age, but I didn't really have anything that worked. Salem offered to lend me something, but I wasn't blessed with big boobs like she was. I looked like a little kid dressing up in my mom's clothes.

She's not dressed very sexy, either, wearing last year's cheer-leader uniform splattered in red paint. Along with her makeup, she looks enough like a zombie that nobody notices how lame I look in comparison.

I'm surprised anybody notices her at all. I feel like I walked into a strip club. There are girls in shoes that have at least five or six-inch heels. They're wearing latex and leather and, in one case, a sheer bodysuit with pasties over the nipples.

"Trashy," Salem decrees under her breath even though she's all smiles for the girl wearing it.

"Hey, where's Hayes?" another girl asks as they pass by.

I can only shrug. He knew I was coming to this—it was sort of an established thing before I agreed to leave him alone and stay out of his way. But I haven't seen much of him except for his presence in history class today. I should be happy about that, shouldn't I? The less I see him, the less chance of him doing or saying something to make me feel bad about myself.

But I miss him, too. I wonder if Mr. Ambrose would pay for me to go to therapy. I'm thinking I need it.

"He texted me. He'll be here soon." I didn't know Franky was right behind me. He winds his arms around my waist before giving me a squeeze. "You look cute."

Salem rolls her eyes dramatically. "Cute. No girl over the age of ten wants to be called cute."

I have to agree. "She's not wrong. But thank you. I wasn't going for sexy or anything." I'm sure it will be easier to deal with Hayes when I'm dressed this way, too. Otherwise, he might get all weird like he did at the last party. Should he rule so much of my life, so many of my decisions? Probably not. But I can't help it.

Just like I can't help feeling a little jaded now. There are girls making out in one corner of the kitchen, and another porn playing in the backyard. Now there's portable heaters out there, and I guess the pool is heated, too, since people are swimming. I think one of the couples might actually be having sex in the water.

It doesn't even shock me anymore. I guess I'm finally getting used to this life. I don't know if that's a good thing or a bad thing. I don't know if I want to be like some of these people. All they care about is finding the next experience, the next chance to feel something. Of course, I could be overthinking it. It wouldn't be the first time I've done that.

I'm surprised at how many of the guys are dressed up. A few

people are wearing masks that hide who they really are, but of course if a person wants to drink, they have to take the mask off. I keep expecting one of them to be Hayes, but I haven't seen him yet. I wonder what's taking him so long and hope he didn't pick tonight of all nights to do something crazy.

I need a night off from worrying about him.

After a couple of drinks, though, I don't care as much. Salem even convinces me to dance a little, and it actually helps loosen up the tension I'm carrying around. It doesn't matter that I'm not great at dancing—few of the people around us are, but nobody cares.

One of the football players dances up on her from behind, but she laughs it off and plays along. I can't help remembering her warning about them, but right now she seems fine with it. Somebody comes up behind me, too, and I roll my eyes.

"Back off," I call out over my shoulder. "I don't need you poking my ass." I barely even sound like myself.

But he doesn't stop—in fact, he puts his arm around my waist and pulls me closer. From one heart-stopping second, I think it must be Hayes. I can't see much of him, but he's wearing a mask that makes his head look like a skeleton.

I touch his bicep and stiffen in surprise. It's not nearly as muscular as Hayes's. "Get off me," I mutter before driving an elbow into his stomach.

He doesn't react to it, instead lowering his head to speak into my ear. "I don't think so. We have business to take care of."

I know the voice. Now, I regret drinking because everything in my stomach wants to come back out. I'm still swaying back and forth to the music, and Salem hasn't noticed. Oh, my God, I hope she doesn't notice. I hope she doesn't see him.

"I told you. I don't have anything to give you." All I want to do is scream, but I can't. Because I don't know what he's going to do.

"And I told you we could work something out. Unless you want your brother going to prison."

"He's not my brother." I can't believe we're having this conversation in the middle of a party. Nobody knows, nobody notices.

They're all too busy having fun while I'm standing in the middle of a nightmare with a rapist's arm around my waist.

"But you sure as hell cared a lot about him staying out of trouble. I feel you could be motivated under the right circumstances." With that, he yanks me away from the makeshift dance floor, his arm still around my waist. How is nobody seeing this? I want to scream, but I don't dare. I don't want Salem to know he's here. What might that do to her?

I don't know where we're going. Everything goes by me in flashes—people, dancers, girls waiting in line for the bathroom. We reach the kitchen, then go through a door off to the side. It's cool and quiet, especially compared to the noisy party. Logan closes the door before letting me go.

My head swings around as I look for a way out. Where's the light switch? I stumble toward the door we came through, my hands outstretched, but he pulls me away. It smells like gas in here, exhaust. We're in the garage. It's still too dark to see, but now I can make out the outline of a few cars.

"We're gonna settle this now, you and me." He tears off his mask and runs a hand through his flattened hair.

"Why bother with the mask? You look plenty scary without it."

I regret it when he rushes at me, closing his hand around my throat. This isn't like the way it is with Hayes. Hayes might intimidate me, he might even scare the shit out of me, but this guy is trying to hurt me. Now I know the difference.

"And whose fault is that? Give me one good reason I shouldn't go to the police right this very fucking minute and identify him as the motherfucker who did this to me."

"You're a rapist," I grit out despite the pain and my limited air.

"Says you." He shoves me away and I land against a set of shelves, but stay on my feet. "Video evidence says otherwise."

"Right. Good luck finding anybody who will provide those videos from the concert. People have short memories. I bet most of them are already deleted."

"Tell yourself whatever you need to." He lunges for me again, and the alcohol must slow me down because he catches me before I run. Where am I running to? I don't know how to get out of here.

He presses me against one of the cars, the door cold under my back. "Here's how it's going to be. You're going to give me what I want, or else I'm going to the cops tonight. Understood? Hayes is going away for a long time after what he did. And you know that little slut can't say anything about it. Stop pretending."

"What do you want?" I ask. Even though I know.

"You're gonna put my cock in your mouth, and you're gonna suck it real good. And I'm going to come on your face, and you're gonna thank me for the privilege." He runs a hand over my boobs, and I have to bite back a whimper. "Or maybe I'll come on these tits instead. That way, I won't mess up your Halloween makeup. See? I'm not such a bad guy."

"You mean it? I suck you off, and you won't go to the police and report Hayes?"

"If you do a good job," he reminds me with a grin. It's sickening, even more so because of his messed-up face. "Now, on your knees, like a good little kitty."

What am I supposed to do? He could just as well go to the police after this, for all I know. But if he was going, wouldn't he have gone by now? Can I even call him on it? Do I want to push my luck?

I don't think I can. Oh, my God, I think I have to do this. Even though I know he won't stop with only this. Even though I know he'll find me again and want more next time. *Hayes, I'm doing this for you.*

I lower myself to my knees, fighting like hell not to cry. I don't think I'm going to win that battle.

He chuckles as he undoes his belt, then unbuttons his jeans and lowers the zipper.

All of a sudden, the room gets bright, almost blinding. I blink, confused, stunned, while Logan whirls around with his dick in his hand. Salem was right. It's huge.

I look up to see Theo standing on the other end of the garage, and he's holding his phone in front of him like he's recording.

"Here's the thing about this being my house: I know all the entrances."

"Get the fuck out of here!" Logan shouts.

"Like I said. My house." I get on my feet and brush off my knees and thank God for him. "What do you think you're doing out here? Because I know you weren't just forcing an underage girl to perform oral sex on you in exchange for not going to the police, right? That's pretty serious."

I've never seen him like this. He's not joking, not even a hint of a smirk. He's a lot more like Hayes when he's in one of his dark places, his eyes stormy, his face a mask of barely contained rage.

"Okay, fine. I guess I have to go to the cops then." Logan shrugs, arms extended to the sides.

"No. I don't think so." Theo puts his phone in his pocket, advancing on us. I back away because something tells me this will not be pretty. "You're coming with me." He pulls something else out of his waistband—and I barely bite back a scream at the sight of a gun. He has a gun! Theo?

"You're going to go back inside," he growls, and Logan's eyes go round when Theo circles him and presses the gun to his lower back. "Right now. March. Morgan, would you open the door?"

Like I have a choice. I scramble ahead of them, opening the door and scurrying into the kitchen. Theo pushes Logan inside, one hand on his shoulder while the other maintains its hold on the gun.

"Okay, man. I get it." Logan's starting to sweat, but Theo doesn't show any sign of strain. Instead, he takes Logan into the center of the kitchen, where a group of football players and another of guys I recognize from the basketball team are gathered around a couple of kegs.

"Hey, guys!" Theo shouts, his voice ringing out over the music and chatter. "See this guy? He just tried to coerce Morgan here into giving him a blowjob out in the garage so he wouldn't accuse Hayes of beating the shit out of him."

I'm horrified and embarrassed, but that's nothing compared to Logan's obvious horror.

Especially once the guys move toward him.

Theo backs away, and in a flash, he tucks the gun in his waistband. "I'd run if I were you," he says to Logan, who makes a break forward, fighting his way through the crowd on their way to the kitchen to see what's going on.

"Take him outside!" Theo calls out. "No blood on the floor, please. I don't want to explain it." He's so cool and calm. I barely recognize him.

I fight my way through the crowds of confused people and finally make it out to the front of the house, where a circle of guys are beating the shit out of somebody in the middle. I'm disgusted, but I can't look away. Two of them pick Logan up by his shirt and drag him to a truck.

I look around, confused, and find Theo watching from behind me. "What are they going to do to him?"

"Don't worry about it. Things like this have a way of sorting themselves out." He looks at me, and his brows draw together. "Are you all right? That's the real question."

"I'm fine." I'm not. I'm sort of scared of what this all means now. "How did you know to be there?"

"I saw him dragging you away. I didn't know who it was with that mask, but you looked like you were trying not to piss yourself." He puts a hand on my shoulder, and I can't believe how comforting it is after what he just put in motion. "Would you really have done that for Hayes?"

"Yes. I was going to."

"Why?"

"Because he's part of my family now. And I don't want him in trouble." I bite my lip, unsure. "So you know what he did?"

"You mean showing up at school with a swollen fist the day after somebody was beaten half to death?" Still, he shakes his head. "He wouldn't like it if he knew you were going to do that for him."

"Somebody has to look out for him."

"I guess you're right. He's not always so good at doing that himself." He looks across the lawn. I'm pretty sure there's blood on the grass. "That piece of shit will get what he deserves. Don't worry about that. He'll never bother anybody again."

I don't even want to know how he can be so sure. Something tells me there's a lot more about his family, I don't know. I don't want to know either, just like I don't want to know how he got his hands on a gun out of nowhere.

"Come on. You look like you could use a drink. I know I sure as hell could." He takes my hand and leads me back into the house, and it's almost like nothing ever happened.

Just when I think I understand my new friends, they make me question everything I thought I knew.

CHAPTER 30

My heart sinks when I get home from school on Thursday and see Mr. Ambrose's car in front of the house. I knew they couldn't stay away forever, but I couldn't help hoping they would. I should be happy my mom is home, shouldn't I? I mean, in a normal world, I would be. But nothing about my world is normal.

I can only hope Bridget has Lucy under control, or else I'll be the one who takes the blame. I can't forget the way Mom made it sound when we were on the phone on Monday. I was sick as a dog, but I remember that much.

"Morgan! Mommy's home!" Lucy runs at me the second I'm through the door.

"Is she?" It's amazing she can be so happy. I hope she never loses whatever allows her to be this way.

"There you are." Mom comes gliding down the stairs, looking tan and glowing. "Where's your brother? His father already texted and told him to come straight home after school."

I don't have a brother. "I don't know. He doesn't drive me, remember?"

Her smile slips. "Already with the attitude?"

"I'm just saying. I don't know why he isn't home yet."

"Well, he'd better get here soon, because we have an announcement to make."

I guess this is my fault, too. I settle for going to the kitchen for a snack while Lucy follows me, chattering about her day. Usually I'm able to pay attention and actively engage with her, but I'm a little too distracted right now. I wonder what they're waiting to tell us.

I don't have to wait long.

The front door swings open and a moment later, Hayes's voice echoes down the hall. "Okay, what's the big news?"

I don't know why, but I'm filled with dread as I leave the kitchen holding Lucy's hand. Hayes looks at us and I frown, shrugging.

Mom emerges from the study, smiling again. "Come on in. We wanted to talk to you."

Lucy and I get there first, with Hayes following close behind. The first hint of this being a bigger deal than I imagined is the bottle of champagne on ice.

Mr. Ambrose is all smiles as he waves me closer. "This is a celebration. You're both underage but certain situations call for a glass of champagne. Lucy, I have apple juice for you." He hands her a glass, and she accepts it with a solemn expression.

I look over my shoulder to find Hayes standing in the doorway, scowling. "Can we get this over with?" he says. "No offense, but I have a lot of homework to do."

Mr. Ambrose only chuckles. "Trust me, this is worth it." He hands me a champagne flute before offering one to Hayes, who accepts it but hasn't stopped scowling—if anything, his scowl deepens.

Mom exchanges a look with Mr. Ambrose. "Do you want to tell them?"

Oh, no. A flash of intuition tells me when I'm about to hear. I shoot a panicked look toward Hayes, but he's too busy glowering to notice.

Mom holds up her left hand, where even more diamonds are than before. "We eloped! That's why we extended the trip. We decided to get married on a whim."

My mouth falls open. "Married?"

Lucy squeals. "You got married! Mommy, I was gonna be the flower girl!"

Mom laughs indulgently. "We'll still have a ceremony and a big party, baby. Don't you worry about it. You'll be the most beautiful flower girl there ever was."

"This is for real? You really did it?" I can't wrap my head around it.

"We did. I've never been happier in my entire life." Mom wraps her arms around Mr. Ambrose's waist—no, my stepfather's waist—before giving him a peck on the cheek.

I look at Hayes again, and he wears the expression of somebody who just stepped in dog shit.

"There's more." Mom's chin trembles like she's about to cry, even though she's still beaming. Her eyes sparkle with unshed tears as she looks from one of us to the other. "Our little family is going to grow. I'm pregnant."

I feel like somebody punched me in the stomach. "Wow, this is great. A new brother or sister?" I look down at Lucy. "A new baby in the house. Isn't that exciting?"

"I'm gonna be a big sister?" She bounces up and down on the balls of her feet. "Can I take care of the baby?" The adults laugh and I manage a brittle smile.

Hayes does better than that. He drops his glass on the floor, where it shatters. Lucy shrieks in surprise and ducks behind me.

"Hayes, what's wrong?" his father asks.

"What's wrong? Can you seriously ask me that?" His face is turning red, his lips pulled back over his teeth. "This is a fucking joke, right? No way you actually married her."

"Hayes, don't be unfair," Mom pleads in her sweetest voice. "Now we're really, truly a family. And you'll have a little brother or sister to love."

His hands flex, and for one nauseating second, I think he's going to strangle her. I honestly think he's going to hurt her—and I know what he's capable of. "Dad, this is a mistake. You've made the biggest mistake of your entire fucking life."

"That is enough from you," his father barks, stepping away from Mom so he can stand toe-to-toe with his son. Glass crunches under his shoes. "She is my wife. Your stepmother, and the mother of your sibling. You are going to treat her with respect, or you are going to leave this house for good."

"Fine," Hayes laughs. "Then I'm gone. I'd rather live anywhere than pretend anything about this is right." He stomps out of the room while I stare with my mouth still hanging open.

"No, wait." I turn to Mom, who looks stricken. "Somebody has to stop him."

"It won't be me." Mr. Ambrose turns to Mom. "I'm sorry, Christine. This was supposed to be your big moment."

"Don't worry about it," Mom murmurs. "He'll come around. What about my babies?" She turns to us, and of course I know better than to show my dismay or the sense of dread these sudden announcements have planted in my chest.

Meanwhile, I can't stop wondering where Hayes will go and when he'll come back. He can't leave for good, can he? This is all too bizarre.

I drink my champagne if only because I know what will happen if I don't. No wonder Mom didn't get a glass of her own. A baby. It's not like I didn't know it was possible, but I still didn't expect it. I almost feel bad for the kid.

I feel worse for Hayes. I don't know why. He's the one who threw a fit and said he was leaving. And he did. The thing is, I'm sure his dad thinks he'll come back, but I'm not so sure myself. I don't think Mr. Ambrose has any idea who his son really is.

I duck out of the study when one of the housekeepers comes in to clean up the mess from the shattered glass. I'm already texting Salem before I reach the stairs.

911. Hayes left, serious blow up. Let me know if you hear anything from him.

I send a similar text to Theo and Franky once I reach my room. No specifics, just a warning that he might show up.

What if he doesn't come back?

What if he actually kills himself this time?

I don't want to believe he'll do it, but I can't pretend the danger isn't there. I saw what he was like in the car after we left Theo's. He honestly didn't care if he died. He would have even taken me with him. He was that determined. And now that I know for sure what's happening to him, I know what a dangerous, twisted place he's in. All he needs is the confirmation that my family is now a real, permanent part of his life—and a baby on top of that. He already hates our parents being together. Now, there will be a baby to remind him of it.

I dissolve into tears, curling up in a ball on my bed, clutching my phone in case a message comes through. As a last-ditch effort, I text Hayes.

Please, don't do anything to hurt yourself. Please, go somewhere safe. Let me know you're okay.

I don't expect a response. I only hope he reads it.

It feels like the whole world is ending. What a joke that we were supposed to be happy about the announcement.

I must cry myself to sleep, because the next thing I know, something hits me in the face. I jump, eyes flying open, startled out of a murky dream.

Only to find my mother bending over me, reaching behind me to grab what bounced off my head. She holds it up in front of my face and I recoil in horror at the sight of the Plan B box. "What is this? What the hell do you think you're doing?"

"You went through my trash?"

"How else am I supposed to know what you're sneaking around doing when I'm not here? You little slut."

"You don't understand—"

She lunges, stopping with her face close to mine. "I understand everything. You take advantage of us not being here. You go around fucking anybody who will give you even a little bit of attention.

Then you go off and buy this?" She throws the box at me again, but at least this time I can deflect it.

"It's not like that."

"Like hell it isn't. I will be damned if I let you ruin this for me the way you've ruined everything else!"

The bedroom door creaks open a little and for a second I think this is it. This is where the truth finally comes out. My new stepfather is finally going to see what his wife is all about. Even though I know she'll blame it on me, it's for the best. He needs to know.

Instead, Lucy flies over to the bed. "Mommy, no!" she whimpers.

"Get out of here," Mom snarls, pushing her aside.

"Stop yelling, Mommy! Don't hurt Morgan!" Mom whirls on her, and I see that look in her eyes. The one that says she's going over the edge.

I scramble off the bed to put myself between them. "Leave her alone!"

"Don't you talk to me that way." Pain explodes across my cheek when she backhands me. Lucy bursts into tears, so Mom takes her by the arm and yanks her closer before smacking her across the ass.

"I'll give you something to cry about." She shoves Lucy away hard enough that the poor thing bounces off the side of the bed and lands on the floor. I throw myself over her, covering her with my body.

Mom only snorts in disdain. "Look at you. Pathetic. I'll kill you before I let you get in the way. Just remember that." Only once she closes the door do I look up. She's gone.

"Are you okay?" I whisper to Lucy, whose soft whimpering tears at my heart.

Her eyes are big, filled with fear. "Mommy was hurting you."

"Oh, sweetie. I'm okay." I sit up before gathering her in my arms and holding her close. "Remember, I told you before. If Mommy is mad at me, I need you to stay away so you don't get hurt."

"I forgot."

"I know, sweetie. Thank you for trying to help me." I rock her a little until her crying turns to sniffles, my face throbbing the whole time. Stupid me, thinking we were past this now. We never will be. It doesn't matter who she marries or how much money she has. She'll never change.

And now she's about to have another baby. I won't be here to protect this one, or to protect Lucy. I can't help Hayes, either.

I've never felt so helpless in my whole life.

CHAPTER 31

"What happened to you?" Salem winces when I get in the car. She's staring at my face, which doesn't hurt as badly anymore but looks uglier hours later.

"Don't worry about it." She reaches out, her fingers almost touching the bruise, but I turn my face away before she can. "Please. Don't touch."

"Was it your mom?"

My throat tightens. The only thing that stops me from breaking down is when I remember Hayes. He's out there somewhere. He needs help.

"It doesn't matter," I say. "Have you heard anything?"

"Not since I just talked to you before I came over. I texted a bunch of people, but nobody saw him." She pulls out of the drive-way, and I can only hope Mom doesn't find out I left. I don't need a bruise on my right cheek to match the one on my left.

"Where else could he be, do you think?"

"I don't know. We can check down at school. Maybe he's there. But I doubt it."

I can barely breathe. My chest is so tight, and my heart has raced faster with every passing hour. It's been five since he left, and I don't know how much more I'm going to handle before my heart gives out completely.

"So that's why he left?" Salem asks. "Because they got married and they're having a baby?"

"He lost it. He really hates us."

"He just, you know." She flaps her hands around before putting them back on the wheel. "He blew up. He'll get over it. He'll probably spend the night at some place, and tomorrow he'll come home after school, and everything will go back to normal."

"I don't know. I don't think so."

"Why? Why aren't you telling me?"

I want to tell her. Finally, so I don't have to carry this around inside me anymore. But it's still not my story to tell. "He's going through a lot of stuff he doesn't want anybody to know about. I only know about a little of it. He wouldn't even tell me everything."

"I swear to God. Men. I think they're being strong when they hold everything inside." She's not wrong, but she still doesn't know the whole story. She can't imagine his shame.

I keep my eyes peeled for his car while she drives me around town. I hate thinking about him wandering around, seething and aching.

"This is impossible," I say. "He must have gone somewhere he can stay for the night. He won't be hanging around town."

I take out my phone and send a text to Franky and Theo. *Can you please help us look for Hayes? I'm really worried about him.*

"Fuck this," Salem huffs. "Let's go to Theo's first. He's closer. I'll drag him out by his balls if I have to."

"Thank you for helping," I offer.

"You don't have to thank me. And no offense, but I'm not doing it for you. He's going through shit. This isn't like him, running off like that. I'm worried, too."

We reach Theo's in record time—and what I see on pulling up in front of the huge house makes me want to scream.

"He said he didn't know where Hayes was!" I shout, pointing at the familiar car sitting next to the house. He parked it at an angle, like he was in a hurry. "I'm going to kill him for lying."

"Take a breath. He probably made Theo promise to pretend he didn't know where he was." Still, there's an edge in her voice like she's just as mad as I am.

I'm out of the car before she puts it in park, running up to the front door.

I jam my finger against the bell. "Theo!" I shout, even though he probably doesn't hear me inside the huge house. I punch the bell again and again since that's the only thing he'll hear, and I need to vent my anger somehow.

The door swings open to reveal a scowling Theo. "For fuck's sake."

"I know he's here. He should have parked in the garage if he was trying to hide. Why did you pretend you didn't know where he was?" By this time, Salem is behind me, and I can almost feel her anger mixing with mine.

"He made me swear. What am I supposed to do?" He runs a hand through his hair, his forehead creasing. "It's not like I did it to fuck with you."

"I need to talk to him."

"I don't think that's such a good idea right now."

"Then let me do it," Salem suggests. "I'm not a part of any of this."

"Any of this?" Theo's head snaps back, eyes narrowing. "What do you mean?"

"I'm not part of the family, you know? If he's freaking out because of the wedding and the baby, I'm an outsider."

Some of the confusion drains from his expression, but not all of it. His eyes dart back and forth between us. "I don't think that's the whole problem." He shifts his weight from one leg to the other, thrusting a hand into his pocket before glancing over his shoulder.

That's when it hits me. Why didn't I see it before? Something must have happened today at school between Hayes and Coach Greg. Finding out about the wedding and the baby alone wasn't enough to make him go off the deep end like this. It was only the straw that broke the camel's back.

"Do you know?" I ask Theo. "You do, don't you?"

His head swings around, eyes wide. "You know about it?"

"Know about what?" Salem demands. "Dammit, would everybody stop being so cryptic? What am I missing?"

"No!" It's a roar coming from deeper inside the house. I look over Theo's shoulder to find Hayes jogging down the hall with fury written all over his face. "No, you will not. Get the hell out of here. I don't want you here, either of you!"

"We just wanted to make sure—" Salem begins, but he cuts her off.

"I don't fucking care! Both of you, stop fucking around in my life." He jabs a finger at me. "This is all your fault. You and your fucking family. You ruined everything, my whole fucking life!"

"How?" I ask, and I don't care that I'm crying. I can't help it. Let him see what he's doing to me, let them all see. "All I ever wanted was to help you. Remember? I just wanted to be your friend."

"I don't want you to be my friend. I don't want you. I don't want your mother. I don't want any of it. Get it through your fucking head. What do I have to do? Do I have to kill you?"

Theo steps between us, a hand against his chest. "Wow, hold on."

"Get out of the way." Hayes shoves him aside before advancing on me until my back is against the doorframe. "Go away. Stay away. Get out of my life. I wish I never set eyes on you."

I can barely see him through my tears, can barely breathe as I sob. "Hayes, no..."

"You should have let me do it. Why didn't you fucking let me do it?" He leans in close, vibrating with rage. "Why?" he roars.

"I'm sorry," I sob, even though I'm not. I don't want him to die. "Please, let's talk about it."

"What is there to talk about? My life is over. It's all fucking over."

"I don't understand."

"And you never fucking will. So damn clueless. You think you're helping, but all you do is make things worse." He takes a breath like he's about to say something else, but pauses, eyes narrowing as he studies my face. "What happened to you? Your cheek?"

I raise a hand to it, about to explain, but he shakes his head. "Don't bother. I already know. I'm surprised it took this long, but they've been out of town so much of the time."

I flail around in my head, trying to come up with a way to get through to him. There has to be a way. "If it's bothering you like this, if it's really killing you inside, it's time to finally tell somebody," I whisper. "Or go to the police. Somebody. You don't have to go through it alone. You have people who care about you. Don't you get it? I can't stand to see you doing this to yourself."

When I reach out, hoping to touch his face, he slaps my hand away and snarls. "You're so fucking naive. You honestly think it's that simple? Wake the fuck up. If it was, don't you think I would have done that by now?"

"What are you talking about?" Salem demands. "What's happening? Is somebody hurting you?"

"Go away," he growls, and she recoils with a gasp. "Both of you. Stupid bitches. You don't have any idea what it's like."

"What what is like?" she counters, but he only shakes his head. I've only ever seen him look so disgusted when he's dealing with me alone. If he's treating Salem the same way, I know he's in the worst possible place. And dammit, it's ripping my heart to pieces.

"Fine, then." Salem takes me by the arm and starts pulling me away. "Come on, this isn't helping."

"Hayes, please!"

He only stands there in the doorway, fists hanging at his sides, watching Salem pull me back to her car.

How can he be like this? Why does he keep pushing me away?

Why does he still hate me?

Once I'm in the car, I cover my face with my hands and let it all out. All the pain, frustration, helplessness. Salem sits beside me, silent, her head propped up on her hand as she stares up at the house.

"Are you going to tell me what's happening now?" she finally asks once my sobbing turns to soft weeping.

"I can't. I'm sorry, but I can't do it. But I guess Theo knows about it, too. That's what I was so worried about. I'm afraid he's going to hurt himself."

"Fuck."

"I just don't get it. All I ever wanted to do was help him. I know he's hurting, but every time I've tried to get through to him, he only hates me for it." I dig through my bag for a tissue, but I don't think an entire box would be enough.

"Is that how he treats you at home?"

"That's not important right now."

"But it is. I've never seen him like this. How long has this been going on for?"

"That's really not what matters. I know why he's doing this. Why he acts this way. He's in so much pain. And he doesn't think there's any way out. And now, with the wedding and the baby, he's losing it. That's all it took. I'm afraid he's never going to come home."

"He has to," Salem insists. "How could he survive otherwise?"

"That's the thing," I confess in a whisper. "I don't think that will matter if he does what I think he wants to do."

Her mouth falls open, but she snaps it shut right away. "No. Absolutely not. He would never do that. Theo will make sure he's okay. He has friends who will take care of him."

"I wish I could be so sure." Because I know how close he's come. If it hadn't been for me finding him on the bridge, he might have killed himself months ago.

One thing I know for sure: after what happened today, he's not coming home. Not so long as we're living there.

Because he hates me.

And even though I know he does, that hasn't stopped me from falling for him.

Salem starts the car and pulls away. I don't have anything left in me. Neither of us says a word as she drives me home.

CHAPTER 32

The house is quiet when I get home. If Mr. Ambrose is worried at all about where Hayes went, there are no signs of it anywhere. I hear him in his study when I go to the kitchen for water to hydrate after all this crying. He's typing on his keyboard, pounding the keys, but that's how he always types.

What's Hayes going to do? Is there anything I can do to help him? A big part of me wants to knock on the study door and tell my stepdad everything I know. Maybe that's what I need to do. I wanted to keep Hayes's secrets, but not if he might do something drastic. Something preventable.

At least I know for right now he's safe at Theo's. I text Theo on my way to the stairs, just in case.

At least let me know if he leaves, and where he plans on going, if so.

He must've told Theo about what's happening with Coach Greg, but Hayes interrupted us before I could find out for sure. Maybe he'll have the guts to say something to somebody who could stop this, since Franky clearly doesn't.

Lucy's in bed now, sleeping. I'm as quiet as I can be when I check on her. Hopefully she forgets what happened earlier, but I doubt it. I've never forgotten the things Mom has done to me, even back when I was this age.

I lean over her, brushing her away from her forehead before kissing her smooth skin. "You're gonna be fine," I whisper, even if I'm not sure how to make that happen. I used to look forward to the day I moved out and went to college, but now it only makes me afraid for her. It's obvious Mom has no plans to change her ways. She can marry all the rich men she wants, but that will never make her a better person.

And if Mr. Ambrose finds out, and this arrangement ends, she'll only get worse. I don't even want to imagine it.

I carry my phone around with me as I go to my room, only putting it down to change into pajamas. I take it to the bathroom, leaving it on the counter while I wash my tear-stained face. I keep glancing at it just in case a message comes through, but so far there's nothing. Looks like this is another night where I won't be getting any sleep.

I'm starting to wonder if life was better back when we were at the hotel. Before we moved in here, before I started at school. It seems like everything only got worse since then. At least Lucy was happy when we were there, though, I know most of that had to do with me trying to make the whole thing an adventure instead of what it really was: an eviction without a backup plan. I guess Mr. Ambrose was the backup plan.

I don't know what makes me do it. Maybe I need to connect with different times to escape the time I'm in right now. I open my photos app and scroll through. Most of the pictures are of Lucy, of course. In the pool, in our room the day we pretended we were down at the spa. I took a picture of her wearing one of the complimentary bathrobes, with her hair wrapped in a towel turban and cucumber slices over her eyes. It makes me laugh a little, something I wouldn't have done otherwise.

The rest of my photos are in the cloud, saved in our account. I guess I'm desperate for something to lift my mood, so I pull out my laptop and log in. Now I can look back on the last few years. Lucy's first birthday party, the cake I made for her. Her first steps. Bath time, which was always her favorite. She was so little—she's little now, but compared to these pictures, she's a big, grown-up girl.

I want so much for her to feel happy and safe. To feel loved. What should I do? Stay here forever? Go to school nearby, so I don't have to move out? But that would mean living with my mother for at least the next four years, too. Can I stand that?

Especially when she has a new baby to spoil? A reason to ignore Lucy even more than she already did? Bridget's nice, but she's no replacement for a mother. I wish I didn't feel so guilty, but I know how bad things could get. What if Lucy thinks I abandoned her?

This isn't making me feel better anymore. I close out my folder, which takes me back to the main account. The only other folder consists of Mom's stuff since Lucy's too young to have a phone, obviously.

I'd close the entire window if it wasn't for the thumbnail preview in front of Mom's folder. It stops me, freezes me in place. I don't even blink.

I can't be seeing what I think I'm seeing. It's tiny, the pic, but it's familiar—because I've seen it before. Both on a screen and in person. Hayes's erect dick.

The dick pic from last weekend. It's in Mom's cloud account. He sent it to... her? Which means she must've been the one who asked for it?

No. Not my mom. My brain won't accept it. This can't be real.

But it's here in front of me. The files are from her phone. It must have been her.

I wouldn't click on the folder if a sick, twisted certainty wasn't settling into my bones. I need to know I'm not imagining this. Even if it's awful, I have to see it. Hayes is the one who's been suffering through it. I can't turn away now when he's the one who's falling apart because of what I think I'm about to find.

I wish I was wrong, but I'm not.

So many photos and videos, and they're all of Hayes. They stretch back months according to the dates, since the summer. Shots of Hayes sitting by the pool in his swim shorts. Hayes swimming. Hayes coming out of the pool. There's a short video of him drying off.

And one of him in the shower.

"Look at the camera," she murmurs in a sweet voice. I can't see her, but I'd know her voice anywhere. "Turn around so I can see that gorgeous cock, baby." He keeps his head down, moving mechanically, coming to a stop once he's fully facing her.

She moans in approval and zooms in on his dick, hanging flaccid. "Stroke it for me. Get it hard, baby." He's slow to take it in his hand, slow to stroke it. She zooms out. He's still looking at his feet, but he's getting hard. Just like she wants him to.

I'm going to throw up, but I can't stop watching. I have to know what she's done.

"I can't wait to taste it," she murmurs. "I want your cum in my mouth. Can you give it to me?"

He only grunts in response.

She sets the phone on the counter, angled toward the shower, then steps into view and drops the towel she was wearing.

"No, no," I whisper, but that doesn't stop her from opening the shower door and kneeling in front of him, taking his dick into her mouth.

"Oh, my God." I can't watch anymore. I stop it before anything else happens.

But I don't close the folder. My hand's shaking, but I keep navigating through the files. I can't stop now. It's like a perverted obsession. I need to see all of it.

C. I thought it stood for Coach, but now I know better. It stands for Christine.

It was her all along. And now she's his stepmother and he'll never get away from her. All these weeks, I assumed he was being abused at school. I never considered it might've been happening right here at home. That explains his happiness when our parents went away, and his attitude when they came back.

She asked him for a dick pic while she was away with his father.

Now the memories come flooding back, and all of them look different now that I know the full story.

The way she touched him that first night, when we moved in. I thought she was trying to get him to warm up to her, but now I see it was the caress of a lover. No wonder he pulled away like he did. No wonder he doesn't like to be touched.

The way he flipped out when she suggested he call her Mom during dinner. She even made a point of asking him for a hug. She was screwing with his head right in front of us, and there was nothing he could do to stop her. Not with his father watching, thinking everything was great, and we were all going to become a family.

He wanted to jump off the bridge the morning after a weekend Mom spent with his dad. Were they here at the house? What did she do to him that weekend to make him want to end his life?

Tears course down my cheeks, but I keep looking through the contents of Mom's phone. Now I feel like I owe him this.

There's another video, a longer one this time. Recorded in what I recognize as the master bedroom. The phone was propped up on the nightstand.

My mother is lying in bed wearing a skimpy camisole and a thong. Her eyes are closed, her body basically on display.

Hayes walks into the frame. He's naked, stroking his dick with one hand. With the other, he reaches out, running his fingers over her hip. She rolls onto her back with her eyes closed and he caresses her boobs through the satin before pushing it up to expose her. He bends down, still stroking, then takes one of her nipples into his mouth.

She opens her eyes and gasps before pushing him away. "No! Hayes, what are you doing? Don't do this!"

Instead of running away, he climbs on top of her. I force myself to watch him forcing her, holding her wrists over her head and rubbing his cock over her crotch even though she twists and fights.

He reaches between them to yank down her panties. She begs him to stop. "Why are you doing this? You have to stop! No! You can't!" He covers her mouth with one hand, and she weeps behind it while he forces himself inside her and fucks her hard. Mercilessly.

Then he finishes, grunting as he does. Her whimpers soften until she goes silent and limp. He lifts his hand from her mouth.

She waits a second—then smiles and runs her hands over his chest. "Well done. You made me come with you. Next time, I want you to eat my pussy before you fuck me."

He bolts up from the bed. "I'm going to throw up." He stumbles to the bathroom and slams the door. The sound of his retching is followed by my grinning mother reaching over to stop the recording.

I can't believe I just saw that. I can't believe it happened.

I sit and stare at the screen long after the video's over. I knew she was fucked up, but I could never, ever have imagined this. Obviously, or else I might've seen it before now. It's so obvious. She and his dad started dating over the summer. I assumed the abuse started during swim training, but it started because she came into Hayes's life.

All the times she's tried to be the loving mother. I only thought it was a sick joke before this. Now, it's sicker than anything I thought she was capable of. I used to think she was a neglectful mother. Self-centered, impatient, even violent.

I didn't know she was evil, too.

What must that have been like for Hayes? She must've told him all kinds of sick things to get him not to tell his dad. That he'd be crushed, that he wouldn't believe it, that their relationship would be ruined. Maybe she'd even try to blame Hayes for it if he came forward. I wouldn't put anything past her now.

I have to make a decision. Somebody has to stop this.

Is it going to be me?

CHAPTER 33

*I*t's obvious, right? Now that I've seen the proof, I have to do something about it. This is evil. It can't keep going on. So why am I still frozen at my desk?

Because this isn't some true crime movie or TV show or anything like that. This is my life. Lucy's life, too, and she means more to me than I do.

When our stepfather finds out about this, the marriage is over. The relationship is over. Nobody could see this and want to continue being with the person capable of it. According to the dates on some of these files, Hayes was seventeen when this started. He didn't turn eighteen until August. She was preying on him when he was still underage.

My own mother. How could I come from somebody like her? I feel so dirty and sick. No wonder Hayes hated me for being naive. I would have hated me, too, knowing I came from the person who ruined his life and made him want to die.

But what happens to Lucy? What happens to me? We'll be out on the street. I can't support her. She'll end up in foster care. I might lose her completely.

I grab the small pillow out from behind my back and throw it across the room, but that's not good enough. I go to the bed and punch the pillows as hard as I can, teeth gritted, and every time I land a blow, I imagine my fist hitting Mom's face. How could she do this to all of us? Hurting Hayes, abusing him. Neglecting me and Lucy. Hitting us.

And then she still walks around here like some kind of queen, like the perfect mother.

By the time I don't have the strength to punch anymore, the sad truth is obvious. If I don't come out and say something, I'm no better than she is.

So even though it might mean losing everything, I take the phone off my desk and text the only person I can think of going to. It should be his decision in the end. I can't make it for him.

I know who did it, I text Hayes. *I know everything now. What do you want me to do about it?*

For once, he doesn't leave me waiting. Immediately, the ellipsis appear under my message.

Wait there. Don't do anything. I'm on my way.

Even now, relief washes over me. I don't have to make the big decisions. I can leave it up to him. Still, I continue pacing my room, trying to come up with a plan for what to do when the inevitable happens, and we get kicked out. Maybe I could ask Salem if we could stay with her for a little while? Or one of the guys? They live in these massive houses with staff and everything. We wouldn't have to take up much space. Lucy knows how to behave herself. I can't believe I even have to think about this. Should I start packing?

Ten minutes seem to stretch on for hours, but finally I get another text. *I'm not coming in the house. I'm parked at the foot of the driveway.*

I slide on a pair of shoes and grab a sweater before running down the stairs and out the door. The sight of Hayes's car is almost enough to make me cry. He's safe. He didn't do anything drastic.

He won't look at me when I get in the car, staring at the wheel instead. "How do you know?" he asks as soon as I'm settled in.

"I was in our cloud account and found all the stuff that got uploaded from her phone."

"And what do you want?"

Not what I was expecting. "I want to know what you want me to do."

"Spare me. Let's just get down to it. How much is it going to take for you to keep your mouth shut?"

"No, you don't understand—"

"So you're not going to make it that easy?" His head snaps around, his eyes bloodshot. Has he been crying? "What do I have to do, then? Do I have to actually go through with it this time? Do you wanna take a little drive? Is that what it's going to take to keep you from telling everybody about it?"

"No! You're all wrong. I would never!"

"Yeah, right. Sorry if I don't believe you, but we're talking about your disgusting bitch of a mother. Don't pretend you don't want to protect her."

"I don't want to protect her! Please stop assuming you know what I'm thinking. It made me sick, what I watched. Knowing what she did to you. I am so sorry I didn't see it, but I didn't think… I mean, I know who she is, but I didn't know how bad…"

I lean against the seat, exhausted and heartbroken. "I'm just so sorry."

"I'll fucking kill you if you tell anybody."

"Why are you treating me like your enemy? I only want to help you. Hayes," I insist when he replies with a bitter laugh, "don't you understand? I love you."

The word hangs heavy in the air. I didn't mean to say it, and now I'm too surprised to say anything else. Surprised and horrified. He threatens to kill me, and I counter with the fact that I love him?

It broke the tension, anyway. "How can you say that?" he mumbles, looking down at his lap. "Especially if you saw… everything."

"That's what I'm trying to make you understand. I want this to stop now that I know. It doesn't change how I feel about you. If anything, I want to protect you even more."

"I told you before to save your pity." He slams the heel of his hand against the wheel, but it doesn't scare me. I'm not afraid of him anymore.

"Why didn't you ever tell your father? He never would have married her. I'm sure of it."

He's breathing too fast, like somebody who just finished a workout. Is he going to explode? I'm afraid so, but I can't get out of the car. I can't leave him now.

"There's a video." His voice is so tight, so flat. "She made it look like I was raping her."

I close my eyes, my insides twisting at the memory.

"She told me that was how she wanted it. Before that, she only said she would tell Dad if I tried to stop her. She said she would blame it on me and say I seduced her, and I would end up out on my ass without a penny. Plus, would make him miserable, all that shit. I guess she decided she needed some extra insurance, so she set up that video. She told me she could cut it down to make it look like I was responsible for all of it. She would take it to the cops, and I'd be arrested for rape. My life would be over."

I ache all over, literal pain. Just when I thought she couldn't get worse. "I am so sorry. And I'm so sorry I didn't understand."

"Franky actually walked in on it once. I made him swear not to say anything to anybody, but he keeps trying to get me to do it myself. And I can't. It'll be my word against hers, and I know whose side Dad will take when he sees the video after she fucks with it."

"But I've seen it now, too. I could testify. And I would if you wanted me to."

"Against your own mom?"

"Yes! That has nothing to do with it. She has to be stopped."

He shakes his head before letting out a long sigh. "It's not just that. Do you know what it'll be like? Coming out and saying I let her do that to me? It's bad enough when a girl is abused or raped or whatever. Everybody always blames it on her." He places a hand against his chest. "But me? A guy? A fucking athlete? If I wanted to, I could've stopped her. I could've hurt her. But I didn't because I was weak and confused and conflicted and ashamed. You don't know what it feels like until it happens to you."

"But it's not weakness to come forward. It's strength. Maybe if more guys spoke out about stuff like this, it wouldn't be so shameful. It happens to boys and girls, both. You're right, there's this ugliness around it. Maybe if another kid in your situation hears you were brave enough to speak up, it'll make them brave, too. I'm not saying you owe it to anybody, but it's just something to think about."

He turns slowly and eventually looks me in the eye for the first time since I got in the car. "You're really encouraging me to do this?"

"If it's what will make you feel safe, yes. You should do whatever will end this in a way that you'll be safe. I'm behind you, no matter what you decide."

"But what about you? What about Lucy? What if they get divorced?"

"I'm sure they will. And if there's any justice, she'll end up in prison."

"But what happens to you guys?"

"I don't know," I admit. "But I do know I'm not going to sit by and pretend I don't know what's happening just because I want to protect my sister. I can't sacrifice one of you for the other one."

"You could end up hurting her instead."

"I'll figure it out. I'm going to do everything I can to make sure she doesn't end up separated from me. It's only a few months until I turn eighteen. If I could find some place for us to stay and, I don't know, get a job after school, I could save up some money until graduation and figure it out from there. I'll adopt her if I have to."

"You would do that for me?"

"I couldn't live with myself otherwise."

He goes silent and I wait with my heart in my throat. What's he going to decide? I'm with him all the way, but that doesn't mean there isn't a big knot of fear in the pit of my stomach that gets bigger with every heavy breath he takes. He might still end up deciding to say fuck it and end his life just to avoid the humiliation he thinks he's going to face. All I can do is hope I got through to him, that he really understands.

He takes a deep breath, then lets it out slowly. I'm on pins and needles, ready to jump out of my skin. "Okay," he says with a firm nod.

"What does that mean?"

"It means I know what I have to do."

CHAPTER 34

"**Y**ou're sure you want to do this?" I can't believe it's Hayes asking me that question rather than the other way around. I've brought my laptop down from my room, ready to present the evidence. He looks like he just saw a ghost, his face pale, drawn.

"So long as you're sure."

"I guess I have to be."

"I'm with you no matter what happens."

He squares his shoulders before turning in the direction of the study. Here goes nothing.

He walks into the room without knocking and I follow close behind. His dad's jaw drops when he sees Hayes. "I thought I told you, I don't want you in this house if you're going to disrespect your new stepmother."

I'm waiting for Hayes's cue, prepared to destroy his father's life and mine with it. For one painful moment, I think he's going to back down. He even falls back a step. His whole body is tense, his breathing erratic.

"You can do this," I whisper, looking up at him. "I'm with you."

His jaw tightens. "Dad, there's something I've been keeping from you. If it hadn't been for Morgan accidentally finding the proof, I don't know if I ever would have said anything. I didn't want to ruin everything when you were so happy. I didn't want to blow everything up."

Mr. Ambrose lifts an eyebrow. "All right. What is it?" He looks at me, then eyes the computer in my hands. "What did you find?"

One more glance at Hayes. He nods, so I go to the desk and leave the computer in front of Mr. Ambrose. "It's our cloud account," I explain in a tiny voice. "I wasn't trying to snoop. I was only looking through my old pictures. But I couldn't ignore what I found."

"It started over the summer, right after you two started dating. Dad, I'm sorry." Hayes's voice breaks, and all I want to do is go to him. I just want to hold him. But I'm too afraid right now. I don't know how he'll react with his emotions all over the place.

I back away from the desk when Mr. Ambrose starts going through the files. I've never seen a man look so horrified, especially not him. He's always got everything together. "Is this some kind of sick joke?"

"No, Dad," Hayes replies in a voice heavy with emotion. He's creeping closer to the desk, while I move further away. I don't even feel like I should be in the room. "This is what she's been doing. At first, she told me you would never believe me, and you would throw me out and it would ruin my life, so I didn't say anything. And then she tried to make it look like I forced myself on her and she told me she'd have me arrested if I ever told. So I didn't say anything, but now... the wedding... the baby..." His breathing is erratic, his hands clenching and loosening, color rising in his cheeks.

Mr. Ambrose waves his hand like he can't hear anymore. "I don't know what to say. I can't believe... I never imagined... How could..." He stands, snapping the laptop shot. He's looking all around, and it sounds like he might hyperventilate.

I shoot a panicked look toward Hayes, who goes to his dad. "Are you all right? Dad, I'm sorry. I'm really sorry."

"You? You're sorry?" When Mr. Ambrose reaches out and pulls Hayes in for a hug, I can't help but burst into tears. Hayes cries quietly against his dad's shoulder, while Mr. Ambrose murmurs in his ear. I can't quite make out the words, but they sound a lot like "I love you" and "I'm sorry" and 'We'll fix this."

"I should have been more present in your life," he says, letting Hayes out of the hug but holding him at arm's length. "I should have been there for you. I should never have made it so you'd believe for a second I wouldn't be on your side. I'm sorry about that. I'm sorry you went through this because you didn't think I would believe you."

Hayes sniffles, staring at the floor. "I'm so ashamed of what happened and what I did."

"We'll get you help if you need it. You can talk to a therapist. I'll even go with you if you want. Whatever you want to do."

Hayes nods, swallowing hard.

I watch as Mr. Ambrose's hands tighten around Hayes's biceps. "And she'll never see the light of day again. I promise you that, too. But you're going to need to talk to the police and make a statement. It might get ugly. I'll do everything I can to make sure it doesn't, but I can't promise."

"I can accept that—on one condition."

"What is it?"

Hayes looks at me over his father's shoulder. "You have to promise to take care of Morgan and Lucy."

"Hayes!" I gasp.

He ignores me. "Morgan backed me up all the way. She knew if you two got divorced and her mom went to jail, she could end up on the streets with Lucy. But she still wanted to do the right thing. She shouldn't be punished for this. Neither of them should."

Mr. Ambrose turns to me, teary and splotchy faced. "Morgan, we don't know each other very well yet, but I would like the chance to change that. Thank you. You have nothing to worry about. You and Lucy always have a home here. It's the least I can do after what you've done to help my son."

I drop to the sofa with my head in my hands. It's almost too much to believe. I didn't know until right now how terrified I still was. How unsure. How much I doubted I could protect my sister. "Thank you," is all I can manage to say.

"I will tell you, I have plans to annul the marriage."

"I don't blame you."

"But we'll work something out. You have nothing to worry about, you or Lucy." He looks up at the ceiling. "I want her out of my house," he growls.

"What are you going to do?" Hayes asks him.

"Call the police, of course." He lowers his brow, his lips pulling up over his teeth. I've never seen him look so much like his son. "But first, I'm going to need a word with her."

Oh, shit. I jump up from the sofa when he starts for the door.

Hayes catches up to him, holding him in place with a hand on his shoulder. "Let me go first. Let me be the one."

His father gives him a tight nod. "Right. You should get the pleasure."

Hayes takes the lead, his father behind him with me on his heels. I can't believe this is happening. I can't believe I don't feel the slightest bit conflicted. She might be my mother, but this is what she deserves. She's gotten away with it for too long already.

We reach the upstairs hallway and walk single file to the master suite. The door is closed. Hayes taps on it with his knuckles before opening it. I can't see inside, but there's a light on somewhere, so Mom wasn't sleeping.

I hear her voice. "Oh, this is a nice surprise," she purrs. "Did you come to welcome Mommy into the family? You know how dangerous it is with your father downstairs."

I shoot an embarrassed look at Mr. Ambrose. He's barely holding himself back.

"No. I only wanted to see you first, so I could tell you it's over. This is all over. Say goodbye to all of this because you'll never see it again."

"Honey, have you forgotten already? Do I need to remind you of what will happen if you tell anybody about our relationship?" She almost sounds compassionate. How twisted can one person be?

Obviously, Mr. Ambrose has heard enough. He marches into the bedroom, flinging the door open wide. "You disgusting, filthy bitch."

I peer in just in time to see her scramble to a sitting position. She fumbles with her nightgown, and I wonder if maybe she started exposing herself when she thought it was only Hayes coming to visit.

"Sweetheart, what are you talking about?" she has the nerve to ask.

"Don't you ever call me that again. Don't you ever pretend there was ever anything normal about any of this."

"What are you talking about? What did he tell you? You told me yourself. He can't be trusted. He's unstable."

"That's not what I said, and you know it. He was behaving in an unstable manner, and now I know why. I've seen it with my own eyes, Christine. You've done well at hiding who you really are, but you weren't smart enough to keep the evidence from being uploaded to the cloud."

She looks around wildly, like she's searching for an excuse, and finally her gaze falls on me. "You wretched little shit. What have you done?"

"Don't talk to her like that," Hayes warns. "Somehow, even with a mother like you, she ended up being a better person than you could ever be."

"You don't know what you're talking about. None of you do."

Mr. Ambrose barks out a laugh. "I know what I saw. I want you out of that bed and out of this house. I'm turning you in, Christine."

There it is. I was waiting for it. That horrified victim face she's pulling. "I'm your wife! I'm going to be the mother of your child!"

"Are you sure about that?" he counters. "Because I'm not. You announced to me over the weekend that you're pregnant and raised that big stink over wanting to be married before the baby comes. You've never offered proof you're pregnant—and now, even if there is a baby, I have to wonder if the child is mine. Who else have you been with when I was out of town?"

"Nobody! I'm going to have your child. I would never lie about that."

Hayes steps forward. "Are you sure it's not mine?"

Oh, my God, it keeps getting worse. I think it can't, but then it does. No wonder he freaked when she said she was pregnant.

Her mouth falls open, her eyes as big as saucers. Her head snaps back and forth between Hayes and his father. "I—I mean—"

Mr. Ambrose shakes his head. "Maybe you'd better hope it was a scam. Get dressed. We're going to the police station."

"No, please. Please, it won't happen again. I'll do anything it takes. Let me make it up to you. Let me make you happy. You know how happy we've been."

"It was a lie, all of it. And if you were on fire, I wouldn't spit on you."

Her gaze falls on me and she pivots to a new strategy. "My babies. What about the girls? What's going to happen to them?"

"Already taken care of. They'll be better off without you." He makes a big deal of checking his watch. "Either you get out of that bed and get dressed, or I call the cops and have them pick you up at the front door. We can do this quietly, or we can do it the hard way. But we are doing it."

I can't stand to be in this room anymore. I go out to the hall, leaning against the wall, fighting for every breath. My mother. I hate her, she sickens me. She's never been a decent mother. Not a role model, none of it. Just the same, my heart feels heavy.

Hayes meets me out there. "Are you okay?"

"Me? Are you okay?"

"No, but I might get there, eventually." He flashes a sweet, vulnerable smile, and my heart skips a beat. In the end, this was all it mattered. Making sure he's safe from her.

His dad steps out next. "We're going down to the station. You don't have to come."

"I don't think I want to," I admit. "I'll stay with Lucy."

"Good idea. She's lucky to have a sister like you."

I give Hayes as much of a smile as I can manage before heading down the hall. He's got his dad taking care of him. I don't have to worry.

Lucy's fast asleep, lucky kid. Now that it's all over, or at least my part of it, I can't stop shaking. Even though we're safe, I know it's not going to be easy. Hopefully she's young enough that none of the kids she'll meet will have any idea who she comes from, but I can't avoid that. Word's going to get around. Hayes is still more important, so I don't regret coming forward.

That doesn't mean I feel very confident as I lift the blanket on Lucy's bed and snuggle in next to her. The way we used to when she'd have a nightmare, back when we were at the hotel. "Everything is going to be fine," I whisper, holding her tight before closing my eyes.

For the first time in a long time, I'm able to fall asleep right away.

CHAPTER 35

"$\mathcal{M}$organ. Wake up. How come you're in my bed with me?"

It's morning. Sunlight streams into the room through the gauzy pink curtains. "I guess I fell asleep. I just wanted to give you a hug."

She rolls onto her side to face me and gives me an impish little smile. "You want to pretend we're in a cave?" She pulls the blanket over her head before I answer, so I have no choice but to follow along, right? She sort of owns me.

"Do you want to tell secrets?" she whispers.

"You know something? I want to tell you something important, instead. It's real serious, so I need you to listen."

"Okay."

"If anybody ever hurts you, I want you to know you can come to me and tell me. If they ever make you feel uncomfortable or if they tell you to never tell anybody, don't listen to them. You come to me. I will always believe you."

"I knew that already."

"Yeah, but it's easy to forget." I kiss her forehead before pulling the blanket back down to my shoulder. "You know what, I really want to play, but I need to check something first."

She gasps. "Morgan, you're not at school! It's Friday!"

"Oh, gosh. I forgot." I actually did, too. When you find out your mother is a sexual predator, you forget about school. "I think it'll be okay. Let's get up and figure out breakfast."

She scrambles out of bed and goes to the bathroom. I open the bedroom door to find Bridget on her way up the stairs.

"I was just about to come in and get her," she says.

"I sort of fell asleep in her bed. She's up, taking care of business." I try to smile, but it's shaky.

"Mr. Ambrose is down in the kitchen with Hayes." She slides me a look I can only interpret as sympathy before heading to Lucy's room, where I hear her enthusiastically warn my sister to hurry or there won't be any pancakes left. I guess Mr. Ambrose had to give her at least a tiny heads-up that Mom won't be around.

I hurry down to the kitchen so I can beat Lucy there. Obviously, nobody is going to want to talk about this in front of her, and I'm dying from curiosity. I hear the men talking as I trot down the stairs and into the sunny room.

They look like two men who haven't slept, both of whom need a shave. But they're talking, actually sitting down together and talking. There's none of that stiffness I've seen in them before.

They turn when they hear me come in.

"I didn't want to interrupt," I offer, even if that's not technically true. I didn't know they would be sitting here like friends though. Mr. Ambrose looks over my shoulder, and I shake my head. "Lucy's upstairs."

"I'm happy to follow your lead when it comes to what she does and doesn't need to know," he begins. "Obviously, certain things she never needs to hear. But Mommy can be on vacation or on a long trip. Whatever you think she'll accept."

"Okay." I bite my lip, glancing at Hayes. "So, she's not coming back."

"They're holding her on $250,000 bail, and I sure as hell don't plan on paying a cent of that. She can figure it out for herself."

"I gave a statement," Hayes explains. "It wasn't as bad as I thought it would be. It actually felt kind of good to get it off my chest. The cops were nicer than I thought they would be."

"It's probably not the first time they've seen something like this," his father reminds him. "You don't have to be alone."

"If you're happy, I'm happy, too." I say, pouring myself a cup of coffee, even though I don't really like the plain kind. I need the caffeine. "Not to change the subject, but what about school? I forgot today was even a school day."

"I already made the phone call when we got home. You're both excused for the day." Mr. Ambrose gets up and walks slowly around the island before coming to a stop in front of me. "I can't thank you enough. I know what a difficult decision you faced last night. I'm getting a better idea of the person you really are, and how much you've carried on your shoulders. I want you to know you don't have to worry about that again."

"Thank you. I just want to make sure Lucy is taken care of. I'm glad she will be."

He heaves a sigh. "Now, if you'll excuse me, I need to instruct the housekeepers to clear out half of my bedroom." My heart still hurts for him a little bit. She had him completely fooled. If I didn't think it would be insulting, I would remind him he's not the first man she's tricked into thinking she's better than she is.

I look down at my coffee, a little nervous now that I'm alone with Hayes. "How are you really? Like, how are you feeling?"

"Honestly? Like I am the luckiest fuck who ever lived."

I lift my head, surprised, and it doesn't look like he's joking. "Seriously?"

"Yeah, seriously." Hayes gets up from his stool and makes a slow journey to where I'm standing. "I tried so fucking hard to push you away. You reminded me of her. And you being here reminded me she was here."

"I wish I had known."

"What could you have done about it?"

"I might have stopped bothering you."

"It wasn't your fault. I wish I could explain how it felt. You're my angel. You saved my life. You gave me a reason to stay on the bridge instead of jumping off. I was determined to do it before you came along with that stupid iced coffee and that story about fishing with your dad."

It's embarrassing to remember. "I can't believe you remember that."

"How could I not? You saved my life that day, like I said. And I admit there have been times since then that I've hated you for it. You stuck with me after all that. And you took a huge risk. For me."

"I couldn't have lived another day knowing what I knew. No way."

"Because you love me. Did you mean that?"

"So much. I knew I met the real you that day on the bridge. All I've wanted all this time is to get back to that person."

"No matter how hard I try to hide him from you."

"No matter how hard you tried."

He runs his hands up and down my arms. His touch is soft, but electric. "Even when you know about what I had to do? You still feel the same way?"

"It wasn't your fault. None of it has to matter."

"Like I said." He lowers his head like he's about to kiss me. "I'm the luckiest fuck who ever lived."

The sound of Lucy's feet slapping against the stairs reminds us where we are. This is going to be awkward, living here with him and wanting him the way I do. The look in his eyes right now tells me he wants me, too, even as we separate ourselves. How are we going to make this work?

All I know is, I want to. So much.

"There you are." Charlotte bustles into the room at almost the same time Lucy does. "Who's hungry?"

* * *

I LEAVE my bedroom door unlocked before getting into bed.

Hayes doesn't disappoint me. It's been a long day, with his dad looking into therapists and with the cops coming by for additional information while Bridget kept Lucy out of the house. I've barely been able to have a few minutes with him since breakfast.

It's a relief when he opens the door and creeps into the room. "You awake?"

"What do you think?" I pull back the blanket and pat the mattress.

He slides between the blankets, wearing nothing but his boxer briefs. The feel of his smooth skin and that faint scent of chlorine are comforting.

"How are you doing?" I settle in with my head on his chest. His heart's pounding hard, but it slowly eases.

"I feel like I got run over by a truck, but it's better than I've felt in months."

"It makes me happy to hear that."

"How are you?" He strokes my hair, his mouth close to my ear. We have to be quiet. Nothing matters more than that.

"I'm okay. Really." I snort, shaking my head at myself. "You'll laugh at me, but you've been a big part of my life since I met you. I only think about you… all day, every day."

"Come on."

"I do." I look up at him, so he knows I'm serious. "Most of the time, I was wondering why you acted like you did. Why you hated me so much."

"I'm sorry for that."

"I know. You explained it. You didn't have to. I understand now that I know the whole story." I have to wince. "You know, I thought it might've been your coach who was doing it."

"Is that why you were sneaking around that day at practice?" He groans. "He was only checking my Speedo. If it's even a little loose, it creates drag in the water."

"It didn't look that way."

"To a non-swimmer, no. And you already had the wrong idea." His arms tighten around me. "Theo told me what you did, or almost did, at the party before I got there. I've been wanting to talk to you about it, but it didn't seem like the right time."

"It's fine now."

"Don't ever do anything like that for me again. I'm serious." He presses a kiss against the top of my head. Nothing has ever felt this good. "I'm not going to let you get hurt because of me. You mean too much."

"I wanted to protect you."

"I'm the one who's going to protect you." He lifts my chin, then cups my cheek in his hand. "I never knew how to show you the way I felt. I'm still not sure it'll come out right. I have a lot of shit to get through and work out."

"I understand."

"But I want to start by saying I meant everything this morning. You're my angel. You saved my life every day. Sometimes I hated you for that, but deep down I couldn't stand away because I loved you." He runs his thumb over my lips, now parted in wonder. "I love you."

He's made me cry before. More than once. But never for a reason like this. "I didn't think I would ever hear you say that."

"The only reason I can is because of you." He rolls us both over until I'm under him, on my back. "I'm sorry for hurting you before. I was only trying to hurt myself. I'll never do that again."

"I believe you."

He shakes his head a little. "Sometimes I wonder if you're real. You can't really be this understanding and good. You can't want me after… everything."

"I do." I kiss him as hard as I can, like that will help convince him. "I'll always want you. Just like I'll always love you." I slide my leg against his.

"We have to be careful with this. How are we going to make it work?"

"I don't know," I admit. "But we'll figure it out. Maybe no sneaking around in each other's rooms."

He starts to get up, but I tighten my grip. "I didn't mean right now!"

"I'm fucking with you," he whispers with a laugh. "We could always try the high diving board again, you know."

"Yeah, we wouldn't get into any trouble if somebody walked in, right? Maybe you need to learn to control yourself, is all."

He growls. "Unlikely. But I'm willing to try."

For now, that's the best I can hope for. No matter what comes after this—and I know it won't be easy—we'll have each other. That's more than enough.

EPILOGUE

ONE YEAR LATER

There's nothing like waking up to a hot, naked man between my legs. "Mm…" I moan, rubbing my eyes once I know I'm not dreaming. It's morning, and we're in bed, and Hayes is a few inches away from going down on me. "You're in a hurry."

He nips at my inner thigh before kissing the same spot. "Remember, we have stuff to do today. Do you want me fantasizing and groping you under the table instead?"

He's right, but I wouldn't try to stop him even if he was wrong. We've been together for a year, but it wasn't until we moved out and started college together that we could really start acting like an actual couple. It's like we're catching up for lost time.

Not that Hayes's dad didn't figure it out way before graduation. By then, the marriage was annulled. We were officially stepsiblings for hardly any time at all. It was still a little weird, but he tried to be understanding. Maybe it was almost losing his son or finding out all those terrible things happened without him ever knowing about it, but he's worked hard to be a better father.

We've always kept it from Lucy, however. She's a smart kid and always has been, but she still thinks of Hayes as our brother and his dad as our father. She understands Mom's not coming home, she just doesn't know why.

The worst part might've been how unsurprised she was when I finally told her. Not even all that upset. Like it was going to happen someday.

Now we're meeting up with her and Hayes's dad for lunch later. I'm looking forward to it—but right now, what matters more is what's happening here in bed.

Like the feel of Hayes's tongue gliding over the seam of my inner thigh and my shaved pussy. I close my eyes to focus on the sensations, sighing and running my fingers through his hair. Every lick feels better than the one before, all of them combining to make me writhe and groan.

He laps at my lips next. I know they must be wet by now, thanks to what he's already done to me. When I try to push against his tongue to force him deeper, he only pulls back with a chuckle.

My fists twist the sheets. "No fair."

"I didn't know we were supposed to be playing fair." Another lick, feather-light, just to drive me crazy. "You think it's fair I can't think about anything but this pussy twenty-four-seven?"

"Is that all you care about?"

"Of course it isn't." Another lick lights me on fire. "I think about your ass…" Lick. "Your tits…" Another lick.

"Fuck," I moan, desperately grinding my hips.

"That, too. A lot." He opens me with his fingers, parting my lips before finally giving me what I'm dying for. The tip of his tongue flicks the tip of my clit, and my body jumps.

"I could do this all day." He sighs. "One tiny lick at a time."

I open my eyes and look down at him, head between my thighs. "Or you could just make me come now so I can suck your dick."

His eyes meet mine, his mouth lifting just enough from my throbbing pussy to speak. "Yeah?"

"But you better hurry. This offer won't last long." I haven't closed my eyes yet before he plunges down to feast on me. And he does, groaning, grunting like an animal while he plunders me with his tongue. Now my hips jerk wildly as I ride out the intense pleasure shooting down my arms and legs and rippling through my core.

"Just like that… oh, yes, Hayes… I'm going… I'm gonna come…" I arch my back and let out one last cry before riding out the waves of bliss. The tension melts, and I fall back against the bed with a happy sigh.

Here's the thing about promising a blow job: you can't pretend you didn't, not when your boyfriend's already hard and dripping precum.

I move, ready to put myself between his legs to return the favor, but he takes hold of my hips before I can. "I want you on top of me. I'm not finished eating."

Yes, I like it even more this way. Hovering over his mouth, riding his face. I've come a long way since those early days when I didn't know anything about this. Hayes has encouraged me to figure out what I like and how I like it. He gives me the confidence to take what I want.

Right now, I want to come again. It's like an addiction. Being with him, just the two of us, with no need to hide or hold back anymore. It's amazing we both make it to class.

I straddle his face while taking his dick in my hand. He pulls down on my hips until I'm properly sitting, then buries his tongue in me. I respond by burying him deep in my mouth until his head presses against the back of my throat.

We find our rhythm together, moving in reaction to what the other one does. Soon, he's pumping his fingers in and out of my pussy in time with my head bobbing, licking my clit with every stroke.

When he takes it between his lips and sucks, I moan with him in my mouth. Yes, that's good, that's perfect. I grind over him, forgetting what I'm doing for a minute to focus on what he's doing to me. On what's going to happen soon if he doesn't stop—only he'd better never stop because fuck, it's perfect. I'm so close again.

I let him slide out of my mouth but stroke with my fist, moving up and down over his spit-slick shaft. "Yes… I'm gonna come. You're going to make me come again…" He groans when my juices flow, his tongue sliding inside me to pick up every last drop.

"Forget that." He moves me off him, but keeps me on my hands and knees. I spread my legs wider, lifting my ass for him to take me. He slaps a hand against my right cheek, my left cheek, making me hiss before impaling me from behind.

It's like he was made for me. Like we were made for this. I push back against him with every thrust, and soon, our bodies are slapping together. We're not making love. We're fucking, rutting like animals, taking from each other.

He buries a hand in my hair and pulls until I'm up on my knees. One of his arms wraps around my stomach while he holds my throat with the other hand. "You like it when I fuck you this way?" he asks against my ear.

"Yes!"

"When I take this pussy? Who does it belong to?"

"You," I sob, lost in a haze of pleasure.

"Who? Who owns your pussy?"

"You do!" His teeth sink into my shoulder, and I cry out in pain and pleasure. "Yes! Yes, fuck me!"

He thrusts upward, pounding me, punishing me. And I love it. I want nothing more than this. Him. Us.

"Come with me," I gasp, so close again.

He moves faster, deeper, harder, closing in on release. I move with him, wanting it for him as much as I do for me. His breath catches in a familiar way, and I know he's on the edge. My muscles clench and tighten around him until the tension explodes one last time.

I come with him wrapped around me, sweating and panting in a tangle on the bed. His lips rain soft kisses over my shoulder, neck, and back.

"I'm glad we got that out of the way," I whisper. "Before we have to go out in public."

"It's all your fault. You're too hot while sleeping, all stretched out and naked."

"Should I start wearing pajamas again? So you don't have to get all distracted by my nakedness?"

"I'll burn them if you do."

This is the best part, I think. Better than the sex itself. Holding each other like this, joking, loving each other. The two of us in our own little world. After everything we've been through, I think we deserve it.

"Come on." I don't want to, but we have reservations later, and one of us has to be the mature one. "We've got to get ready. I'll jump in the shower if you need to rest, big guy."

"Who says I'm going to let you shower alone?" He rolls out of bed behind me. "We're going to be out and behaving ourselves for hours. I have a lot to get out of my system."

How am I supposed to argue with that? I don't bother trying.

Of all the things Hayes Ambrose has taught me, the one thing I need most to remember is how pointless it is to argue when there's something he wants.

I just so happen to be lucky enough that he wants me.

Obsession Duet
Cruel Obsession
Deadly Obsession

* * *

The Moretti Crime Family
Savage Beginnings
Violent Beginnings
Broken Beginnings

* * *

King Crime Family
Indebted
Inevitable

* * *

Diavolo Duet
Devil You Hate
Devil You Know

* * *

Dark Lies
Perfect Villain
Beautiful Monster
Cruel Beast
Savage Vow

* * *

Doubeck Crime Family

Vow to Protect

Promise to Keep

Bound to Darkness

Bound to Cruelty

Bound to Deception

* * *

Breaking the Rules

Kissing & Telling

Babies & Promises

Roommates & Thieves

* * *

Standalones

Her Mafia Bodyguard

Hitman (*part of Heaven & Hell*)

ABOUT THE AUTHOR

J.L. Beck writes steamy romance that's unapologetic.

Her heroes are alphas who take what they want, and are willing to do anything for the woman they love.

She loves writing about darkness, passion, suspense, and of course steam.

Leaving her readers gasping, and asking what the hell just happened is only one of her many tricks.

Her books range from grey, too dark but always end with a happily ever after.

Inside the pages of her books you'll always find one of your favorite tropes.

She started her writing career in the summer of 2014 and hasn't stopped since. She lives in Wisconsin and is a mom to two, a wife, and likes to act as a literary agent part time.

Visit her website for more info: www.beckromancebooks.com.

To stay in touch with J.L., subscribe to her newsletter here. If you'd like exclusive, early access to ebooks, paperbacks, and other exclusive content subscribe to her Patreon. You can read the first couple of chapters of the next book there now!

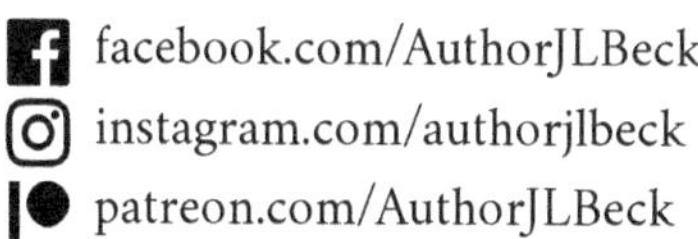